8/17

the ART of FEELING

the ART *of* FEELING

LAURA TIMS

HARPER TEEN
An Imprint of HarperCollinsPublishers

HarperTeen is an imprint of HarperCollins Publishers.

Library of Congress Control Number: 2016961848

ISBN 978-0-06-231735-3 (trade bdg.)

Typography by Ray Shappell

17 18 19 20 21   PC/LSCH   10 9 8 7 6 5 4 3 2 1

First Edition

To my parents, Brenda and Jerry, and my sibling, Evan—
the most solid family anyone could ask for

Chapter One

NAVIGATING MY HIGH SCHOOL HALLWAY
has gotten a lot scarier since the crutches.

I stand to the side of the classroom door, letting the flow pass by. I'm a tractor with a thirty-miles-per-hour max on a seventy-miles-per-hour highway. The three-o'clock bell stops ringing, but nothing gets quieter because everyone in the hall is shrieking to be heard over everyone else.

I could take a chance and dive in. Or I could miss the bus. But missing the bus means calling my brother, Rex, and I'd rather pull out my toenails with tweezers.

And then it's like a cartoon, how fast it happens.

One second I'm battling for space between a chubby kid with Mentos breath and a skinny kid with Doritos breath, and the next I'm on my butt, my metal-and-plastic extra legs skittering across the dingy linoleum. Everyone nearby takes a collective breath: *someone knocked over the girl on crutches.*

"I'm *so sorry,* Sam. Are you *okay?*" says this poor sweating freshman. He's a guy, so everyone is giving him the brutal-beast look, which is slightly worse than the clumsy-idiot one that the girls get.

If I was sadistic, I might pretend to cry and laugh about it later. Instead I flash him a winning smile. Or as winning as a smile can get when it comes from a girl on the floor whose left leg is an inch shorter than her right and twists instead of bends. "I'm fine."

"Are you *sure*—?"

"Yep."

"But are you *really sure*—"

"Like two hundred percent sure."

"I'm so sorry," he repeats, handing me my crutches. It should be a rule that when somebody hit-and-runs your mom's Toyota into a ball of tinfoil with both of you inside, you get to pick a new superpower. I'd choose invisibility. Instead I got hypervisibility. Everyone stares as it takes me way longer than it should to get up.

"Don't even worry about it," I say to the crowd, absolving them, my face burning. None of them is friendly enough with me to stick around. I prop myself against the wall and fake play with my phone, waiting for the pain to whiplash up the six-month-old cracks in my leg.

Lots of things make people anxious. Heights, spiders.

Pain is just supposed to *hurt*, not make my heart pound like I'm about to be in a car crash. It's not even a sharp hurt—more of a dull ache. The problem is that pain means glass sparkling on the pavement, bright enough to sting my eyes.

Forget invisibility. Invulnerability is the best super-power.

I wrestle my pill case from my baggy jeans, untwist one side, and pop half a Vicodin. It's a tired sort of feeling, not wanting to hurt anymore.

When I look up, the last bus is disappearing beyond the glass front doors. This is a great opportunity to find out if they'd suspend a girl for bashing in the trophy case with her crutches. But I already know the answer. Perks of surviving a firestorm of glass and steel: I could run naked across the drama stage while screaming every swear ever written down, and Principal Chase would give me a Snickers bar in her office and ask me how I'm doing.

I search my phone for people to call other than Rex. Dad's at work. My sister, Lena, is at her internship in Northton, a two-hour drive that she always manages to stretch into four. Dr. Brown said I could call whenever, but judging by her phone consultation rates, chartering a private jet would be cheaper.

There's Kendra, Amy, Erin—my old group. They don't understand how friendship works outside the lacrosse team, and I haven't figured it out yet either. The dead-mom thing got me a temporary free antisocial pass, redeemable for five (5) ignored party invites and six (6) months avoiding the lunch table; but I forgot to check the expiration date, and now I accidentally have no friends. Which is inconvenient. You need them for group projects. And rides home.

It's three fifteen. There's a seventy percent chance Rex is high, a ninety percent chance that if I call he'll come get me anyway, a one hundred percent chance that if he's high I won't get in the car, and a one million percent chance that if I don't get in the car we'll fight about it.

I walk down the hall and punch the handicapped button next to the front doors, the one I still feel lazy for using even though I'm supposed to. The light blinds me for a second. The kind of light that makes broken glass glitter like diamonds.

And then I spot my ride. He's zipping around the corner of the building—magazine-blond, Polo-wearing, baby-blue-eyed Anthony Moore, who got a full scholarship to Yale and sells prescription pills even though he's too rich to need either. He used to be best friends with Rex and me, back in elementary school when people called him No-Moore because he wouldn't stop crying on our fourth-grade field trip out of town.

I swing after him, but he disappears past the art department Dumpsters. His home office. He should hire a hot secretary to pop out like a stripper from a cake: *Would you like some Adderall with your Xanax?* He'd love to offer Vicodin for dessert, but I'm strict about the *As Needed* part of my prescription. Pills are more common than Altoids in Anthony's crowd, and the staff is in denial because this is a nice upper-middle-class town in the whitest state in the country, and there's a J.Crew half a mile from the school, and no one in salmon-colored shorts could ever do *drugs*.

By the time I reach Anthony, panting because my lacrosse muscles disappeared after the hospital stay, he's stopped in front of someone. A tall, thin someone with messy dark hair. Eliot Rowe.

It's like seeing the sun next to the moon. The new Anthony is all glow-tanned perfection and a *Mad Men* aesthetic. Eliot is pale mystery, sharp-cheekboned stares, and supercilious slouching. Alone in the cafeteria, alone always. He moved here just after Alani Herring (mother of Lena; Reginald, i.e., Rex; and me, Samantha, i.e., Sam) died in a car crash.

Eliot and Death showed up together. Two stamps on the memories of everyone who attended Forest Hills High in the worst year of my life. For a while he was the most interesting phenomenon in the world to everyone except me, because of the funeral or whatever. I owe him for splitting the spotlight between us the second he walked through the doors.

I creep close enough to hear Anthony say, "I don't appreciate being spoken to like that," in his coffee-soft polite threat voice. It sounds fake to me, especially when I remember No-Moore sniffling on the playground, but it tends to convince everybody else.

Eliot smirks, mutters something—and then Anthony's fist smashes into the side of his face. Jesus. I jump and almost fall for the second time today. "Anthony," I say loudly.

He ignores me and picks up Eliot by his shirt. I've seen what happens next, and maybe later Eliot will be together enough to stagger home alone, if he's lucky. "Anthony, I need a ride home."

He groans. "Five minutes."

Blood paints a broad streak down Eliot's shirt collar. His silk shirt collar. Who wears silk shirts? Slutty vampires is the first and only thing that pops into my head. "Leave him alone," I say in my best Rex-and-Lena-are-fighting-again-but-if-I-say-it-like-it's-not-a-big-deal-it-won't-be voice.

"The hero act's cute, Samantha Herring." Anthony uses everybody's full name, probably because Rex and I don't like ours. "Call Reginald."

"Rex is busy." We're having this conversation like blood isn't dripping down Eliot's neck. Except Eliot's not making any "Ow fuck" facial contortions. Instead, he's watching me with amusement. It's actual amusement. "I mean it. Leave him alone."

"You've aroused my curiosity as to how this is your business," Anthony says. "I mean I'm *intrigued*, like *fascinated*, as to how this is your fucking business."

That's the new Anthony.

He cocks his fist again, and I take a breath. I may have to walk on sticks now, but I've trained with the lacrosse team long enough that I also know how to swing one. Anthony yelps a very un-Anthony yelp at the *crack* my crutch makes across his shoulders. He drops Eliot and makes a lunging move at me. I can't believe it. I hold out the crutch, the world's least-effective sword.

He's breathing hard. "If this is your new boyfriend, Reginald is going to hit him way harder than I ever would."

"If you hit me, Rex will hit you way harder than he would ever hit my nonexistent boyfriend."

"I would never touch you," he says, hand-over-heart offended, like he didn't just dive at me with a vertebrae-separating expression. "Jesus, Sam. We grew up together. You're my *friend*."

I'm electric everywhere, shot with adrenaline, like when I used to catapult the lacrosse ball into the net (*GO SAM GO*). But the switches haven't flipped in a long time. I thought even the backup generator was dead. You don't realize that you haven't been feeling anything until you feel something again. "Go home, Anthony."

Anthony pauses, then turns and scuffs up dust with his shoe into Eliot's face. "Don't start daydreaming about how this is the end of it."

Eliot goes on smirking from his sideways position in the dirt. Finally someone else appreciates how stupid Anthony sounds when he plays mafia.

He jabs a thumb at me. "You've officially pissed me off."

It slips out: "Sure, No-Moore."

For a second I feel like a dick, even though he deserves it. But he surprisingly doesn't murder me on the spot. He just turns and saunters away toward the parking lot.

So much for my ride.

Eliot hops up, straightens his torn shirt, and looks at me. I hate his eyes immediately. They're hard and crystally, like they light up in the dark.

Some people are socially incapacitated. You feel bad for them, you're glad it's them and not you, but nothing's going to change them. Sometimes you wonder—not in a mean way, just curiously—whether or not they'll be alone forever. And if they ever wonder, too.

I've never talked to Eliot, so the specifics of his social incapacitation are a mystery. But since he moved here, we've had that silent awkward connection that exists between the two people at school with no friends. It's not so bad being a loner if there's another one who's weirder. I get the urge to nod at him in the hall, or shake his hand like we both know the steps to a secret handshake.

The first thing I ever say to him is "Nice slutty-vampire shirt."

"Thanks," he says.

I suffer from a coughing fit and stare at my crutches in lieu of eye contact. "So what'd you do to piss off Anthony?"

"I piss off everyone. The details don't matter."

"I'm curious."

"Have I *aroused your curiosity*?" he asks, his voice startlingly deep and deeply amused. "I warned him not to sell his pills here at school anymore. Someone's going to narc on him."

"No one narcs on Anthony."

"He broke up with Trez Monroe a few months ago. She's an ESFJ—you know."

"What?"

"An ESFJ—the Myers-Briggs personality type—so she's obsessive when it comes to other people. She's been shooting him death looks every time his back is turned." He rattles it off like an equation.

Trez was a loner during the No-Moore days, too, until she got hot and they started dating. She's been a social butterfly ever since, but she's also one of those people who won't meet my eyes since the crutches. "You're not friends with Trez. How do you know what Myers-Briggs personality type she is?"

"I know the Myers-Briggs type of every person in this school."

Ookay. "Kendra Baker?"

"ENFP."

"Jasper Barnett?"

"INFJ."

The Myers-Briggs types are like Hogwarts houses. Fun for Tumblr, but not really science. Yet Eliot's talking like a professional researcher. I resist the impulse to ask which type I am. "Guessing Trez's Myers-Briggs type doesn't mean she's going to narc on Anthony."

"It's not a guess. People are predictable."

"You didn't predict Anthony punching you in the face."

"Yes I did." He's smiling faintly. Is he joking?

"Why'd he hit you, if you were just trying to warn him?"

"Possibly it was my phrasing."

"Which was?"

"'It takes a special kind of idiot to do something illegal

in the same place at the same time every day.'"

I choke laugh. "I'm gonna say it was your phrasing."

His smile gets less faint, stretching the cut on his lip.

"Does that hurt?" I ask.

"No."

"Looks like it hurts."

"It doesn't."

Is he high? But his eyes are clear. His face is angular, full of shadows and smirks and secrets, but no pain, and I know what pain looks like.

"It's amazing that you noticed all that about Trez. I figured—" —*you didn't know anything about anyone here since you're alone,* but I slice it off.

"Is that what you think?" he asks suddenly. "That it's amazing?"

I nod, surprised by his new tone.

"That's not usually how people feel."

"You haven't called me a special breed of idiot yet."

"Fair enough. Though you are one, for getting involved."

"You're welcome." I frown. "Is that why I always see you in the detention room? For insulting people?"

"One of the reasons." He pushes his thick hair away from his forehead, exposing a widow's peak. It's weird how natural this conversation is. Even with Kendra and my old group, I was forcing it. "I guess I'm supposed to thank you."

If anyone sees me here, I'll be deported from the realm of no-friends-but-friendly-enough-with-everyone to the land of nobody-speaks-to-me, but his smile makes me wonder if that's a stupid thing to care about.

"No one's ever done that before," he says, almost to himself. Not in a sad way, more like *Ah, the lab mouse is displaying unusual growths.* Still, I feel sorry for him.

Then his eyes narrow. "So why? You don't like to draw attention to yourself. You're aggressively boring. Normal. And you've been on the waiting list for a new set of friends ever since you had to quit lacrosse, so I have no idea why you'd jeopardize your application by standing up for me."

Now I know the specifics of his social incapacitation. "Fuck you," I splutter because I feel like I should.

"Maybe you just don't like to watch people get hurt because your mother died in that accident."

He says it so casually that it takes me a moment to feel it.

"You were in the car with her, weren't you?" he continues. "You couldn't prevent her death, so you get involved when other people are in danger. Like I said, people are predictable."

I pull my crutches up from where they've sunk into the dirt. There's a dull ringing in my ears. "I have to go."

For a millisecond, his expression is bewildered. "I didn't mean—"

"Right," I mumble randomly, and swing away from the Dumpsters with my ears sandwiched between my shoulders.

I could phone Rex. Maybe he's sober. Or maybe I'll walk. I'll walk, and screw any doctor who tells me I can't.

★ ★ ★

When I get home, Rex is halfway to oblivion on the Vicodin train, a ticket he won on the last guilt trip he took me on. Rex is well traveled. Without ever leaving the house, he's become an expert in being anywhere else.

I maneuver through the front door to find him spaced out in front of a football game, on the hideous striped living-room couch (original owner: deaf eighty-year-old on craigslist). Tito, our equally hideous tiny mutt, is nestled under his chin. Rex used to look like a handsome version of me, if I was the guy that strangers always think I am. But sadness ruined his face.

"Kendra gave me a ride," I say before he can ask. My leg throbs, and glass splinters in the back of my head. The anxiety is remote and immediate at the same time.

Rex ignores the fact that I'm sweating and limping and sees what he wants to see. "Kendra? The hot one?"

"She's my age, you pedophile."

"Oh, gross," he moans.

Tito topples off Rex's chest, wobbles to me, and bashes his head ecstatically into my leg, his eyes puddles of doggy joy. Since Mom died and Lena moved out, he no longer believes that humans walking out the door will come back. Whenever we return, he acts like we were presumed dead in battle.

"Stupid dog," says Rex with tremendous love.

Rex got kicked out of Forest Hills in his senior year for hiding Oxycontin in the charger compartment of his laptop case. He's spent ninety-nine percent of the subsequent seven hundred and thirty days zoned out on the couch with

Tito. Since Mom died, it's become incredibly depressing.

Since Mom Died. I think it so often that it deserves an acronym. SMD.

Too bad it doesn't spell out anything.

Smid.

I remember that Rex and I are having a conversation and quip, "You just said a girl the same age as me, your sister, was hot. That's basically incest."

"Girls your age shouldn't have giant tits. That's her fault."

"I'm sure she grew her tits out specifically to annoy you."

"Hhhh," breathes Tito, hearing something close to his name. Lena named him after a Hawaiian character in a cartoon she liked when she was little, since Mom was half Hawaiian. I don't think Tito is a real Hawaiian name.

"Seventeen is fetal. They should all be titless like you."

I wait until Rex faces the TV to flip him off. Then I raid the kitchen. Now that Dad has sole reign of the groceries, the cupboards are stuffed with Cheetos, SpongeBob mac 'n' cheese, and those gummy bear dinosaurs made for five-year-olds. Dad prescribes junk food for himself like antidepressants, devouring endless bags of chips after we go to bed and stashing the evidence in the garage so we don't notice.

In the days after Mom died, we lived on pity casseroles. It's not that Mom did the cooking—Dad did. Before. We do always have lasagna, though. Somebody still leaves a warm lasagna on our porch once a week, wrapped in tinfoil. Dad thinks the neighbors take turns.

Suddenly Tito falls on my foot. This is normal. He has epilepsy, and the pills we feed him, wrapped in slices of Kraft cheese, produce a constant state of mild sedation—hence the drooling, Darth Vader breathing, and falling down. I kiss him and set him on his paws. The fact that Tito is the best dog ever is the only thing Rex and I agree on.

"Anthony punched some kid today," I yell into the living room. If I was more aggressive and less on crutches, I might've punched Eliot, too. He's punchable.

"Who?"

"Some kid." Some random stupid kid who can't hurt me with a couple random stupid words. When I think about Mom, I can fix it so it's nothing. But when people bring her up out of nowhere . . .

But even Aggressively Boring (the truth) doesn't bother me as much as it should. Being offended takes too much emotional energy. And it's almost nice that someone has something to say about me other than *THAT'S the girl whose MOM got KILLED.*

"I told you to stay away from Anthony," Rex yells back.

"As if I'd be scared of somebody who cried at your tenth birthday party because he lost at Mario Kart." I sift through junk food for something that contains nutrition.

"He has issues."

"Luckily he can afford a therapist." Unlike us and Dr. Brown's low-income co-pay discount. I grab a bag of chips and try to sneak through the living room past Rex, but he whips up like a manic security guard.

"How's school?" he demands.

"Fine."

"C'mon, Sam."

I throw my hands up. "There's pencils and teachers and stuff."

"Any guys bothering you?" He cracks his knuckles.

"I thought I was titless."

"Some guys are into that."

All I'd have to do is breathe Eliot's name and Rex would eat him alive. "Boys don't bother me, Rex. It's like in zombie movies when the people cover themselves in zombie guts to hide the fact that they're not zombies. Boys miss the fact that I'm botherable."

But the Vicodin train is leaving the station. His gaze drifts over my shoulder, and he sinks back into the couch. I have no idea how he tolerates that couch. The mystery stains were there when we bought it.

"I'm almost out," he mumbles.

All aboard for the guilt trip. I count the swans in our faded wallpaper. "I'm not giving you more."

"You don't know what it's like."

Not just a guilt trip, a guilt vacation, an all-expenses-paid stay at a guilt resort. His last resort. "It's illegal," I say like a brat.

"They're for pain, and I'm in pain." He buries his face in one of the throw pillows. They don't match. Mom got them off craigslist from a chiropractor with five ferrets. They're scratchy and smelly, like Tito, like the rest of our furniture. But SMD, the steady flow of weird secondhand stuff has stopped. We have to preserve what we have.

"You know what's illegal?" he adds. "Pulverizing some-body else's car and driving off."

My leg aches. I move toward the stairs.

"I want to talk about it," he says to the pillow.

"I don't," I say to the stairs. He doesn't usually go straight from acting-like-Mom to asking-me-about-Mom.

"You got to be there with her."

I submit a request to my brain to please *not* pick up the orange lamp (origin: waitress from craigslist) and smash it on his skull. But I'm already pissed off, courtesy of Eliot, and my leg still hurts. "You're jealous, is what you're saying."

My voice is flat and sharp, like pavement with glass glit-tering on it. He flinches. Tito whines.

"Maybe next time it'll be Dad, and you'll be the one in the car and then won't you be so lucky." And I run (hobble) upstairs and slam my bedroom door.

I'm a terrible person, I guess.

To punish myself, I stare hard at everything in my room. It's full of lacrosse gear—sticks propped against the wall, cleats under my bed, photos from last year's game against Brighton—because I like to be reminded that now I can't do the only thing I was ever good at. Other than the glass, I don't remember the accident. I had nothing for the police. And nothing is all I want. Nothing is safe.

I find my emergency bottle of Vicodin in my sock drawer, dump half the contents into a Ziploc, and return to the stairs long enough to lob the bag into the living room. "Sorry," I bellow.

Back in my room with the other kind of guilt, I switch on my broken lava lamp (origin: craigslist hippie), hurl my crutches on my bed, and grab my notebook. Family counseling is this weekend. Dr. Brown gives us homework, which is unbelievable, but Lena—who now comes down only for the appointments—lectures me if I don't do it. I'm supposed to write down my goals.

I make a fake list for Dr. Brown and an honest list for no reason at all.

LIST #1

Make new friends

Do good in school

Heal with my family

LIST #2

Make new friends without having to actually hang out with anyone

I'm doing fine in school, fuck you

Kill Rex, avoid Lena (not hard), avoid Dad

Kill Dr. Brown

Never talk to Eliot Rowe again

When the honest list has enough murder victims to get me interrogated if it's found, I rip it up and poke the shreds into a Coke bottle, where they drown in the muddy liquid at the bottom.

Chapter Two

THE ONLY INTERESTING THING THAT HAPPENS the next day is that Anthony gets arrested.

I leave English to pee and stick my head into the hall just in time to witness him being marched down the hall by a cop and Principal Chase. The news rockets around school, pinging off lockers, breaking windows. Anthony's gang sulks in a mob. Trez darts between classes with her books clutched to her chest, feverish satisfaction in her expression. Eliot was right.

Every year, at least one student is caught with pills, enough of an epidemic for an auto-expulsion policy, but it's supposed to be the ones with bad posture and no extracurriculars. Rexes, not Anthonys. This event is right up there with my accident and Eliot moving in.

I try really hard to care. I'm not jaded. I *want* just a zap of the electricity from yesterday, a plug-in to the energy. But as my next lectures are drowned out by everyone buzzing, as my teachers flop at their desks, I keep dissociating, the whiteboard blurring and smearing across the room in a stretch of nothing.

The truth is, I'm blank most of the time. Static.

Sometimes I think I've used up all my emotions.

On Friday, the first words anyone addresses directly to me are these:

"Punch me."

I'm loading books from my locker into my bag, and the suddenness makes me jump. Books topple. Before I can tackle bending over, Eliot Rowe stoops.

"What?" I ask.

"I said punch me. Or hit me with your crutches. Judging by Monday, you might prefer the latter." He tips the books back into my locker. Up close, he's startling: his high cheekbones, hair so dark it's almost blue, the smirk that makes it impossible to tell if he's being serious. He seems even less human with the mottled bruise on his vampire-pale cheek. Next to me, he's probably even more exotic. I look like a twelve-year-old boy with baby cheeks, and my short hair is the kind of brown that you can't compare to chocolate or coffee because it's not the shade of something delicious.

"Mind if I ask why?" Four days have passed since

Monday, I realize—time passes without me noticing nowadays—and he hasn't spoken to me at all.

"You're a lacrosse player—"

My leg throbs. "Was."

"The point is, you're physical. I was going to apologize for what I said on Monday, but it'd be easier if you got rid of your anger the quick way. Then we can move on."

I gape at him. "Move on where?"

He pauses, then shakes his head. "Nowhere. Never mind."

Something about that saddens me. "I'm not going to punch you."

"Sure, men are more socialized to deal with anger by hitting things, but I think you'll find it surprisingly liberating."

"Are you joking? Or is this like some kind of fetish thing?"

He snorts. "I just hate apologizing."

"Nobody hates apologizing that much."

"I hate lying," he corrects himself. "And I don't really feel that apologetic. It's not a secret, about your mom."

"And what about calling me boring?"

"Point taken. You're not boring. You do interesting things like stand up for me."

The halls are mostly deserted, like they usually are by the time I get to my locker. Nobody to overhear. "You were right about Trez," I say, changing the subject.

He rolls his eyes. "Of course I was right about Trez."

Then a momentary silence in which he seems to remember something. "I'm sorry for your loss, by the way."

He doesn't give me warning signs. No forehead wrinkling, no hand on my shoulder. He just adds it bluntly.

"Are you?" The platitude always annoys me, but I've never been rude enough to be a jerk about it. Now he'll either call me out or grant me concessions. People let you be mean when you're grieving. Funerals turn a lot of us into assholes.

"Not particularly," he says instead. "I'm sorry in theory, but I didn't know your mom and I barely know you."

Which is why it annoys me. "I thought you hated lying."

"I meant I usually don't bother."

I sag against my crutches. Talking to Eliot uses up a week's worth of emotions. I can't decide if I'm annoyed or amused, but the last one is the least amount of work. "Does that mean I'm special?"

"We'll see." He leans into my locker, his sharp shoulder pressing into the orange metal in a way that looks painful. It's definitely possible that he's been messing with me since he opened his mouth. "Mainly it means I owe you."

"You don't owe me."

"A ride home, at least."

"I don't—" I start, but through the glass doors at the end of the hall, I see that the last bus is disappearing. "Oh."

"I'll take that as a yes."

The only thing left to do is follow him.

★ ★ ★

Eliot drives like he's taking his license test as he pulls out of the lot. His Porsche (!!) is practically new, loaded with that new-car smell they aerosol on the upholstery. I stroke the white leather, the enameled wooden dashboard. Before Mom died—BMD—I liked cars. Now driving feels like a dentist appointment: scary but too necessary to avoid.

"My brother's," he says before I can ask.

"He lets you borrow this?"

"Using the term *lets* broadly." He rolls down the window and takes out a cigarette.

"Smoking's bad for you."

"When has that ever stopped anyone?" Smoke swirls above his head. "Driving is worse for you, in terms of how likely you are to die from it. Yet here we are."

I don't say anything. A pulse of pain courses through my leg, and my chest aches with something similar.

Eliot grimaces. "I can't avoid every mention of car accidents forever."

"Most people can." Usually I hate it when someone blunders into topics like accidents or crutches and acts like they've set off a trip wire, but what if it's my expression that makes them think they have? Maybe my face isn't as blank as the rest of me.

His grimace deepens. "I reiterate my offer to punch me."

"What is it with this weird joke?"

"Not joking."

"Yes you are," I say, scowling.

Silence forms. I wait to slide back into blankness like

always when I'm not being forced to pay attention, but instead I'm practically caffeinated, microfocusing on Eliot's elbow propped against the window. It's cold for March, but he has no jacket.

"How's your face?" I find myself asking.

"Expected worse. Anthony's an ENTJ—the Maverick. Charismatic, elaborate, perfectionist. He knows how to get people to do what he wants, and he's violent with whoever threatens him because it's the fastest way to send a message."

I picture No-Moore in third grade with peanut butter–smudged cheeks. "Then why did you warn him?"

"I like him." He grins. "We have a lot in common."

One cares more than anything that everyone thinks he's cool, and one makes sure everyone thinks he's weird. "So you knew he was going to punch you and you let him because . . . ?"

"I'm the type to say things. If others don't like it, they can handle it however they want."

I can't politely phrase the question on my tongue: *What's wrong with you?* There has to be a name for it, some diagnosis with a Wikipedia page. But apparently I'm not the type who says things. Instead I ask, "Which Myers-Briggs thing are you?"

He looks at me sideways. "Guess."

"Um—"

"Not *now*. You barely remember what they are. Do your research first."

"Okay?"

2 3

"This is the longest conversation I've had with anyone from school," he notes suddenly. "Thanks again for Monday. You're good with those crutches."

"You're good at making people want to punch you."

His smile's surprisingly genuine. It's crooked, breaking the symmetry of his face. I can't figure out if I like him or not. If I do, that's concerning.

And then I'm saying, "I had self-defense lessons two years ago. My sister made me take them with her. I can teach you how to block."

"That would involve spending time with me."

"Well . . . yeah."

"Interesting," he says. Then he sort of laughs.

"What?"

"*Interesting* isn't usually a word I use to describe people."

It'd be so easy to dislike him. Liking him has to be against the rules.

"Are you going to ask what type you are?" he says.

He was obviously waiting. "Fine. What type am I?"

He stops at a light, tips his head languidly against his seat, and gazes at me. His eyes are neon. I shift away.

"ISFJ. The Defender," he says finally.

"I haven't taken the quiz."

"It's not a *quiz*," he snaps. "And self-administered personality tests are nonsense. An assessment needs to be objective, and you can't be objective about yourself."

"You're guessing my personality type after five minutes with me," I point out. "It's not like you know me better than I do."

"It is like that."

He's not a loner because he doesn't talk—it's because of what happens when he *does* talk. "What's my favorite color?"

"Trivia," he snorts. "Look, you're exposed to all kinds of information that warps your perspective. Old versions of yourself that haven't been you in years, private thoughts you judge yourself for. You're in the worst position to give yourself a fair assessment."

"Nice theory," I sniff, mimicking my sister. "Why does my personality type even matter? It doesn't tell you anything about my life."

"Of course it does. You don't visit your mom's grave with your family, do you? ISFJs don't like people to see them upset."

I work around the thickness in my throat. "That's creepy."

His hand tightens on the wheel.

"And also kind of brilliant. Are you, like, a genius?"

"More or less," he says happily, slowing to let a tailgater pass. "Though the teachers here would disagree. They wouldn't notice intelligence if it told them their classes are a waste of time."

"I'm sure it has."

"You just have to watch people. They don't hide as much as they think. Like your expression."

I inspect my face in the rearview mirror. Same heavy eyebrows, stupid snub nose.

"You have an injured look." He taps ash absently out the

window. "You see it with traumatized people. Don't worry, it's not obvious."

How can I be traumatized by something I can't remember? I take the antidepressants, I go to school, I'm fine. I open my mouth, but I'm distracted by the fact that the street we're on is unfamiliar. I realize I never gave him my address.

"We're making a stop first," Eliot says. "I need your help with something. Nothing much. Just drug dealers."

"You mean Anthony and his group? Remember Monday when he punched you in the face?"

"That's why I brought you."

"Wait, what?" Sure, Sam, get in the car with the freaky dude who says he hates lying and owes you one. I guess "The Defender" makes him think I'm a bodyguard. "Number one, I can't fight anyone off for you. I'm on crutches—"

"Which is convenient. Otherwise you'd be weaponless."

"*Number two.* What are you meeting with them for?"

"Anthony asked me to. And I was curious."

I've never been stunned into silence before. There has to be a medication he's supposed to be on.

"If you really want me to, I'll take you home," he says.

"And you'll have a nice chat with Violence-Before-Words Anthony, who probably thinks you're the one who narced, because you're curious."

"Correct."

"I'm not coming."

He's not my responsibility. And after what happened at school, surely Anthony is in jail, or under house arrest, or whatever happens to people who get arrested—just not around to harass Eliot.

But his friends are. And they're worse than Anthony, some of them. They'll do more than punch him once if they think he got Anthony arrested.

"Never mind, I'm coming," I growl at the exact moment he says, "Yes you are."

He smirks maddeningly and adds, "ISFJ." I'm tempted to change my mind, but he parks before I can.

Anthony's neighborhood is full of huge white houses spaced apart with hedges so the neighbors' marital disputes don't interrupt each other. His friends are rich kids who realized they could make more cash selling pills to high schoolers than going to college. One of them owns the house on the corner—his parents moved to Cancun and gave it to him. I used to pick up Rex here when he was too blitzed, when Anthony was a freshman and Rex started trailing after him instead of the other way around.

Eliot knocks. It's fascinating, watching an insane person do insane things. Like a TV show. Except I go blank during shows, and right now my brain is 100 percent accounted for.

A guy with red-rimmed eyes and a Beer with Me T-shirt answers. "What do you want?"

"I'm Eliot," says Eliot.

"So?"

"Anthony asked me to meet him." He steps sideways. "This is Rex's sister."

I wave weakly.

Inside, it's clear that a bunch of insane twentysomethings have unleashed their hormone-and-drug-influenced life choices on this house. An empty birdcage perches on top of a million pizza boxes, a scraggly dude puffs on a hookah and stacks beer cans, and a black cat shreds the curtains. Spray-painted on the wall are the words *DON'T LET THE COPS IN OR THE CAT OUT*. But I don't see any of Anthony's crazier friends.

Beer with Me Guy points at Eliot, the stairs, and then me. "Rex's sister, you are welcome to refreshments."

He indicates a spilled box of Cheez-Its and a bottle of Mountain Dew on the scarred coffee table. Eliot strides upstairs before I can remind him I'm his bodyguard. When I follow, the guy stops me. "Business only."

I sit on the couch. A patch of unidentified wetness soaks my jeans and I jerk back up. The bearded guy on the other end, who I thought was sleeping, clears his throat with hazy recognition. "'M sorry for your loss," he says.

I crush a Cheez-It under my toe and text Rex:

Are you upstairs in this dump?

He responds: I'm at Tito's vet appt, what dump

Anthony's friend's house, I text.

wtf are you doing there

Protecting Eliot, apparently by being downstairs while he gets murdered upstairs. I guess Rex hasn't heard about

Anthony's arrest. They've been phasing him out ever since he became nonfunctional. The moron's not even a good drug dealer.

I'm counting beer cans (thirty-three) when Anthony himself comes down the stairs, smiling a lot for someone who was recently hauled out of school by the cops.

"I thought you were in Guantanamo Bay," I say. Everyone else either cowers or sucks up to Anthony, so I avoid both.

"Thank you for your concern, Samantha." He halts at the base of the stairs. "This is an eighteen-and-up establishment."

"I'm making sure you don't punch anyone in the face."

He laughs softly. "You're Eliot's security now?"

"Not on purpose."

"Go home, Samantha Herring." These days he talks to me like I'm way younger, even though we're both seniors.

"He said you asked him to meet you, and he said yes for no reason that I can figure out."

He goes practically incandescent with pity. "He's here to buy."

I squash a few more Cheez-Its. The mystery of Eliot is solved, and there's no diagnosis. He warned Anthony because he was afraid of losing his source. He dragged me here because even though he's a rich pill-abusing kid, the rich pill-abusing crowd hates him.

When someone is rejected by the whole world, including their own group, there's usually a reason for it.

I'm weirdly disappointed.

"He said he hated lying," I mutter like an idiot.

"Never trust anyone who says they don't lie. That's just insurance." He rubs my shoulder, even though I'm supposed to be on his shit list. "Rex always bragged about how you were too good for this. Don't waste that on a guy like Eliot, acting like he's proving something by being such a freak."

I haven't felt this stupid since Lena told me what a blow job was.

His grip tightens. "When we were little, I always thought of you as my baby sister. What kind of good brother would let his sister hang out here? I'll give you that ride home."

I sink into the moldy couch. I never get to yell at people, and Eliot's not even a family member or a friend—just an ex-possibility. "I still don't trust your driving skills after you rammed Rex's plastic truck into our doghouse."

I mean it friendly, but his face sharpens. He snatches keys off the top of a broken grandfather clock and bangs out the door without a word, the echo ripping around the house.

What the hell was that?

In the kitchen, it sounds like someone is putting a chain in a blender. After a minute I realize it's heavy metal music. I take advantage of Beer with Me's absence to go upstairs, a clunky affair that I'm glad the dude on the couch is too stoned to register. I open the only closed door. It's the luckiest time I've ever opened a door, because two of Anthony's crazier friends are holding Eliot. Or rather,

3 0

one of them is holding him and one seems to have recently stopped hitting him.

And I understand why they turned on the music.

And that Anthony is full of shit.

"Put him down." My voice shakes. I wish it wouldn't.

"This is how we handle these situations," says the first guy, who was a senior when I was a freshman and got expelled for choking someone.

I yank out my keys. Before Lena left, she loaded my key ring with three things she said every woman should have: pepper spray, a whistle, and a penknife. The second guy laughs, presumably at the five-foot-four girl on crutches wielding a one-inch knife. Which is fair. I'm not the type you rely on for protection.

But maybe Eliot hadn't had anyone else to ask.

"It's fine," says Eliot with mild irritation, like I offered him a drink too many times. Blood trickles from his lip.

"I'm calling the police," I say hoarsely.

"I don't think you should do that," says the first guy.

"Then put him *down.*"

He does, shrugging. Eliot crumples soundlessly to the ground.

"If he's dead, you killed him. I'm telling Rex," I gasp, which comes out exactly as ineffectual as you'd expect.

The first guy sighs. "What do you care about this asshole?"

"He's my friend," I lie.

The second guy shrugs again, and they both step around

me. I wait until they've left. Then I stagger on my crutches, breathing deep like Dr. Brown said, before lowering myself to the floor beside Eliot.

He opens his eyes. They stand out like alien beacons against the blood. "Sam."

"Okay. Good. Good. I can't carry you. Can you get up?"

"Yes," he says, but doesn't move.

I do the deep breathing. "Okay." By balancing on one crutch, I drag him upright. He pulls away stubbornly, but then he either slips or collapses and we both crash down.

"I'm sorry," he whispers.

"You hate apologizing, remember?"

Somehow I get us downstairs. Eliot doesn't wince once. Anthony's two friends are gone, probably worried that I actually will call the cops.

"I'm bringing you to the hospital," I say as soon as we're outside.

"No hospital. I'm fine." His voice is normal. Zero pain.

"Give me your address then."

"Not there either."

"Then where the hell do I take you?"

"Your place."

Dad's not home yet. Rex is at Tito's checkup with the vet. It's doable. But— "Why do you want to go there?"

"You'll look after me," he says.

I stare at him, but he doesn't say anything else. Swearing, I unlock his car and dump him in the backseat. Then I climb in front, shoving my crutches over my lap. I have my permit, but haven't gone for my license SMD. My bad leg isn't the one I use to drive, but the accident messed with my driving abilities in other ways.

Only the sight of Eliot in the backseat is enough to make me turn the key.

Chapter Three

AT HOME, MY DRIVEWAY IS EMPTY. FOR A second I don't know how I ended up driving this car with this boy in the backseat, like I swapped lives with someone without noticing. "Eliot, we're here."

There's a bloodstain on the seat. He gets out, unsteady but upright. I lead him inside. Back when I had friends and they'd come over, I'd launch into explanations for our mismatched furniture, but this isn't the moment for craigslist war stories.

It's the first time a boy has been in my room, but Eliot probably doesn't qualify as a boy in the *boy* sense. I shove aside dirty clothes on my bed to make space. I've taken care of enough injured teammates to know what to do. "How's your head?"

"More functional than most."

"Are you dizzy?"

"What about you? Are you all right?"

"Answer, don't ask."

"Typical ISFJ, playing doctor."

"Oh, Jesus. Tell me what just happened. Do you remember?"

"You were there."

"*Eliot.*"

"I may not have thought it through. But that's a rarity, I promise."

"That is so obviously a true thing you just said." I shine my phone flashlight in Eliot's face. He squints. Regular dilation. "I don't think you have a concussion. Does anything feel broken?"

"Just my dignity."

"It'll recover." I dip a clean sock in the glass of water on my bedside table and wipe blood off his jaw.

"Thank you," he says quietly.

"I think you'd better just shower. It's on the left. Clean towels are on the rack by the sink."

"Does your dad know you're inviting strange boys over to shower?"

Only the strangest. "I'd like to think you move to acquaintanceship after saving someone twice."

He stands. I expect him to finally flinch—he hasn't even said *ow*—but nope. Is he hiding his pain for my sake? "I feel the need to point out that I was right again. About bringing you." He addresses the wall. "You're a decent bodyguard."

"Maybe you could pay me back by avoiding stupid situations."

"What else is there to do around here?" he says, the smirk returning, and leaves. A minute later, there comes the sound of water running. I lie across my bed and listen to my heartbeat slow down.

Anthony was lying. Eliot doesn't take pills. He doesn't have to be an ex-possibility.

Except he didn't tell me where we were going. I was supposed to find a new friend to keep me safe—socially anyway. Someone with a spot at their cafeteria table who doesn't abuse the word *sorry*. Eliot fulfills this requirement, but he's also a lunatic.

Eventually I realize it's been ages since the shower turned on. If he passed out and I have to administer CPR to his naked body— But then he steps into the room, bare chested.

"Could you relocate my shoulder?" he asks casually. "And lend me a clean shirt?"

I can't speak. He's covered in scars. Old ones, new ones, jagged ones, thin white ones patterning his sides and stomach and everywhere else. And his shoulder looks wrong. It's swollen and pointy.

He should be in the hospital. He should be in *agony*.

"I thought you might know how since you know sports injuries. If not, I can show you."

"What—you—? You definitely need to go to the hospital!"

"It's easy. Easier for someone else, though, which is why I was hoping—"

"How are you not screaming in pain?" I can't believe I didn't take him to the *hospital*.

"I don't feel pain."

"What?"

"I have congenital insensitivity to pain with anhidrosis."

"What?" I repeat.

"It's a problem with my nerve fibers," he says impatiently. "Now I'm going to lie on the floor, and all you have to do is—"

"Insensitivity to pain with what? Are you serious?"

"It's a rare condition." He looks tired. So tired that I stop the questions from flying out of my mouth. He has to be lying, right? Invulnerability to pain isn't a rare condition— it's a superpower.

Still stunned, I say, "So you lie down and—?"

I end up sitting with my good foot in his armpit. It's the least sexually compromising setup in the world, but if Rex comes home, he'll find a way to make it inappropriate.

"Now pull on my arm," Eliot instructs.

"It'll hurt."

"It won't."

His skin's warm and soft from the shower. I privately catalog the tiny scars on his fingers, his palms. Where did they come from? Most don't look neat enough to be self-harm, which means he's either been cage fighting lions or he's incredibly careless.

After a minute of steady pulling, with Eliot gazing

at the ceiling like he's at the dentist's, there's a pop. He straightens.

I pinch his ankle. "That doesn't hurt at all?"

He frowns. "No."

My most wanted superpower is real. I choke on a laugh. I can't help it. "That's amazing. You're so lucky."

"Yes, very lucky. Thanks for the joint relocation. I should be going."

"Wait, I want to talk to you." I feel an obsession hatching, like the time Rex took me to Anthony's middle school lacrosse game and I tracked the ball from start to finish. But then Eliot's frown deepens, so I reroute. "About your death wish. They could have killed you. They dislocated your *shoulder*."

He rotates it experimentally. "They were holding me like idiots, that's all. They wouldn't have done any permanent damage."

"You don't know that."

"I did. I brought you."

My annoyance is vaporizing in the face of his inability to take care of himself. "You're saying it's fine if they beat you up, but as long as they don't kill you—"

"I don't feel it. It doesn't matter. And it's hilarious how pissed off they get when they realize they can't do anything to me."

He has a point. How do you hurt someone who doesn't care what you think of him, doesn't care what you say to him, and doesn't care if you attack him?

He sighs at my expression. "People hit something and they feel better. It's convenient to be something that doesn't mind getting hit. I wanted Anthony to get over his issues."

"I figured you had an ulterior motive for going, but considering that you're smart I assumed it was a good one."

"Isn't it?"

"He thinks *you* narced and got him arrested, not Trez. There was this freshman last year—all he did was steal a couple pills. He ended up in the hospital." It's usually not hard to laugh at Anthony playing mafia, but I'm realizing how dangerous he might actually be.

He picks up a plastic toy from my dresser. "My Little Pony. Interesting."

"It's from when I was— Forget it. You can't let people treat you like a human punching bag just because it doesn't hurt. It'd be easier to avoid pissing them off."

"Easier for some."

"Just be nicer."

"People waste their lives trying to find the right thing to say."

I groan. "Why didn't you tell him it was Trez?"

"I imagine I can handle the retribution better." He holds the toy horse up to his face and imitates its vacant wink. I can't stand looking at his scars anymore, so I go down the hall and pillage Rex's room for one of his least-favorite shirts. When I get back, I throw it at Eliot, along with a point. "Health problems. You'll have them when you're older if you let people beat you up."

It was Mom's end-of-debate card: eat the spinach or you'll have health problems when you're older. Stretch before practice or you'll have health problems when you're older. Take the fish oil or YHHPWYO. Except having health problems when you're older doesn't matter if you get creamed by a car at forty-five.

The shirt is too big on Eliot. He's not muscled-thin, but angles-thin, breakable like something beautiful made of glass. "My life is a health problem."

"Come on." I chuckle. "Not feeling pain, that's not a health problem—that's a miracle."

He stiffens. "I don't want to get so old I can't think. My goal is to live efficiently. And that means cutting out stupidity like saying things I don't believe to people I don't respect, and—this conversation."

I fold my arms. "Has it ever occurred to you that people would be upset if you died?"

"No," he says, surprised. "It's not a factor."

"Why not?"

"Because nobody would be upset."

I say the automatic thing: "I would be upset."

He squints. "You would?"

"Yeah," I say defiantly.

"You'd put flowers on my casket and wear a black dress and listen to a minister call me an upstanding citizen?"

"I'd order a hundred baskets of flowers and carry the casket and get ordained as the freaking minister if it would convince you not to be so dumb."

He stares. Then he tips back his head and laughs, wet hair trailing moisture into his eyes.

This funeral could be way less hypothetical if Anthony continues his campaign of revenge. But there's one person who might be able to convince him not to put Eliot in an early grave, and luckily that person is me.

Rex gets home after dark. The only person with less grace than me on crutches is Rex when he's high. I listen to him crash into the living-room cabinet, mistake it for someone named Jeremiah, and threaten to kick its ass. I'm readying for intervention, because if he sticks his fist through the glass, I'll have to drive him to the emergency room, but then his bedroom door bangs shut.

Dad arrives even later. He moves like he's haunting his own house: silent, but filling every inch. He pads upstairs, and I launch myself into bed just as he peeks into my room. I fake sleep-breathing. His gaze is like a screw tightening until I'm about to scream, but then he leaves, shutting the door softly behind him.

I scroll through my phone under the covers. Eliot is the first new contact I've added in months. I type "disorder where you can't feel pain" into Safari, and after ten minutes of reading, I'm listing all the working limbs I'd trade to undo saying he was lucky.

Over half of all sufferers die before the age of three. The rest often do not make it past twenty-five years. . . .

. . . can't sense heat or cold, so heat stroke and febrile seizures are common . . .

Most people with CIPA have some form of mild mental problems, but not all. . . .

. . . statistically the most fatal kind of the seven types of hereditary sensory and autonomic neuropathy . . .

No wonder he claims he doesn't want to get old. It's probably easier than facing the fact that he might not have a choice.

I spend another minute energetically hating myself, and then I google his full name. I'm struck by an article captioned with a picture of a dark-haired little boy with a swollen eye and his arm in a sling. He's grinning like he just won a fight.

Six-year-old Eliot Rowe is one of about a hundred people worldwide affected by a rare genetic disorder that prevents him from feeling pain.

"Infections, injuries . . . we never know something's wrong unless it's obvious from the outside," said his mother. "He broke his elbow and we didn't realize for two days. Once he almost chewed off his tongue. Not to mention all the tests. . . . It's beyond exhausting."

As a baby, he rarely cried. Researchers have studied him and are attempting to develop more effective painkillers via gene sequencing.

"It's fascinating because we get to observe the

relationship between physical and emotional pain," noted a psychologist who has been working with the family. "Will his emotional development be stunted?"

Eliot's older brother, sixteen, offered a counterpoint: "When our dog got run over, he cried for a week."

"A normal kid who touches a hot stove once will never do it again," continued his mother. "Eliot doesn't understand what the problem is. He looks at us like we're crazy when we tell him no."

Children with the condition often experience repeated injury. Pain serves an important evolutionary purpose: it teaches avoidance.

"What do you think when you see someone in pain?" we asked Eliot. He shrugged and said, "Ow."

"What is ow?"

After seemingly thinking about it, he couldn't answer us.

Oh, Eliot.

I text him: I'm sorry.

He responds in seconds: It's fine.

What are his mom and brother like? The brother's twenty-seven now. Obviously they've never figured out how to keep Eliot safe. That's probably impossible.

I google "Myers-Briggs." I'm supposed to be guessing which type Eliot is, but I don't even remember what the letters stand for. I find an infographic. *E* stands for Extraversion, and *I* is Introversion. *S* is for Sensing, which apparently means you like things more concrete, versus *N* for Intuition, if you're more figurative. . . . I rub my eyes. Eliot's definitely introverted anyway. Then there's *T* for Thinking, and *F* for Feeling. . . .

Which one did he say I was—ISFJ? I read the description: **Loyal, responsible, forgiving, pragmatic. Devoted caretakers who enjoy being helpful to others.**

That sounds more like my sister than me. Or at least how she'd like to be. All the summaries sound like ways people would like to view themselves. No wonder everyone loves personality types. It's probably nice to see something good and decide that's what you are.

Eliot saw something good in me, apparently. But he doesn't know me. I scan descriptions for one that sounds more accurate, but none are. Where's the type for *mentally checked out and usually in a bad mood*?

I can't decide which one is Eliot's. Which is probably because I don't know him either.

But I do know one thing, and it's that the blankness that I usually feel went away the second I got into his car and it hasn't come back.

Chapter Four

THE NEXT MORNING, I BANG ON REX'S DOOR with my crutch. "Wake up, sunshine."

"Dear sweet baby Christ," I hear him groan loudly. "It's Saturday."

"I need Anthony's number."

There's a curse, a crash, and he appears. I scream.

"What?" he says, like he's not plastered in mud, like his eyes aren't a supervillain shade of red, like his nose isn't broken.

"I think your nose is broken."

He swears and gropes for the bulbous thing in the center of his face. "I fell."

"You should get that looked at. Seriously."

He ignores my plea and swipes a bottle of ibuprofen from

his dresser. "Why do you need Anthony's number?"

Dr. Brown told me that grief is like a dying lightbulb. Sometimes it's dark for an hour, sometimes it sputters for a day, and sometimes it seems fine before giving out when you least expect it. I feel the tears in my throat. Before the accident, Rex was a morning person.

"Aw, shit, Sam," he says guiltily.

I scrub my face. "I just need the number."

He wavers between being a dick and ignoring my tears, or being an asshole and noticing them. The first wins, but he tries to make up for it by turning up the dial on Big Brother Mode. "Tell me why you were at that house yesterday. Is Anthony trying to get with you? He knows you're off-limits."

"First, you don't get to decide who I'm off-limits to. Second, *ew*. Third, fucking *ew*. And fourth, I'm not telling you why I need his number, but you're giving it to me because you owe me."

"For what?"

"For not doing this." I lean back toward the stairs. *"Dad!"*

Rex tenses all over like a cat and hisses like one, too. "Shutupshutup—"

"Give me the number," I hiss back in similar cat fashion.

"Like hell—"

"Dad!" I bellow. "You better come up here."

"What's wrong, Sam?" he calls back faintly from the kitchen.

Rex grabs my arm. "No, shut your mouth—I just have to clean myself up—"

"Da-aad—"

"Fine, fuck you, fine," and he shoves his phone in my face.

Dad's head appears at the bottom of the stairs, and Rex hurtles back into his room. There's flour on Dad's shirt. My heart sinks. He's cooking, which means he's trying to Make Changes, which means he's going to bug me to go back to physical therapy.

"Sorry. Thought I saw a spider," I say in my singsongy for-Dad voice.

"Oh." He sags in relief, not remembering that I've been the spider killer of the house since I was seven. He puts on his Since Mom Died smile. It doesn't fit his face right yet. "I'm making pancakes. Tell Rex to come down when he's ready."

Rex never eats breakfast, but grief made Dad forgetful. He forgets I don't like Chinese food, that I'm allergic to strawberries. But I don't mind the blank slate. It's a chance to remake myself into someone who suits him better.

I chase Rex into his room, which is as messy as mine, except my trash can isn't full of tissues and I don't have a poster of a model humping a car. He glowers at me from his bed like a hungover gremlin. "You're not allowed in here."

I find Anthony's number on his phone and put it in mine as he tears through his room for clothes, unearthing a bag of pills in the process. He's kept his habit secret from Dad, though it's not hard. He'll go downstairs in twenty minutes with a clean-shaven face and a funny story about tripping over Tito to explain his nose.

He surfaces with chili-pepper-patterned boxers clenched in his fist. "I thought I told you to stay away from Anthony."

I bathe him in my haughtiest Lena glare before leaving.

The kitchen is full of good smells that shouldn't make me feel this sick. Dad is stirring batter. Three glasses of orange juice are on the table, surrounded by four chairs. I swallow. It takes me five seconds to work my face into my own SMD smile, which is my number-one tool for dealing with Dad and which I have perfected through trial and error.

"Sam," he says. There used to be lots of ways he would say my name: a happy "Sam!" or "Sam-antha Herring" if I stayed out too late. Now it's just the careful—

"Sam, what kind of pancakes would you like?"

"Chocolate chip, please!" I beam. Everything I say to Dad is dangerously close to being a musical number.

He upends a bag of Nestlé chips into the bowl. Mom would have said, "Everyone wait. I'm getting a vision of the future—it involves dental visits—" and the lightbulb flickers, but it's against the rules to cry in front of Dad. He'll think I'm falling apart again, and I'll go crazy trying to act like I'm not crazy.

"I thought we could have a family breakfast." He pours batter into the pan. There's a mug of coffee next to the blender, which nobody uses anymore—Mom was the smoothie person—but caffeine can't disguise the bags under his eyes. "I was hoping Lena would get here early, but she's stuck in traffic. She ought to be here in time for our appointment, though. Did you do your list of goals?"

I nod and pull out a chair as Tito nudges my leg. There's no traffic on Saturday mornings—Lena is just an expert at timing her arrival so she doesn't have to spend any more time with us than therapy mandates.

"Dr. Brown is very good?" Dad was always a nervous up-talker, but it's gotten worse SMD.

"Yeah, really good."

The pancakes look exhausting, like slabs of flesh. I yell for Rex, but the shower is still running. Traitor.

"How's school?" Dad's scared it's awful and I'll be honest about it.

"School is *amazing*. And I hung out with Kendra yesterday."

It's not that Dad is inherently fragile. It's that he's so terrified of me being fragile that it makes him fragile. It's my fault. I spent the winter in my room with the lights off, and he's still scanning the sky for the bomb that will send me back inside my bunker. But I've learned that coming out of your room doesn't mean you have to come out of your own head.

"I'm glad you still spend time with those girls. I was worried about that because you had to leave the team. . . ." He rubs Tito's ears. "Things are going well?"

"So well." I start counting the swans in the wallpaper. I've gotten up to seven hundred and fifty-four. One day I'll know exactly how many there are.

I take a bite of my pancake, which is mostly chocolate. People say grief turns food to ash in your mouth, but it's just that you get sad when food is good. Like, *She'll never taste this*, or *She'll never see how pretty the sky looks today*, until everything nice makes you want to cry.

Dad opens the vitamin cupboard. Mom's expired supplements are in the back. She hated the way the pills felt going down but said she planned on going hiking with her great-grandchildren. People who think flaxseed oil will make them immortal should be warned: it's not worth it. Switch to junk food like my dad. Your Omega-3 intake doesn't matter when a car hits you.

Dad wordlessly gives me my antidepressant bottle. I take one pill and hand the bottle back and he puts it away, a practiced gesture that both of us pretend is happening to someone else. He tosses Tito his cheese-wrapped pills, too. This whole family is medicated.

"So I was thinking it might be good to make some changes around here," Dad starts. "I called the doctor, and he says he has a physical therapy appointment open—"

"Breakfast was delicious, but I gotta run," I interrupt. "I'm meeting with Kendra for a group project."

"What class?"

I miss not having to worry about being a good liar. "Biology. Frog dissection thing. Can you give me a ride? We're meeting at McDonald's."

We both hear the joke Mom would have made, like a

record playing, about how a dead frog soaked in formaldehyde is probably more nutritional than a Big Mac. SMD, our conversations are full of moments of silence for the comments she'd have contributed.

He places the dishes in the sink and says, a little confused, "Grab your jacket."

The car ride is only slightly awkward, a teaser for the ride we'll all take to the therapist's office later. I blank out the way I should have in Eliot's car yesterday, and Dad doesn't bring up physical therapy again.

The McDonald's in our town is semifamous. They were going to tear down a town landmark, this old Greco-Roman house, but Mom was part of the protest. They ended up putting their restaurant inside the original building, so there's waxy floors and a soda machine in a house that looks like it belongs to an heiress. BMD, Rex worked here, but now he can't even hold down a job at McDonald's.

As soon as I have my greasy bag, I call Anthony.

"How did you get my number, Samantha Herring?" he asks immediately, which means he had mine.

"We have to talk about yesterday. Meet me at McDonald's—I bought you a Big Mac. You used to beg my mom for these, remember?"

"I'll have to pass, due to the unfortunate shortage of shits I give."

I crunch a fry audibly. "These fries are so fresh. Like ridiculously. And all crispy—"

He yawns into the phone. "I haven't had breakfast."

Anthony's one weakness is fast food. Fifteen minutes later, he walks in behind a mom and her kids. He's on the phone. I wave his Big Mac meal, and he saunters toward me, still chatting.

"I talked to Principal Chase. She loves me—she's suspending me for two weeks, no expulsion." Silence. "No, Mom, I'm not expecting you to fly—" Then he stops talking and stares at the phone. His mom must have hung up. He glances up and recovers. "How can I help you, Samantha?"

I squash the anger in my stomach. "Leave Eliot Rowe alone."

"I can't leave someone alone who I haven't touched since Monday." He grabs the bag, not bothering to acknowledge his lie from yesterday.

"Your friends hurt him because you told them to."

"Do you know why I sell pills?" he asks. "I don't need the money. But people need medicine, which means they need me. Not everyone is lucky enough to have a problem they can get a prescription for. So when Eliot Rowe puts my business at risk, he's putting my clients at risk. You've known me a long time—I'm not a bad guy. I'm just ensuring this never happens again. Looking after the people who've come to me for help, because they respect that I'll come through."

He smiles at the girl behind the counter who's been checking him out. His appearance is disorienting sometimes. You want to believe the best of people who look that good. It's like brainwashing. "Eliot didn't narc."

"I know you're smart, and you know I'm smart, so we can talk facts, correct? And here they are: I don't store anything in my locker. Obviously. But Principal Chase found weed there on an anonymous tip. I don't even fucking sell weed."

"He didn't do it," I snap.

"Do you know what loyalty is when you give it to people who don't deserve it? It's stupidity. Stay smart, Samantha."

The best way to deal with Anthony's silky voice is to throw up a blank wall, which is good, because I'm a walking one. *"It wasn't him."*

"Then it's a fascinating coincidence that I got arrested the day after he threatened me."

"He wasn't *threatening* you—" I'm about to bring up Trez, but I remember what Eliot said about her not being able to handle the retribution. I squeeze my leg under the table.

"If Principal Chase wasn't as willing to make exceptions for top students, this could have affected my Yale acceptance." He's sipping his soda calmly, but a shiver runs through me.

"Drop it or I'll tell the cops what your friends did."

"Then I'll tell them Rex sold me the weed in my locker," he says easily. "Are we done with this game?"

It's not Dad's reaction I imagine but Lena's. Rex isn't underage anymore. He could go to jail. I know Anthony's different now, but somehow I thought we'd always be safe from him. "You'd do that to him?"

"You'd call the cops on me?" He sounds genuinely

wounded. "Eliot gets your loyalty after a week, and I don't have it after years?"

He's actually making me feel guilty. "It's not like we even still talk at school."

"I'm a certain person at school." He doesn't say *but*, but he doesn't need to. I don't fit that person anymore. I fit No-Moore, and Anthony's so desperate not to be him that he's become the opposite.

"I care about you, Sam," he says softly after a minute.

I shift. "Just don't hit Eliot anymore. He has a health problem."

He rips open a ketchup packet with his teeth. "He looks fine to me."

I'm not going to get anywhere. I should have realized that from the beginning. I hook my crutches under my armpits and stand.

"Don't burn yourself out for Eliot," he says. "People like him don't care about anyone else. They're not programmed to."

"People like him?" Past the toy display case, the mom stares at me. I guess I was loud.

He bites the last fry in half. "Retards."

I am so grateful that he hasn't finished his drink.

"Fuck!" He jumps up as I plant my crutch back on solid ground. Luckily he's wearing a nice shirt. The brown Coke stain spreads fast. His eyes lock on me, and I get this shooting feeling, like I'm prey and he's a predator. Our history doesn't mean I'm safe.

"Careful, Anthony." The mom is still watching us.

"Attacking the girl on crutches, it's not a good look."

"I regret that you did that." The scariest thing about Anthony is how easily he switches from tropical warmth to Antarctic cold. I don't know which is real. No-Moore wasn't capable of either.

"I regret that you didn't get hot coffee."

I swing out of McDonald's, feeling like such a badass that I don't even care I'll have to hide out in the J.Crew across the street for whatever stretch of time is a believable amount for a biology project.

When they come for me, Lena is driving. She parks in a handicapped spot, which annoys me even though we have the card. Rex is so slouched in the backseat that all I can see is the one piece of hair that always stands up no matter how often Lena presses it down.

"Samantha!"

When I was twelve, I didn't speak to Lena for a month because she refused to call me Sam. Then I gave up. Everyone gives up around Lena. She puts people under siege.

She gets out of the car and hugs me. She's pencil thin in her pencil skirt, with a pencil behind her ear. "How are you doing?" she says with neighborly sympathy instead of she-was-my-mom-too empathy.

"Fine," I say into her giant boobs, the only nonpencilly part of her.

"How's school?" she fires off.

"Fine."

"I am truly interested in your life, Samantha."

"I learn stuff; there's teachers." What do people want you to say when they ask how school is? School is school. They went there, too.

She steps back. SMD, I feel swoopy when I look at her, probably because she's a twenty-three-year-old skinny version of Mom. Same softness to their cheeks that echoes my total roundness, same warm tint to their dark hair, same greenish eyes. But today, Lena's face is buried under an inch of chalky concealer two shades too light. And there's something else—

"Are you wearing contacts?"

She squints self-consciously, which is the first time I've ever seen someone successfully be self-conscious about their eyeballs. "The glasses felt too *intern*. I want my boss to know I'm aiming higher."

Her irises are mud brown. "They're colored contacts."

"They look more practical." She frowns haughtily at the curb. "Can you get into the car? I keep telling Dad to get a minivan with a lift."

Which I'm sure the minivan-with-a-lift fairies will pay for. "I'm not paralyzed."

My tone freezes her. I freeze back. Rex-versus-Lena fights are a well-worn path, but BMD, Sam-versus-Lena was uncharted territory, and we still don't have a map. I used to keep out of her way, and she used to have other charity projects.

She busts through the silence. "Let me help you." And she completely unnecessarily opens the door for me and half hoists me inside.

"Hello, my-sister-who-is-not-an-invalid-and-does-not-need-to-be-treated-like-one." Rex glares out the window like it's the window's fault he's sober.

"Reginald—"

"*Rex*," he says with his teeth mashed together. He's the only one who does not give up around Lena.

"To my-brother-who-is-not-a-carnivorous-dinosaur," Lena says waspishly, "please move over so I can make room for our noninvalid sister's *crutches*."

"How was the bio project, Sam? Frog dissection, wasn't it?" asks Dad in the voice of ultimate defeat.

"They still dissect frogs?" Lena cries. "But I wrote a letter to the administration my senior year."

"Damn, a letter to the administration. They're probably still holding each other and pissing their pants." Rex wedges himself deeper into the seat. "They're frogs, Lena. Frogs."

"Frogs are living creatures."

"Not these ones," I reassure her.

We drive off to a hearty discussion about the ethics of frog dissection. Halfway there, Dad intervenes with the only topic (Tito) on which the Herring family can reach a firm consensus (good, great, awesome). "How was Tito's appointment yesterday, Rex?"

"Doc wants to up his medication dose. He's worried another seizure might kill him since he's so old. It'll be eighty a month instead of fifty."

Dad sucks in air, at the price or Tito's mortality, I don't know. As far as I'm concerned, Tito is a universal constant.

"Eighty a *month*?" says Lena.

Rex's eyes flash. "Is there an issue?"

Lena opens her mouth, but even she doesn't dare. Lena was the one who convinced Mom to adopt him. She was volunteering at the shelter, and nobody else wanted him because he was so ugly. He somehow figured out that he owed his new home to Lena and followed her everywhere. But SMD, for no apparent reason, Lena acts like Tito is a smelly stray who wandered into our house.

We spend the rest of the ride in silence. By the time we get there, I would consider jumping off the high gray roof if it wouldn't depress Dad. Once again, Lena acts like extracting me from the car is a medical procedure, and I distract her by making a deal with the devil and asking about her internship.

"It's going *really well*!"

A pigeon takes flight at the shrill noise and meets an untimely end via the building's front window.

"The level of professionalism is amazing. Coming from an undergraduate environment, it's a wonderful change. It started as an online magazine, so it's not facing the same problems a lot of paper magazines are."

"I'm glad you're happy." Dad's so sincere it makes my heart ache. Lena gives a small smile and looks away.

"Did that pigeon just die?" Rex whispers to me.

"I'm jealous of it," I whisper back.

We wait in the lobby, Rex and Lena sitting like a before-and-after ad for posture improvement training. Dad puts his arm awkwardly around me and hums along with Bach. The lobby, with its stained ceiling and plastic chairs, has given me an everlasting hatred of classical music.

"Reginald," says Lena very politely, "have you been looking at college applications? It's easier than you think to get your GED out of the way first."

"Lena," he says with equal politeness, "go fuck yourself."

"Kids," says Dad halfheartedly. The receptionist spies on us over her stack of manila folders.

I used to be their buffer, but SMD, I'm not sturdy enough to stand between them. Dad's been working our whole lives and never developed the necessary parenting skills, and Mom was too much of a hippie to tell them to shut up. Now when they fight and I don't insert myself as a cushion, Dad's response is silence on a bad day and a weak "Kids" on a good day. Today must be a good day. At least when Lena's on Rex's back about college, she's not on mine.

"I don't think we should enable Reginald by calling him a kid, Dad. He's nineteen, and two years wasted on that disgusting couch is two too many—"

"You're not that much older than me!" Rex snarls.

"I believe that maturity is measured by education and experience, not years, Reginald."

"My name. Is. *Rex.*"

"Let's not fight in front of Samantha," she says in a stage whisper.

"The Herrings?"

Me and Dad whip toward our savior in the doorway.

Dr. Brown is a collection of conflicting parts: bored eyes, a sympathetic furrow permanently etched between her eyebrows, and a thin, angry mouth she's always using to massacre a piece of wintergreen gum. She's the only family therapist within thirty miles who was willing to partially waive the co-pay. She's our only hope.

She herds us to the back of the building. Her room is painted a nauseating banana yellow, and her armchairs look comfortable but aren't. Legos are scattered on her carpet for her younger patients to play with and her older patients to step on.

"So what's new and exciting in the lives of the Herrings?" Her expectations are visibly low. Eliot, I think, and simultaneously vow never to bring him up.

"My boss is considering me for a permanent position once my internship ends," Lena says, almost shyly. Then she'll have an even better excuse to never visit.

"Excellent. Let's all acknowledge Lena's accomplishment." Dr. Brown doesn't have a gentle therapist's voice. It's gravelly, the voice Eliot will have if he lives long enough for his smoking to affect him. Which is exactly why he smokes, I realize suddenly—he doesn't think he will.

"I acknowledge your accomplishment, Lena," Dad and I both say. Rex's spine completes its jellification.

"Has everyone finished the homework assignment?"

Dad, Lena, and I obediently take out our lists. "Memorized it," Rex grunts.

"Why don't we start with Sam?"

I read my fake list aloud. When I look up, Dr. Brown is smiling absently. "Very good. Lena?"

Lena rattles off a list that includes nailing down the job, getting promoted once she's got the job, moving to a more expensive part of the city once she's promoted, and acquiring a cat. "An *older* cat," she emphasizes. "From a shelter." She looks hopefully at Dr. Brown, but all she says is, "Excellent. Rex?"

"A cat. Start of the decline."

Dad and I wince as Lena unsheathes a second sheet of paper. "I didn't think Reginald could be trusted to make an effective list, so I wrote one for him. Number one: get his GED and apply to a community college, at the very least—"

"Lena, first let's hear what Rex came up with."

"Yes, *Lena*," Rex mimics.

Lena rolls her brown eyes—I can't stop staring at them—and leans toward Dr. Brown like they're business partners. "He's intimidated by professional women," she confides in what might have been conceived as a whisper.

Our last appointment ended with Rex storming out. They take turns storming out. Dad is consistent, spending every one with his head retreating into his neck and occasionally raising his hands a few inches when there's no chance anybody will notice. He's never been assertive, but because Mom picked up the slack, I hadn't realized he doesn't know how to be a parent.

It's easy to sit back and watch when I'm blank. The

appointments play out like they're a TV show instead of my life. And Dad doesn't expect me to help, or contribute, just like he didn't expect me to apply to college this school year, even when the deadlines passed and I ended up missing so much school I wouldn't have been able to apply anyway. When something horrible happens to you, people stop expecting you to function, which might be why I stopped functioning.

Rex gives me the can-you-believe-her face. "Replace *intimidated* with *annoyed by* and *professional women* with *my sister the psycho bitch—*"

"Rex," I cut in. Lena made me swear to defend her if he ever used *sexist insults*, Samantha, because we're in this *together*.

"I choose to define *bitch* as a strong woman, so yes, I am a bitch," says Lena scathingly, nodding at Dr. Brown like they're cowriting a thesis on the subject. "Mom was a professional woman. I suspect his attitude stems from unresolved resentment."

Rex's spine snaps back into place. "Our insurance doesn't cover your bullshit, Lena."

Dad rips open a packet of gummy dinosaurs and drops it on the floor. I cough at Dr. Brown, but our savior is picking dead skin from her fingernails, glazed eyes on the clock. When she pays attention, she's okay, but most of the time it's like something is distracting her. Or maybe we're just not interesting enough. To be fair, Lena and Rex's fights make me go blank, too.

"All I wanted was to offer my perspective on what you're going through—" Lena begins.

"You fucked off to Northton the second Mom died, you never call, and you never visit except for these meetings, and then you think you can make up for it by mothering Sam." He snorts so hard his spit flies onto the table. "Your perspective is worth shit."

I wince. Rex is mostly an idiot, but he has a knack for figuring out the exact most hurtful thing to say. Lena paws furiously at the tears in her eyes and then gasps, plucking a contact lens off her cheek. One eye glistens green.

"I don't understand why you insist on being like this." Her trembling lower lip ruins her stiff tone. "I'm going to use the bathroom."

And she storms out.

Dr. Brown at least has the decency to look a little ashamed of her mental vacation. "I'm afraid we're out of time. I'll reschedule for your usual slot."

Dad hurries into the hall to pay the receptionist for our wasted time. Rex slumps after him. I stay. I'm required to have private sessions with Dr. Brown, and I'm the only one who recognizes the injustice of this. "You're also the only one who didn't come out of her room for months," said Rex when I complained, looking guilty. He generally follows Dad's lead in not talking about what Dr. Brown calls my Major Depressive Episode.

"That must be hard for you to sit through." Dr. Brown makes an I-am-your-friend smile. "Things are still pretty rocky between your siblings. Have they always been this way?"

"They fought, but it's worse SM . . . since Mom died." My leg twinges.

"And has your father always been so quiet?" she presses.

Comparing BMD Dad to SMD Dad makes me realize how little I know him. But it wasn't like I really knew Mom either. There's supposed to be time to get to know your parents as people when you're older. "I don't know."

"Shall we change the subject? How about we discuss the pain issue you mentioned? You said that pain bothers you, but isn't that true for everyone?"

Since I am the Most Traumatized, Dr. Brown displayed unprecedented interest during our first solo session, but she returned to clock-watching as soon as she realized what Eliot did the second we'd met: that I am boring. Her desperation for me to have more original issues is kind of depressing. I picture her at a therapist tea party or whatever therapists do in their free time: *This one patient says she doesn't like pain. So much for the fascinating human psyche they promised us in undergrad, amirite?*

"Uh, yeah." I flush. "It's just that pain makes me feel, like, sad."

She leans forward. "Sad?"

"And anxious. Like my chest is being crushed. And then I get grouchy because being sad and anxious is annoying."

"Is this anxiety accompanied by thoughts of your mother?"

I play with my crutches. "I see broken glass sometimes."

"You still remember very little about the accident, correct?"

"Right." I remember grabbing my lacrosse bag that day, throwing it in the trunk without opening it because I was late for my game. I remember talking to Mom about Rex's upcoming birthday as she drove. I remember Rex sobbing in the hospital, and barely seeing Lena except for the funeral, where Dad read a poem about swans. But nothing about the accident itself, just a black hole that swallowed Mom, even though the doctors said I had no head trauma. At least not the kind that shows up in an MRI.

"Since you associate pain so strongly with the accident, it's possible that pain brings back flashes of this buried memory, which naturally makes you anxious. You don't want to relive it. But I'm concerned you won't be able to process your feelings until you let yourself remember."

The problem with grief is that other people stretch it out. Every time someone says they're sorry for my loss or asks How I'm Doing, it's a reminder I'm not allowed to be okay yet. But I felt the feelings, I cried the tears, I did my time. Why bring something back when I could let it disappear?

The truth is, I'm glad I don't remember.

"—homework assignment," she finishes.

"Sorry, what?"

"I want you to write a stream-of-consciousness piece next time you have this pain-related anxiety. Write down whatever comes to your mind. How bad has your pain been lately?"

"Okay," I mumble. "I take ibuprofen twice a day, and I have Vicodin if it's really bad. Mostly it's when I overdo it and the Vicodin doesn't kick in right away."

"The next time that happens, try the stream-of-consciousness exercise. See if it helps with the anxiety."

I learned a while ago that there's no way to get around the homework assignments.

"You've told me you have trouble feeling. Perhaps in order to block emotions about your accident, you subconsciously avoid any feeling whatsoever. But by not letting yourself feel the bad things, you're not feeling any of the good things either."

I have been feeling, when I'm around Eliot. It'd be great gossip for Dr. Brown's tea party: *The girl afraid of pain is hanging out with a boy who's impervious to it. I'll get into the peer-reviewed journals this time!*

Eliot doesn't have to feel the bad things. But I'm not him, and if I have to trade the good things to keep from being like I was this winter, that's fine with me. The good things aren't worth it.

When Dr. Brown realizes I'm not going to say anything else, she rubs her watch with her thumb. "I'll see you at our next appointment. Don't forget about that assignment."

She rolls her chair to her desk and starts scribbling in her notebook. A few seconds later, she looks at me like she's confused that I'm still there.

Chapter Five

MY FRIENDSHIP WITH ELIOT HAPPENS LIKE this:

I find him in the cafeteria on Monday, reading at his usual table by the corner. I used to look for him automatically when I walked in—I felt better about sitting alone when someone else was alone, too. I take a deep breath and plonk down opposite him, my crutches banging against the underside of the table. He raises a hand without glancing up from his book, like I've sat with him every day since the beginning of time.

"ISTP," I blurt. "That's my guess."

He pages through his book—*A Guide to the Myers-Briggs Assessment Test*. "ISTP. Logical, spontaneous, independent. Enjoys adventure. Wrong, but not the worst guess. Why are you staring?"

I rip my gaze from his bruised face. "Tell me how it looks worse than it feels."

"Everything looks worse than it feels for me."

I wonder how his shoulder looks underneath his dark-blue shirt. "What did your family say?"

"They wouldn't care. I don't feel pain."

"They're legally obligated to care."

"I wouldn't presume to know what they're legally obligated to do."

Maybe his family is messed up, too. I shift awkwardly. "Yeah, my family is—"

"You're sitting with me." He cuts me off, his silvery eyes rising above the page. The food on his tray is untouched.

"Oh. Yeah. That's weird."

"At lunch."

"That's what it's called when we get the food and stuff, yeah." If he tells me to leave, I'm going to javelin myself into the trash can.

"Which means you've decided to be my—"

"Friend." I'm petrified. "If that's cool."

I could have picked Georgia Wilson. She knits. Or Zoey—she has a horse. Instead I'm asking the weirdest person I've ever met. But *friend* is a better word for *the person who's going to make sure Anthony doesn't kill you because she's decided it's her responsibility for some reason.*

"You're the strangest person I've ever met," he says so quietly I'm not sure if I heard my own thoughts.

"What?"

"Nothing." He starts smirking. "Never had a friend before. What are the steps?"

If he's not kidding, we're screwed, because I don't remember the steps either. "First, one person has to save the other person's ass from getting kicked, at least twice."

"A textbook beginning."

"And one person has to relocate the other person's shoulder."

"We have all the ingredients. We'll call it an experiment."

Jokes are involved in friendship, right? I used to make jokes. I have vague memories of Kendra and Erin laughing at them, the only time I felt like a real part of the group. "Do you like to . . . experiment?" Oh, what the fuck.

"It's one of the few things worth doing," he says in the voice of someone who has completely failed to pick up on a dirty joke.

"Sorry, that was . . . I was kidding."

"Of course. The experiments in question are assumed to be sexual, for no reason other than that our society is stupid. Are you asking if I like to sexually experiment?"

"Holy shit." Is he torturing me on purpose or not?

"Because sexual experimentation is overrated and an impediment to clear thinking."

"Eliot."

"Yeah?"

"Eat your lunch."

He picks up his fork. "Are you going to be here every day now?"

"I don't know; I haven't worked out the details of the contract yet."

"Do we have to sign it in blood? Because that's perfectly fine with me. You can borrow some of mine if you don't want to prick yourself."

"I think that defeats the purpose."

"Suit yourself," he says, and goes back to his book.

And just like that I'm no longer that girl whose MOM got KILLED, but that girl who sits with ELIOT ROWE. When did THAT happen?

Now that it has, I'm surprised it didn't earlier. It's like the two leftover kids pairing up after all other group project alliances are made. Everyone stares when I sit with him again on Tuesday, and by the end of the day, I'm an encyclopedia of knowledge about everyone who goes to Forest Hills High. What Eliot does is really just an intellectualized version of gossip. He points out the patterns in people like he's charting constellations. He's a paradox—he understands people so well, and still he's alone. He knows everything about everyone, and nobody knows anything about him. For someone so interested in other peoples' lives, he has zero desire to be a part of them. Except mine, for some reason.

"Have you ever thought about studying psychology?" I ask him once after a rousing analysis of Why Georgia Will Break Up with Emory in Exactly Two Weeks.

"Psychologists are hack scientists with antisocial

personality disorders," he says.

I change the subject. "Why haven't you told anyone about your congenital insensitivity to pain with anhidrosis?" I ask, having practiced pronouncing it for an hour last night.

"'There are two possible reactions: jealousy or pity, or the former followed by the latter. Can't stand either."

"Awful," I agree passionately. "Totally unreasonable."

While he watches other people, I watch him. Once I get used to the silk shirts and the scalpel eyes, there's nothing that weird looking about him. He's actually kind of stunning, like an alien model. But there should be something off. His skin should be armor plated; there should be a force field shimmering in the air around him. Something to hint at what his body can withstand. I feel like the only one at the school who knows the superhero's true identity.

Which might make me the sidekick.

On Wednesday, I introduce him to Tito.

I already know Eliot would confuse Dad, concern Lena, and piss off Rex; but I trust Tito's judgment. He's fallen immediately in love with every human he's ever encountered, except the plumber who overcharged us and the girl down the street who stole flowerpots from our porch. If anyone can pronounce Eliot safe, it's Tito.

I make him presentable, smoothing the tufts of fur on his head while he writhes in throes of ecstasy because I've returned from mysterious lands. Then I tuck him into my elbow and awkwardly carry him outside. He and Eliot stare at each other.

"That is the ugliest thing I've ever seen," says Eliot. "When did you take it out of the dryer?"

"It's my dog," I grumble.

"That's a dog?" He recoils.

Tito sniffs his shoe. I hold my breath.

"I'm not an animal person. I'm especially not a this-animal person."

"Maybe he's not an Eliot animal," I retort, but Tito finishes his inspection, finds the goods adequate, and bangs his head into Eliot's leg, proving that he is, in fact, an Eliot animal.

Eliot tries unsuccessfully to push him away. "What do I press to make it stop?"

"Here's the thing. If you're going to hang out with me, you can't be a dick to Tito. You just can't."

"I can't insult this animal?"

"No."

"Sam." He gestures at the slobbering, heavy-breathing mess that is Tito. "I can't *not* insult this animal."

"Be nice to him," I say sternly.

He crouches, addressing Tito with immense suspicion. "I haven't interacted with an animal since before my brain developed enough to retain consistent memories. I haven't had a friend who owned an animal. I haven't stopped to pet an animal in a park. Do you understand?"

"Hhh," says Tito reassuringly.

"So let's set up some ground rules. You will not bark while I'm around. You will not pee near me. You will not touch my person. You will not—"

Tito licks his face.

I tense. Eliot's unpredictable, and he could be one of those people who fly off the handle at dogs, which would be a deal breaker. But he just sighs, wipes his cheek, and scratches Tito behind the ears.

Maybe choosing Eliot as my new friend wasn't such a bad idea.

"Are you actually dating Eliot Rowe?"

It's the first thing Kendra has said to me in, like, two weeks, and it's unfortunate that I'm drinking from my water bottle when she does. She winces as I mop water from the wet part of my shirt with the dry part of my shirt. Ms. Robbins, the Calc teacher, pretends she doesn't notice and writes next week's homework on the whiteboard.

"I am not," I whisper valiantly, "dating Eliot Rowe."

"Are you sure? Like, five people told me you were."

"Oh, my bad then."

"Cool. I—"

"*Kendra.*"

She shrugs. "Erin told me Anthony punched Eliot in the face the Monday before last, and you started screaming at him not to touch your boyfriend."

The sad thing is that this is the most normal conversation

we've had SMD. "Erin is high twelve-hundred percent of the time."

"Listen, Sam." Her big blue eyes get bluer and bigger—a warning sign. She touches my hand. "I think it's great that you found someone, after—"

"I'm *single*, Kendra. *S-I-N*—"

Ms. Robbins turns, and everyone turns with her. Kendra gets rapidly engrossed in page forty-three of the textbook.

"*G-L-E*," I finish.

Send me to the office, Ms. Robbins. You once stormed out of class because I sneezed during a test. Instead, she bites her lip and faces the whiteboard, underlining the due date for the homework. "I hope everyone brought the worksheets I passed out last class. . . ."

I slump in my chair.

Halfway through class, my text notification—I imagine it wheezing, hoarse from lack of use—goes off. Amy and Erin have both sent me little hearts.

If I'd shown interest in Eliot BMD, they would have held an intervention. Now I could date a serial killer and they'd be so *proud* of me for *moving on.* Aka, becoming someone else's problem.

When the bell rings, Kendra follows me into the hall.

"I think Eliot's perfect for you," she chirps. She's the type of person who chirps. I stop by the water fountain even though there's a bottle of Poland Spring in my backpack, because standing still is better than noticing how much she has to slow down for me.

"You have an understated style, you know? You're the bread and he's, like—blackberry jam. It works!"

Understated. *Bread.*

I lean on one crutch to access the spigot. Whoever designed these assumed all high schoolers are three feet tall. I decide to keep drinking until she goes away.

"You'll have to give me insider details on Mr. Mystery."

Glug, glug.

"Let me know if you need any relationship advice!"

I'll never be dehydrated again.

"It feels like we haven't gotten to talk much since . . ."

SMD.

". . . I mean, lately."

This is how it goes with Kendra and the rest of the team: they try, because they're nice; but they don't know what to say, and they don't realize that saying nothing is a valid option, so they bang into the wrong topics like drunk people in a closet. They can't avoid it—with every step I take on crutches, I'm throwing the accident at them. Eventually we all signed an unspoken agreement that it was easier to not say anything. But Kendra is persistent, probably because her mom tells her to be persistent.

"You're super thirsty," she notes.

I surface. My stomach sloshes.

"Honestly I'm just glad you never ended up making a move on Anthony. I always thought you'd take advantage of having an in with him."

"The only move I'd make regarding Anthony is moving

away from him as fast as I can. Which isn't that fast, because crutches."

She flinches. I said the bad word.

"I don't like Anthony," I enunciate, saving her.

"Oh, good, because he's awful." She sighs.

That's not why I expected relief. "Kendra, you stole his sweatshirt from the cafeteria when we were freshmen and wore it to bed for a year."

"Well, I threw it out." She presses the tip of her tongue against her teeth. "After he and Trez broke up, I thought I'd go for it, so we made out at Erin's party after the Senior Plunge at the lake, but he's kinda—"

"He's a dick. Everyone is forever surprised by this."

"Seriously. I felt sick so I stopped, and he got so pissed, and it freaked me out so I went home."

She actually does look scared. My stomach sinks. "I heard about him and Trez."

"You know how she was out of school for, like, weeks after they broke up? She said she was sick, but my mom knows her mom, and I guess she just wouldn't get out of bed. Hopefully now she appreciates the massiveness of the dick bullet she dodged." She twists her necklace nervously. "Listen, Sam, I overheard a bunch of his friends shit talking Eliot yesterday. They think he got Anthony in trouble. You two stay away from those jerks, okay?"

I'm surprised by a sudden pang. I wish she and the team really had abandoned me because I couldn't play, but I'm the one who avoided the table, who ignored the texts. I was scared of being asked if I was okay because I wasn't, and they had to have been asking because their moms told them to, not because I actually had enough friend credit stored up that it was safe to be an emotional burden.

All she's doing by pestering me about Eliot is circling, looking for a safe place to land. But I've missed too many key developments: her making out with Anthony, throwing out his sweatshirt. The worst part is that I'm not even hungry for details. I left our friendship lying out too long and it rotted, and now the only thing to do is chuck it and start over with something new.

"Thanks, but I'm literally not dating Eliot. I'll see you later."

She wilts, and I leave before I can deal with the fact that it feels like I'm doing something wrong.

I spend the rest of the afternoon worrying. I assumed Anthony wouldn't be a problem until his suspension was over, but I forgot about his friends.

After school, one of them tails Eliot and me to the parking lot.

"What happened to your face, Eleanor? Does she beat you up with the crutches?" Jaden-something is one of Anthony's minor undersecretaries who aspires to be just as much of an asshole someday. He's a sophomore only half an inch taller than me, which doesn't make it better.

"Go away," I growl very intimidatingly, hobbling faster.

"Is this upsetting you?" Eliot asks, like the possibility has just dawned on him.

"No. I love this."

"Just making sure." Without breaking stride, Eliot whirls and begins walking backward, facing Jaden. "So you're an ESFP—the Performer. You're insecure and you like being the center of attention, and you figure if you slip in ahead of your group to fight me or something, it'll raise your status in the hierarchy of pathetic—"

"Eliot," I practically scream.

"What?"

"Car. Now."

Jaden is purple. His shock earns us a head start, but even so, I have to fend him off with a crutch through the window as Eliot starts the car. As soon as we zoom off, we both explode in laughter—mine panicked, his deep and warm. I never laughed like this with Kendra, unmonitored noise just coming out.

Once I can breathe, I repeat, "'Is this upsetting you?' Seriously?"

"How am I supposed to know what it means when your face turns bright red? You could be sunburned or choking to death." Eliot lights a cigarette, obviously pleased with himself.

"Was it not upsetting *you*?" For all the time I've spent as a loner SMD, no one's harassed me before, not even in middle school. I kind of forgot it was a thing that happened to people. My heart's pounding, and Jaden is the least intimidating of Anthony's friends. Am I really equipped to get dragged into it when they all start in on Eliot?

"Was it supposed to be? Can't believe that's what passes for bullying here."

I blink. "Were you bullied before?"

"It's inconsequential if I have or haven't been, because it doesn't bother me. The day I let myself be bothered by a Neanderthal stringing words together in order of how loudly they make his idiot friends go *ohhhh* is the day I launch myself into outer space."

I'm coming to the realization that Eliot can be a little bit dramatic. "Well anyway, you don't need to do that for me. That whole thing with Jaden."

"Friends stick up for each other, at least according to wikiHow."

"You looked up friendship on wikiHow?" I laugh, but at the same time my stomach goes warm.

"You didn't come with an instruction manual. I'm contacting your manufacturer."

Suddenly my phone buzzes. I dig it out of my bag. Before I can say hi, distant shouting echoes.

"Northton has an *excellent* community college—"

Rex's voice surges into my ear. "Please tell me you need a ride home."

"Is that Lena? Why is she home? We don't have counseling this weekend."

Eliot rolls up the window so he can eavesdrop better, which is unnecessary, since Rex starts yelling. "THANK YOU for informing me I'm a failure at life. I DIDN'T KNOW THAT BEFORE."

Eliot looks intrigued. On the other end, Rex lowers his voice and begs, "Save me, Sam."

I mumble an excuse and hang up. My leg is throbbing, probably from speed walking away from Jaden. I force broken glass out of my mind and pop half a Vicodin.

"You won't like my house," Eliot says before I can ask. "And if my brother's back, you'll be treated to a thoroughly bullshit encounter."

He doesn't mention parents. "Believe me, your brother is not worse than mine."

He snorts doubtfully, so his brother must be pretty bad, considering what he just overheard. My stomach hurts at the prospect of going home to a war zone. Hopefully Lena's gone by the time I get back from Eliot's.

Shit. I'm going to Eliot's.

As we drive, the lawns get greener and the fences whiter, like someone's turning up the color saturation the closer we get. He lives closer to Anthony than I do. The house we stop in front of is the biggest on the block, and there's even a gate at the end of the driveway, though it's propped open.

"His work car's not here. The gods smile on us." Eliot gets out of the car and beckons.

When we walk in, I notice that the house is weirdly empty. No welcome mat or pictures on the walls, no lamps or shelves in the front hallway.

He brings me to the living room. I stare. There are cardboard boxes strewn all over the place, some torn open, bleeding clothes. The white couch is still in its factory plastic. The only other furniture is a coffee table heaped with cigarette butts.

"You didn't tell me you just moved again," I say.

He stubs his cigarette out on the wall, adding to a Milky Way of gray marks. "I didn't."

My jaw drops. "You've been here six months and you haven't unpacked?"

"Gabriel thinks that the longer he spends on business trips, the more likely I'll get fed up and put everything away so he doesn't have to do it. He underestimates how committed I am to annoying him."

"Business trips? You've been here *six months*," I repeat dizzily.

He throws himself on the couch, the plastic crinkling beneath him. "Apparently he has a lot of business."

"Your parents can't be okay with this."

"Our parents are okay with anything as long as they're far away from it."

"Where are they?" I'm one more awful revelation away from calling child services. Then I wince at the thought of what Eliot would have to say to child services.

"Half no idea, half maybe Barbados. Or Venezuela. I guess it's closer to entirely no idea." He snickers at my expression.

I want to kill him. "If I knew you were alone, I wouldn't have let you go home after last Friday! What if you had a concussion and died in your sleep? Or what if your spleen exploded and you didn't know because you can't feel pain?"

Horror dawns on me. "Eliot, you're *sick*; you can't live alone."

"'Not feeling pain, that's not a health problem; that's a miracle,'" he mimics.

I wince. Maybe I have been having difficulty seeing Eliot as a sick person, even after researching his condition—he acts more unsick than anyone I've met—but this situation is definitely wrong.

"Besides, I don't live alone. I have a"—he curls his lip—"nanny."

"Where is she, then?"

"I paid her off."

"*What?*"

"Don't worry, she's fine with it—now she has time to paint. She sends excellent emails to Gabriel and my mom about how well I'm doing. Gabriel's the only one who reads them, but I like to make her feel included."

"What about your dad?"

"Divorced when I was nine. He's somewhere." He waves like he can shoo away this conversation. "Who cares?"

"Um—child services?"

"Stop feeling sorry for me. I told you I hate that."

"Well, I hate—whatever this is! Eliot, you need a guardian."

"I absolutely do not, and Gabriel knows that as well as I do."

"So Gabriel's your guardian?"

"You ISFJs. Fixated on whatever you think needs mothering." He lights another cigarette.

"I'm not like that—and you already had one." I snatch his cigarette, searching helplessly for an ashtray.

"I refer you to my previous statement about not needing a guardian." He adds in a mutter, "WikiHow didn't cover this."

I collapse on the couch next to him. "You can't live this way."

"I'm alive, aren't I? Look, a pulse and everything." He presses my hand to his neck, and I inhale sharply. Even the air in this house feels unbreathed. Maybe Eliot's a hallucination, some delayed brain damage from the accident—but his heartbeat is warm and strong against my fingers. I stub out the still-burning cigarette on an open cardboard box lid and get up.

"We're unpacking. Now."

"It's your right to waste your time however you want."

But after five minutes of watching me fumble with boxes on my crutches, he kneels. It only takes us an hour of quiet work to put away the clothes and the spare bedding, and then there's just the cardboard boxes to crush for recycling. They don't own much, these two.

I lift a small instrument out of a box filled with towels. "Gabriel plays the ukulele?"

Eliot coughs. "No."

"*You?*"

"Shut up." He grabs it, but he doesn't throw it in a corner like everything else. He lays it carefully on the couch. There's a gold engraving in the burnished wood: *To Eliot— happy 9th birthday, Mom & Dad*. My stomach twists. How many other things does he care about that he says he doesn't?

Now I understand what he meant when he said he and Anthony had a lot in common. Anthony never knew his dad, and his mom spent every other week with a different guy in a different city—that's why he stayed with us so often. But Eliot didn't have a substitute family.

My finger stabs with sudden pain, and I look down. I sliced it on the edge of the cardboard I was absently tearing open. I pinch the skin, and it pops apart in a ruler-straight mouth, dots of blood swelling until the raw pink crevice has a neat brimful.

Glass sparkling all around me, so bright against the pavement, a spray of light interspersed with flecks of dark red. I feel a hollow shuddering inside me.

"Sam?" Eliot says.

I show him my finger. He makes a disinterested sound and goes back to work.

His world doesn't grind to a halt every time he feels pain. It's ridiculous that mine does, that I'm so affected by a half-inch split in my finger or an old crack in a bone. I should be more than these tiny punctures and fissures.

Eliot doesn't know how free he is, even if there is a trade-off. Would I swap years of my life for the ability not to feel pain?

Yeah, I think. Yeah, I would.

He tosses the last cardboard box on the pile. "Congratulations, I've been successfully bored to death. And the doctors thought I'd at least make it to my twenties."

I suffocate my cut finger in my fist. "It looks way better in here now. And it didn't take long—knew it wouldn't, with the two of us."

"You didn't know I'd help."

"You're not an asshole."

"Years of evidence to the contrary."

"Not all evidence," I say.

The silence curdles into awkwardness. Eliot returns to the couch. I don't think he knows the procedure for dealing with a human being in his house.

"So, I'm starving," I prompt.

He says nothing, his brow furrowed.

"At this point you're basically supposed to ask if I want anything to eat."

He gestures toward the kitchen. "Your ancestors were hunter-gatherers."

I walk across the hall. The kitchen is as empty as the rest of the house. No toaster, no dishes in the sink. The fridge isn't even plugged in. When I open the cupboard, a bug zips out of sight. "Eliot! You don't have any food."

"Keen observational skills are common in ISFJs," he yells back.

"What have you been eating?"

"Eating is a hassle."

I'm back in the living room in a millisecond. "Eating is necessary."

His sigh rattles the house. "Oh, yeah, it's a great time, especially when you're chewing and suddenly your mouth is full of blood—which does nothing to make a ham sandwich taste better. You'd be surprised how similar the texture of a tongue is to most meats. Puts a person off the whole experience."

I try not to be as grossed out as I am. "Does that happen a lot?"

"Not since I was little," he admits. "Trial and error."

"Then you still need to eat. No wonder you're so skinny. This is ridiculous; is there a grocery store around here?"

"Two blocks down. If you're blackmailing me into driving you—"

Before he can finish, I hobble to the front door and angle it open. I can do two blocks. I have painkillers, and Eliot needs food. Once the Vicodin kicks in, walking is okay, but I'll pay for it tonight when it wears off.

The grocery store is a fancy organic one. As soon as I walk in, I stop. I have no idea what Eliot likes to eat.

In the end it amounts to all the cash I have on me, the Omega-3 bread and dried fruit cereal and the other inoffensive stuff I figure he can't mistake for his own tongue. Nothing hot or sharp. The cashier raises his eyebrows at me, and I realize I'm beaming at him. This must be how Lena feels when she shops for us on the weekends she visits, loading the crisper with kale and radishes that go mushy as soon as she leaves. It feels nice to take care of someone.

It takes longer to get back to the house with the bags dangling from my elbows. When I reach the driveway, there's a new car parked beside Eliot's, even sleeker and blacker.

I guess I do get to find out whose brother is worse.

Inside, Eliot is facing off with a man who looks like he's in his upper twenties, except for his hair, which is so thinned out he's almost bald. He has Eliot's height but none of his exotic vampire-ness. Instead, he's practical looking in his gray suit, his tanned wrists setting off the glint of a silver watch. Gabriel.

"Sam, I texted you." Eliot is colder and paler and angrier than usual. I glance at my phone.

Don't come back. Abort mission.

I'm serious. Go anywhere but back to my house.

Are you getting these?

"I couldn't check my pocket with all the bags on my arms," I say.

I mean, a little thanks would be nice.

"Who is this?" Gabriel's voice has rounded granite edges. His eyes are dark, not like Eliot's, but the X-ray stare is the same.

Eliot draws back his shoulders with defiance, and if I'm not crazy, some nervousness. "She's a friend."

"You usually don't bother lying."

"He's right," I snap. At least I think he is.

Gabriel's eyes narrow. "How much is he paying you?"

Eliot might actually have won the worst-sibling competition. Amazing.

"Or do you have any mental deficiencies, beyond the obvious?" Gabriel continues. The family resemblance is becoming clearer by the second.

"She just so happens to like me," Eliot says stiffly. "See? People like me."

"There's years of evidence to the contrary."

I fold my arms. "He's got tons of friends at school."

Eliot shoots me a startled look. Gabriel's laugh is as deep as his brother's, but nowhere near as warm. "So you've got yourself a lapdog! A puppy with an injured leg that you've dragged home. And trained to buy your groceries, apparently."

I open my mouth, but I'm speechless.

Eliot flares, ice turning to fire. "Don't pretend you're interested in my life, Gabriel, because even if you were, you wouldn't be privy to it."

I edge toward the hallway to escape the rapid-fire hail of bullets. "I should probably be heading out. . . ."

"Stay," demands Eliot, at the same time as Gabriel says, "Feel free."

I remain angled at the door, but I don't leave. Gabriel's stare lights me up like I've done something worth his attention for the first time, but all he says to Eliot is "Tell me what happened to your face."

Eliot snorts. His bruises are faded, nearly two weeks old.

"Who hit you? You promised you'd tell me if it was happening again." Anger ripples off Gabriel. I realize it's been here the whole time, filling the room in invisible waves. If what was happening again? Does it have something to do with why they moved here? "If it is, you know what I have to do."

I want to ask what he's talking about, but I also don't want to give him a reason to look at me again. Eliot, on the other hand, glares straight back at him, neither one of them breaking until I'm expecting their eyes to water.

Finally Eliot snarls, "Come on, Sam." But he doesn't wait for me before he snatches his ukulele from the corner of the couch and stalks upstairs.

I'm going to flee, too, but Gabriel holds up a hand. "Wait." He stares at the staircase where Eliot disappeared. "Sam, is it? You really are his friend? Well, congratulations. There's no predecessor to that title."

I feel like I'll be failing a test no matter what I say. "Right. I'll just—I should probably . . . It was, um, nice meeting you."

"Why are you interested in Eliot?" he asks bluntly.

My face burns. "You mean interested interested? Because I'm not *interested* interested—"

He massages his temples, stretching the skin on his scalp until it shines. "Here's some advice. And very large corporations pay for my advice, so I would listen. Stay away from my brother. Have a normal high school experience—go to parties, go on dates, whatever it is you people do."

"Why?"

"Why?" he repeats like he's never heard that particular syllable before.

"Like, why do I have to stay away?" I'm nervous, but even more pissed off.

Silence. Then he sighs long and hard. "Did someone at your school do that to his face?"

It's the weary frustration of someone who loves his little brother, which doesn't fit at all. There's a lot a guardian would deserve to know: Eliot's disregard for his own safety, the paid-off "nanny," his eating habits (or lack thereof). But would telling Gabriel do anything other than give Eliot a reason to hate me?

Screw it—if bluntness is the language they understand, I'll learn it. "Would you care if they did?"

"Of course I care." His eyebrows shoot up. "I'm his brother."

This family makes no sense. Then again, neither does mine.

"I just ask because . . ." I flop my hand to indicate the past ten minutes.

"I was surprised that someone was here," he says in a pretty explanatory tone for a statement that doesn't explain anything. "What's your last name? I assume Sam is short for Samantha."

"Herring," I say automatically before I think better of it.

He starts typing on his phone and proceeds to ignore me for five whole minutes. "Um . . . are you googling me?" I ask.

"Honor roll for three out of the past four years, but no high honors. No awards or recognition, apart from an old article in the *Forest Hills Weekly* about scoring points in a lacrosse game. And your mother died in an accident around the same time we moved here, which explains your leg." He says it exactly like Eliot did: no emotion attached, no awareness of the lance it sends through my chest. "Eliot has little patience for stupidity, and he's of the view that everyone is stupid, so he has little patience for anyone. What's special about you?"

I blink at him. He waits.

"Am I actually supposed to answer that?" I ask after a minute.

"No, asking people questions is how I request that they stand there gaping at me." His phone rings, and he mutes it. "Eliot doesn't *do* people. So what are you?"

"He doesn't *do* me either," I say, and follow up with a strangled giggle. Fantastic. This is exactly how I wanted my first interaction with Eliot's family to go.

"I see. You hang around him because you're too moronic to know better, but that doesn't explain why he hangs around you."

"I'm not a moron! And honestly I don't think you have the right to police his social life when *you* abandon him all the time, even with his condition."

I cover my mouth, but he's staring at me in shock, not anger.

"He told you about his condition?"

I nod, electing to skip the story about relocating his shoulder.

He shakes his head contemptuously. "So you know him enough to know that, but you don't understand him or you'd know why I keep out of his life as much as possible."

My anger makes me feel less intimidated. "Look, he obviously needs someone to keep an eye on him—he barely eats, he—"

"If I 'kept an eye on him,' I'd go blind. He takes it as an

insult whenever anyone tries to parent him, and he gets revenge by doing whatever would make a parent insane with worry. If you think he's self-destructive now, you should see him when he's convinced I'm hovering. If I spent all my time here, he'd kill himself within the week to spite me for attempting to keep him alive."

So he wants to prove he can take care of himself, and he does it by not taking care of himself. "Sounds like Eliot," I mumble under my breath.

Again Gabriel eyes me like I'm a math problem he can't solve. "I have my methods of monitoring him from a safe distance, so if you're tailing him because you think he needs a babysitter, he has one, and you wouldn't be qualified to handle him anyway. I'm the only one who understands what he needs."

I'm going to inform him about the nanny, but he cuts me off. "I know he paid off his caretaker. He visits her house every few days to proofread her fake emails, and she has a chance to evaluate him with his guard down. I left Miami early once I heard about his face." He closes his eyes briefly. "And he sees a therapist weekly. Trust me, he's not left to his own devices nearly as much as he thinks he is."

"He has a therapist?" It must be a really tolerant therapist who'd stick with Eliot. "Then what's his . . ."

Gabriel folds his arms.

"Like, his . . ." I make helpless shapes with my hands.

"Every diagnosis has been suggested to our family before, mostly by first-grade teachers, I might add. But there is no psychology textbook that will tell you how to fix Eliot."

"I don't want to fix him."

"So you must like him. And you wouldn't have had the chance if he hadn't liked you first."

The question hangs in his voice, but I have no answers. I don't know what makes me special enough for Eliot either. What happens when Eliot figures out that nothing does?

"Why hasn't he ever had any friends?" I ask to distract myself.

"His own logic is the problem. When no one likes you, there's two possible explanations: that there's something wrong with everyone, or that there's something wrong with you. The former is safer, don't you think?" He rubs his forehead and looks around. "I see he unpacked."

"We did it together." Indignation swells in me again. "Why did you leave him in a house like that?"

"It's tiresome to keep packing and unpacking. Six months is more than our average for staying in one place. Also, I know how much he wants to stay by how soon he unpacks." He keeps a sideways eye on me. "He usually doesn't bother."

"What do you mean, more than your average?" I blurt. I force my volume down, but my voice still sounds panicky. "You two move that often?"

"Kids your age aren't kind to people like Eliot. What's more, he's not kind to them." Gabriel exhales, and I get the sense he's needed someone to vent to about Eliot for a long time. "Eventually it reaches a certain point, and I have to relocate us before he's hurt."

"But he doesn't feel pain," I say stupidly. It was a bad excuse when Eliot used it, too.

Gabriel scowls at me. "He can still be *damaged*. He wouldn't know he needed to be in a hospital until it was too late; and even if he did, he probably wouldn't go—he'd spent too much time being poked and prodded as a child. I think he felt like a science experiment. Now he thinks he's invincible, because whenever people find out about his condition, that's how they act."

"He doesn't care what people think." *It doesn't matter to him if the whole school hates him—if I protect him, you don't need to take him away.*

He laughs. "Never trust Eliot when he says he doesn't care about something."

"Instead of moving so much, why don't you just homeschool him?"

"Ask me how many tutors he's gone through."

"Maybe if you stayed at home—"

"It takes money to relocate. Someone has to make that money."

"Can't your mom give you money?"

A shadow crosses his face. "She's an ordinary woman, and on top of having a son with a rare medical condition, both her kids turned out like us. She's as involved as she can handle. Which isn't much."

My phone buzzes with a text. I glance at it. Come upstairs.

I shove it back in my pocket. "You wouldn't have to do

all these weird mind games with Eliot if you were just— *nice* to him."

"Try being nice to Eliot when he wants a reaction out of you and see how well he takes it."

Another buzz, and I can't help but check my phone. If you're not upstairs in the next minute I will assume Gabriel has killed you and will take it as permission to kill him back.

Gabriel steps away like he's releasing me from an invisible force field. He clears his throat. "Don't get too attached. Things never stay at a baseline with Eliot. After a while, they always blow up."

"I'll make sure no one touches him again." I ball my fists desperately. "It's just one guy who has the problem. I know him; I can convince him to leave Eliot alone."

His expression is unreadable. He reaches into his wallet and hands me a business card. "My email address, for emergencies. If there are any more issues, it's my job to do what's best for my brother, whether or not normal people understand what that is."

On my way up the stairs, my leg throbs, splintering my vision with broken glass. I grip my crutches hard, stunned at how dry my mouth is. A single thought bursts in me like a firework: I'm not ready. I'm not ready for Eliot to leave and for the blankness to take over again.

I don't know which room is Eliot's, but one door is slightly ajar, ukulele music trickling into the hall. I step inside. He's rigid in front of the window, back to me, playing some jarringly happy pop song.

I'd pictured his room like the rest of the house, barren

as a monk's, but it's strewn with the corpses of ex-hobbies: beakers crusted with dried liquid, an aquarium too scummy to tell if there's anything inside, scattered books about astrology, Slavic root languages, World War II airplanes . . . and Myers-Briggs personality types. There are several unfolded butterfly knives on the carpet.

"Eliot, you can't feel pain and you have knives on your floor."

He plays on, ignoring me.

"We're going to have to talk about the knives."

He tosses his ukulele suddenly on the bed. "You two really hit it off. The only people who talk to Gabriel that long are lawyers—he loves suing people, especially school districts. I assume he's not suing you."

I remember what Gabriel said about being nice to Eliot when he wants a reaction. "We were just having a . . . nice chat about you," I say as calmly and politely as I can.

He tosses himself next to the ukulele. "Stop."

"Stop what?"

"Patronizing me."

I kneel awkwardly on my crutches and gather the knives to hide my mounting irritation. "I'm not, I'm—"

"Ten minutes and he has you talking to me like I have two functioning brain cells. Where'd he install the chip, and do I need a scalpel or a drill to remove it?"

I fill my lungs with air. "I had to talk to him about—"

"*Had* is inaccurate. *Chose to* is better. 'Hey, Gabriel,

people at school think Eliot is weird, he doesn't eat, he needs round-the-clock supervision, and also what did the doctor say is wrong with his brain?'" he mimics.

I should have known he was eavesdropping.

He keeps going. "'Dear responsible Gabriel, your mutant brother needs to be examined and analyzed and picked apart until we can figure out how to make him easier to deal with—'"

I bang a crutch against the floor like a gavel. Gabriel was right—niceness is not the way to go. "Can you shut up? Of course I said something to him; it's the normal thing to—"

"Oh, the normal thing!" he barks. "Why should the normal thing apply to someone like me? You just had such a *nice chat* about what a freak I—"

"I don't think you're a freak!"

Eliot goes silent. He plucks one of the ukulele strings. "Then what do you think I am?"

The same question Gabriel asked is in his voice, only reversed. And I'm so annoyed, I don't even know the answer. Why do I like him? He's abrasive and dramatic and tells me exactly what he thinks, and it throws me off because everyone else has treated me like I'm made of glass since the accident.

I guess that's my answer.

"Why do you have to be something in particular?" I ask. "You're just Eliot."

"That's what people do. They decide what other people are."

"Then . . . you're an idiot."

He relaxes a little. "Fair enough."

Downstairs, a door opens and closes. I glance out the window. Gabriel's fancy car rolls out of the driveway and down the street. "He didn't stay long."

"He's going to eat at the most expensive restaurant he can find around here, and then he'll be back. The more annoyed he is, the more he eats and the more his hair falls out. My goal is to make him fat and bald."

"You hate him that much?"

"Of course I do. He's my brother."

I sit on his blanket and trace the cigarette burns. "He said you moved here because things were bad at your old school."

He grunts.

"He said you might have to move again. To a place where no one wants to punch you." I hope my voice sounds casual. What I want to hear from him is "Don't worry, I'm not going anywhere."

"Anywhere there are humans is a place people will want to punch me."

Then I'll have to defend him from Anthony and his friends since he's clearly not interested in defending himself. If anyone can find a way to hurt someone who can't be hurt, it's Anthony.

I shift, and pain uncoils in my leg. The Vicodin is wearing off. I stretch my leg away from me like it'll stop the poison from spreading to my brain.

"What does it feel like?" Eliot asks. "When your leg hurts."

I pick at the rubber on my crutches. "Shitty."

"Your attention to detail is astounding."

I look at him, but he's staring at my leg like he can see the ugly scars under my jeans, his brow knit. It must be frustrating for someone so determined to understand people not to understand this fundamental thing. But you can't make someone fathom what they've never felt. It's an uncrossable gulf between him and the rest of the world.

"I don't know," I mumble. "It just hurts."

I want to ask him what it's like *not* to feel pain, but I'll never be able to know that either. It's just some magic in his skin that isn't in mine. He's full of magic that isn't in me.

To get my mind off that and his eyes off my leg, I point at the stuff on his floor. "Why didn't you just unpack everything when you were unpacking all this?"

"Those are things I've gotten since we came."

"You went through all these hobbies in six months?"

He shrugs. "When I get bored, I move on. People spend their whole lives wasting time on things that started boring them years ago."

"Uh-huh. So what's next after the Myers-Briggs phase?"

"You," he says, and I can't tell if he's joking.

If not, how long until he gets bored and moves on from me?

Chapter Six

THAT NIGHT, I LIE IN BED LOOKING AT THE calendar, haloed in the blue-white glow of my phone. In three days it'll be Monday, exactly two weeks since I stopped Anthony from beating up Eliot behind the Dumpster, and Anthony's suspension will be over.

My leg pulses quietly in the dark. I've memorized all the different kinds of pain: climbed-stairs-too-fast pain, knelt-too-long pain, did-nothing-but-fuck-you-it's-hurting-anyway pain. Ibuprofen barely helps with I-walked-too-much pain. I could take another Vicodin, but that goes over my daily limit, and what if I'm one extra pill away from turning into Rex?

But there's broken glass in my heart, and I'm exhausted from pulling the white fog over myself to suffocate what the pain brings back.

Abruptly I remember Dr. Brown's homework assignment.

My notebook's on my desk, across the room. She said it could help with the anxiety. I swing my legs over the mattress, reaching for the crutches leaning on my bedside table, but then I let my hand drop.

Even in the dark, it's obvious that my leg looks wrong. It's more rigid, twisted slightly to the side below the knee. An infection in my bone, they said, that never healed. That's where the pain comes from, something secret deep within me.

"Come on, Sam," the physical therapist had said approximately five seconds before I collapsed on the floor in a sobbing heap. "Just two steps without the crutches. You can do two steps."

I stand and balance on one leg, wiggling my bare toes in the carpet, feeling the roughness of buried crumbs. It's a maroon shag—Mom bought it for me on my fourteenth birthday despite Lena's protests that shags were impossible to clean.

So far so good. With the closet door as my goalpost, I sink my weight onto my bad side and take a step.

You're a leg. Do your job.

My leg declines. Pain scissors up my shin and thigh, and I cry out, toppling sideways, my cheek resting on the shag, crumbs gluing themselves to my skin. I imagine snipping through the neurons that connect my leg to my brain, severing each one with tiny sewing scissors. Eliot wouldn't even feel this. But the connection is as strong as ever, and it funnels the memories to me: black pavement, shattered glass glinting white—

I haul myself onto my desk chair, scrabbling for a pen. I write without thinking, the pain bleeding up my leg and through my brain and out my fingers.

The daughter is getting a ride to a lacrosse game from her mom. It's sunny out, but it should be raining. Car crashes make sense when it's raining.

The daughter has two working legs. Her mom has a working heart. The body parts of everyone in the car are doing exactly what they're supposed to.

The daughter worries that the sun will blind her during the game, but she doesn't worry too much, because she's really good at lacrosse. She doesn't know the importance of the time she's wasting—there are questions she should be asking her mom, stories she should be hearing. Instead they're discussing neck pillows.

"I saw a nice one on Amazon. You microwave it," her mom tells her. "I'm concerned about his neck, with all that slouching."

"Rex eats ramen packets without cooking them; he's too lazy to microwave a whole pillow," the daughter says. Her delinquent brother's birthday is next week. "He has everything he needs: couch and TV. He's like his own ecosystem. Plus he says nineteen is a stupid birthday and he doesn't want a present."

"Not turning eighteen, not entering your twenties,"

her mom agrees. "It's an in-between year."

They're ten minutes from the school. The daughter is pretty confident she'll score the winning point against Northton. She's making it a tradition, scoring the winning point, especially when her mom comes to the games. She's usually busy having talks with the brother. Or quietly worrying about the brother. Or consulting friends about the brother. The daughter feels bad that he causes her mom so much stress—to her, her brother is just doing what her brother does—but it's okay, because her sister has made it her new project to take their mom's mind off the issue. She schedules her for lunch dates, nail painting, free art shows. She invites the daughter, but the daughter has practice, and after-practice parties, and after-party sleepovers; and she can't ditch her new social world to hang out with her stressed mom, because she's never had a life like this before, never been so close to earning herself a place. Her siblings absorb all their parents' energy and so she's learned, out of politeness maybe, to absorb as little as possible. That's why she turned out boring. She is liked at school, but not loved or hated. Her brother might be starting an in-between year, but she has an in-between life. Only now she's good at something, really good at it, and it gives her form and purpose. For the first time she can remember, she's not disheartened by the prospect of being Sam Herring for the rest of her life.

"When Rex says he doesn't want a present, he's just

testing to see if we love him enough to get him one anyway. We have to get him a present," her mom says with that weird, firm certainty she's always had about the brother's needs and the sister's needs but never, it seems, her needs. "He's done it every year since he was nine."

"That's silly."

"People are silly, but that's all right. We love them anyway."

After, the daughter wishes that those were her last words. They're solid enough, as last words go. But instead, her mom asks her to remind her to pick up paper towels on the way home, and however hard the daughter tries to pretend that her last words were about her fondness for humanity and not Bounty, it feels like cheating.

The lack of paper towels becomes a problem, after. The neighbors bring tuna casserole and lasagna, but it doesn't occur to anyone to offer paper towels. But paper towels have a specific niche of necessity. Toilet paper coats the countertop in furry white bits, and there's only so long you can wipe things with the same hand towel before it just makes them dirtier. Eventually the absence of paper towels stops being about forgetfulness and turns into purposeful suffering. Privately the daughter swears never to use them again, but after a couple months, the sister breaks the unspoken code and buys them in bulk at Costco.

At the other end of the street, a silver Jeep turns

I drop the pen, and it flies across the room. I guess I technically threw it.

I notice I'm crying. I rub my eyes hard until my brain reassembles, and then I stare down to find two full pages of writing.

A silver Jeep . . .

It's the first detail I've remembered about the accident. Now it's laser focused in my mind: a silver Jeep, the last of the summer heat rising in glinting waves off the hood.

"Any detail will help us catch them. Can you remember the type of car?" the police officer had asked me in my hospital room, and later at the station, over and over again.

The neck of my T-shirt is drenched with sweat. The walls of my room press in on me like a cocoon, inviting me to curl up again for months so the blankness can wrap me in layers of insulation. If I kept writing, would I remember the answers to all the police's questions? A license plate? The face of the driver?

I'm hyperventilating. I slam my notebook shut and propel myself one-legged back into bed, crawling beneath the blankets until everything is black emptiness, and I'm safe as long as I can't see.

I spend the rest of the weekend in hiding, muttering excuses about homework until finally it's Monday morning and I have to go downstairs and have breakfast with Dad.

Every time he asks about school, he acts like he's afraid of the answer, like he forgets I've said "fine, good, great" every time SMD. Grief is a tapeworm chewing holes in the brain, making it so you don't remember things like that and silver Jeeps.

"School's great." I smile like a Colgate ad. I want to tell him about what I wrote Friday night, but what if he wants to tell the police about the Jeep and they hammer me with all the same questions until I wear down to nothing? It took so much effort to block them out the first time that everything stayed blocked out for months.

Dad stirs his breakfast mac 'n' cheese with the wrong end of his fork. A worse sign than pancakes, but a better sign than gummy dinosaurs. Tito sits under his chair with a paw on his foot like he's weighing him down to earth. He can always tell when Dad's floating more than usual.

"When Lena was here Friday afternoon, she said she thought it was time for you to go back to physical therapy," he blurts out of the blue.

When my leg still hurt a month after surgery, they told me I needed physical therapy. When the physical therapy made it hurt more, they told me it was because I wasn't sticking with physical therapy.

"The doctor said the pain won't always be that bad—"

"But it's good to save on the co-pays, right?" I say. That's not fair, and he stirs his mac faster, but he drops the topic.

The silence is like airplane pressure. I ache to be honest for once, about anything—about the silver Jeep, about how pain makes me picture broken glass, about Eliot and how he makes me feel awake for the first time in months. But even BMD, I didn't know how to be honest with Dad. I was supposed to be the easy kid.

Tito trots into the living room and hops onto the couch. I point. "Remember when Mom bought that couch? It smelled horrible."

Dad chuckles absently, carried away by the memory before he can be scared of how I'll handle talking about Mom. "She always said that secondhand furniture came with a piece of the previous owner. If she liked the owner, she brought it home."

"It smelled like it had a literal piece, like a chopped-off foot under the cushions or something."

Dad's smile slips out like a ray of sunlight between clouds. But then our eyes meet, and he closes back up. He doesn't know how to be honest with me either, not since his easy kid became difficult, too, in a different way from Rex or Lena. "Dr. Brown said not to dwell on the past."

The silver Jeep is part of that past, and we can only be safe if it stays hermetically sealed. It's too late for the police to achieve anything with just that detail. All I can do is try to forget Friday night, and never write Dr. Brown's stream-of-consciousness exercise again.

At school, Anthony is back, and it takes about five nanoseconds for everything to go to hell.

If the news about Eliot being a narc hadn't fully spread yet, it was only because Anthony waited so he could witness the effect. It's amazing how fast everyone in Anthony's network swaps Eliot's label from mysterious loner to public enemy number one. The worst part is that Eliot cannot be convinced to give a shit.

"Maybe you should stay home for a couple days," I tell him at lunch, after the fifth person drops off their dirty tray at our table in a gesture that has apparently been coordinated.

"I spend enough time in a boredom-induced coma in that house. Why do that when I could be sitting in a boredom-induced coma here?"

In other words, he's avoiding Gabriel.

"The trays clearly symbolize what a narc I am. It's brilliant. We'll submit it to MoMA as a public art installation."

"I wish you would take this seriously."

"Waste of a wish. I hear you only get three."

I shove the trays to the side. "I'm worried about you."

He starts laughing.

"What?" I snap.

He tapers off, still smiling. "Sorry. I thought that was one of those jokes that friendship supposedly involves."

I think my lung capacity has increased from all the sighing.

On Tuesday, someone empties the contents of the sanitary bins in the girls' bathroom into Eliot's locker. I try to isolate Anthony long enough to ask him not to be a bag of dicks, but he's constantly surrounded by a phalanx of his asshole friends. Once, he winks at me in the hall. Furious energy explodes in me and I yell, "Fuck off, No-Moore."

His friends are smart enough not to laugh, but Anthony's shoulders go rigid. Everyone else at Forest Hills High might see him the way he wants them to, like a handsome tiger only refraining from eating them out of politeness, but I knew him in his kitten days. And it bothers him.

On Thursday after school, I find the results of my outburst spray-painted on Eliot's Porsche, marring the beautiful hood: ELIOT ROWE GET OUT OF OUR SCHOOL NARC.

Eliot tilts his head critically, then dips his finger in the still-wet paint and draws commas after *ROWE* and *SCHOOL*. "Better."

I'm shaking. "That fucking . . ."

"Oh, I'm upset, too. Horrible grammar." He smirks.

"What happens when Gabriel sees this? He said if people started harassing you, he'd—"

"I'll take it to the car wash after I drop you off at your house." He draws a smiley face next to his name.

"They're not going to stop—"

"This really is new to you, isn't it?" He's looking at me curiously.

The fact that it's not new to him makes me so sad I can barely say anything the entire way home.

On Friday, I confront Trez Monroe.

Every so often in high school, people go through a chemical mutation. They change from anime kids to Wes

Anderson kids, fan-fiction kids to poetry kids, Christian kids to sex kids. Trez picked the most color-coded one: pastel kid to witch-Goth kid. She used to be a poster child for Anthony's type: blondes with tiny noses, light on the butt and heavy on the boobs, with a collection of lace sweaters and an Instagram with at least three thousand followers. He's cheated on her with clones of herself since they first started dating. Now she's a poster child for Halloween, but she does it in style: black fishnets, black leather boots, black skater dress with a shredded hem. Her breakup and transformation would have been a bigger deal if they hadn't been overshadowed by my accident, and Eliot moving to town.

I guess I'm in the middle of a transformation, too. Lacrosse kid to I don't know what. Eliot kid?

Trez is in the auditorium, brandishing a clipboard at two freshmen staggering under the weight of a wooden plank painted to look like a ladder. She switched from cheerleading to theater tech, since you have to wear black for that anyway, and she's already stage manager.

"Why not get an actual ladder?" I ask from behind her.

"Because last year somebody fell off one and broke their wrist. Now we just have to make climbing motions—"

She stops when she turns around. I'm used to that, the pause as the other person mentally scans their previous sentence for anything to do with crutches or car accidents.

I swallow. "Trez—"

"It's Trez."

"That's what I said."

"You said *Therese.*" She pronounces it *thur-ez*. Kendra told me that she submitted a complaint when the yearbook committee spelled it *Therese*. Her name is just part of the new version.

"Can we talk in private?" I ask.

"I'm in the middle of something." She turns to the freshmen. *"Lift it higher!"* Their faces, which had relaxed while she was distracted, tighten back up into panic. This isn't the quiet shadow I remember, trailing after Anthony since middle school. When they broke up, she broke up with her old self, too.

I take a deep breath. "It's about what they found in Anthony's locker."

She starts picking compulsively at her jet-black nail polish. "What about it?"

"Let's talk in the costume room."

She swears under her breath, then addresses the freshmen. "Don't you dare break that while I'm gone."

The costume room is a windowless space stuffed with cheap gowns, frayed capes, and assorted animal ears. There's a loft for storage in which the lead actors traditionally bang each other after the final performance. Once we're shut inside, Trez wiggles her fingers through a hole in a musty tuxedo, not looking at me.

"How did you find out?" she asks.

"It was more of a guess." Eliot's guess.

"That I just confirmed." She grits her teeth.

"Don't worry, I'm not going to . . ." But I have no idea what I'm going to do. All I know is that telling Anthony the truth means Eliot will be safe, and then he won't have to move away.

"Anthony's a piece of shit. He deserved it, and I'm not sorry," she tells the tuxedo.

Definitely not bedridden with a broken heart anymore. "I'm only here because of Eliot Rowe."

"He obviously doesn't care what people think, so why does it matter if they think he did it?" Her voice is cold, but there's a tremble underneath. "I quit cheer so I wouldn't have to go to Anthony's games. We are at zero interaction. Do you expect me to just march up to him and tell him it was me?"

I expected pleas for silence, not a challenge. But she still won't meet my eyes.

"You know what he's like." The tremble gets stronger. "He's always acting like you two are old friends, but I see the way you look at him. You know."

"Yeah," I mumble. "I know."

"You know a little. But you didn't date him for five years." She wraps a piece of hair around her thumb until it turns purple. "Eliot's nobody to him. He's pissed, but it's not personal. With me, it'd be personal."

Her tough persona is new enough to crumble easily, even as she tries to cling to it. It's like I'm a bully, dangling this over her head. I squeeze my crutches. "What do you think he'd do?"

"He always knows when there's someone looking at him, and he knows what he wants them to see. But I've been with him when he thinks he's safe . . . and there's nothing there. He's a black hole. Capable of anything."

I shake my head. Anthony might be a douchebag these days, but he's not a sociopath. "That's not how I remember him. Why did you date him for so long if that's what you think?"

She laughs drily. "We're in the same grade; you remember what I was like before I got with him. Why bother pretending? I was nothing, too. He was the first person who acted like I wasn't, and then he got friends, which meant *I* had friends. . . . You don't know what it's like to face going back to nothing after having something."

It reminds me of how I felt when Gabriel threatened to move away with Eliot. I can't shake off a shiver.

"It's not like he was horrible all the time, or even most of the time, and he's good at making you forget what you think you know about him. And I wanted to forget. He'd sound like he meant it when he said he cared, that he was the only person who'd care." Her fishnets suddenly require extensive rearranging. "He has a thing about loyalty. If he knew it was me who screwed him over . . ."

She's right, and so was Eliot. I can't save him from the tiger pit just to throw someone else in.

"It's your choice. Just don't do anything because you feel sorry for me." She paves her expression over with stone, a trick she probably learned from Anthony.

"I'm not going to tell him."

She doesn't thank me. She's just silent for a second, and then she turns to go. "By the way," she says to the door, "I'm sorry for your loss."

It's not until she's gone that I realize she didn't look at me once.

Chapter Seven

GABRIEL LEAVES AGAIN ON SATURDAY. ELIOT sends me a Snapchat of his car rolling away, chipper ukulele music playing in the background.

Even though all I want to do is bury myself in bed where thoughts of silver Jeeps can't reach me, I ask Dad to drive me to Eliot's, telling him it's where we're working on our group project. Last night I had a vivid nightmare that Anthony burned down Eliot's house in the middle of the day. Even though arson's probably not his style, it's safest to stay close to Eliot for now. The fear in Trez's voice when she described Anthony keeps sticking in my head.

I arrive to find him sprawled on his plastic-wrapped couch in a boredom coma. I log his laptop into my family's Netflix account, and we spend the afternoon marathoning

30 Rock, the show punctuated by twanging from the ukulele and Eliot's grumbled criticism of mainstream comedy.

"Why do people on TV like it when someone shuts them
up by kissing them?" he groans after the scene where Floyd
does it to Liz. "You'd think they'd be perturbed."

"It's called a shut-up kiss. It's supposed to be cute when
a guy cuts off your nervous babbling."

"A *shut-up kiss*," he repeats scathingly. "We should
experiment. I'll do it to you, and you can tell me if you
think it's romantic or if it makes you want to punch me
in the face."

He rolls his eyes, and my brain chooses that moment to
register how much his lips look soft and full. But since Eliot
is always joking unless proven serious, I snort and we go
back to the show.

It's dark by the time we're done. I drag Eliot to the
kitchen, determined to teach him how to cook at least one
thing he can make for himself when Gabriel's gone, except
it turns out I don't know how to cook either. We end up
dumping the burned pasta sauce glop on the lawn.

Eliot drapes himself back on the couch, filling the room
with the crinkle of plastic. "What sad attempts at revenge
do you think Anthony's friends will pull next week? Let's
take bets."

"No. Also, get up for a sec."

He obliges. "What's the point of having a friend if you
can't use your superior knowledge of human nature to win
bets and take their money?"

Once he's standing, I strip the clear plastic off the couch and toss it in a corner. "That was the first thing that needed to be done tonight."

"And the second?"

"I just realized that watching Netflix all day is a depressing way to spend a Saturday. We're going out."

A real friend would distract Eliot from the hell waiting for him at school on Monday. And unless I keep things more interesting than Netflix marathons, there's always the possibility he'll drop me like one of his hobbies. "Plus we need food."

Our burned dinner is still sending up tendrils of smoke as we cross the lawn. I'm the one who knows where we're going, so I take his keys and drive. It makes my skin feel a little crawly, but that's all. Maybe I'd have a worse fear of cars if I remembered the accident. "I'm sorry in advance if I crash your car," I say lightly, just to show that I can.

"It's Gabriel's. Feel free."

We grab hot dogs at the gas station and eat them on the fifteen-minute drive to the lake. It's man-made, not a real lake, but there's a sandy bottom. It's a senior tradition for the class to come jump into the water together in September, in the first month of the last year. I was in the hospital at the time.

"Are we going fishing? A perfect cure for boredom, the one sport that's literally just sitting still for hours," Eliot says as I park in the lot and climb out into the cool air. "And they say I'm the genius."

"You're the only one who says you're a genius."

"My opinion on the subject is the only one that matters."

The night is chilly but not windy, and the moonlight tops the lake with cream. The rickety dock is abandoned, water licking at the faded wood. "I just thought we needed a break from your living room, and this would be a pretty place to hang out."

Jacketless in the cold, Eliot leans against the car hood and yawns. During the day he looks out of place, but at night he belongs. "Prettiness achieved. Now what?"

I'm boring him. Suddenly I'm convinced I'm seconds from losing him unless I do something fascinating this instant. "Let's jump in. There's this thing called the Plunge that seniors do here where they all go in together. It's supposed to be a metaphor for graduating. It was in September, so we missed it, but we can do it now. We'll get right back out. Everyone else did it."

Everyone else is full of endings and beginnings, and I'm made of sameness. I haven't gone to any of the senior events: senior dinner, senior night . . . I won't go to graduation parties, or help plan the senior prank, or cheer at the last sports games. But maybe it's okay that I can't hit milestones with everyone else if I can hit them with Eliot. All anyone needs is just one person, right?

He scoffs. "Everyone else is an idiot."

Everyone else, including me. I flush. "You're right. Never mind."

He looks at me and rubs the back of his neck. "Well, hold on."

"No, it was a stupid idea." Other people can pull off spontaneity. I should stick to Netflix. Even when Kendra and the team asked what I wanted to do, I was always so paranoid that everyone would hate my suggestion that I'd be paralyzed by indecision.

"Would you wait for two seconds?"

I open the car. "Let's go home. We'll pick a new show to watch. I'm sorry—"

"Oh, for God's sake." And suddenly he's stripping off his jeans and T-shirt until he's ivory in the moonlight, his scars gleaming like a school of silver fish. Then he sprints away from me and takes a running leap off the end of the dock.

"Jesus, Eliot!" My crutches clatter on the boards as I chase him. For a second, the surface of the water is still and dark, and then he shatters it, piercing the calm with his harsh breathing. His hair is painted down over his face. He looks ethereal, like a beautiful creature in a fairy tale that might help you or kill you, you don't know which.

"Are you okay?" I gasp.

"Water's great. Come on in." He tilts his head back so that his hair floats out like a crown made of seaweed.

I was worried the water would be freezing in March, but what do I know? A big, stupid smile twists my lips and I sit down, abandoning my shoes next to my crutches but keeping my clothes on. I'm not ready for him to see *my* scars in the moonlight.

Eliot beckons, treading water. I stand up on one leg and leap in.

He lied—the cold is like a fist through glass. I break into a thousand pieces but reassemble when I explode through the surface, feeling like I've been put back together better. "Fuck!" I yell at the moon.

"This aggression toward the moon is unwarranted." Eliot is so close to me, beads of water clinging to his lips and hair. He's as pale as an ancient river deity, but he's not even shivering.

"It's freezing!" I wail. I grab his shoulders, propelling him underwater. He bobs up, cackling, and slips out of my grip like a fish. We're both laughing now, and there's water in my nose, and I'm so violently fond of him, of his snarky comments and his dramatics and his unexpected moments of kindness. I'm cold and so warm at the same time.

"I've never done anything like this before, with anyone," he says matter-of-factly. His breath is the only source of heat in the world.

"I-I've never . . ." I can't. I dive underwater and pop back up. "Been this f-fucking cold! H-how a-are you not shivering right now?"

"People with my condition can't sense extreme temperatures. We don't shiver or sweat. We're prone to hypothermia and heat stroke," he says, still matter-of-fact. At my expression, he backpedals in the water. "Calm down. I'll get out—"

I practically hurl him onto the dock, and then I roll out

after him, seizing my crutches. No way it's the moonlight tingeing his lips blue. The rest of him is so white I can almost see the blood darting in his veins, thousands of tiny, delicate rivers.

Once we're in the car, I switch on the heat full blast. If he dies of hypothermia, it's my fault.

"Stop freaking out. I'm fine," he says impatiently.

"Just because you look fine doesn't mean you are. You need to take care of yourself, or you could die! You can't keep forgetting you have this condition." For once, I barely notice my leg twinging with the cold.

"I thought I was lucky to have it."

I press my palms into my eyelids. "I'm sorry. That was stupid."

"No. You're right. I didn't realize until I met you—I *am* lucky." He stares out the window at the moon. "You're in pain every day. I don't even know what it's like to have something hurt. It's ridiculous of me to act like that's not lucky."

"Your condition is dangerous. It's not a good thing." I'm hot with shame, even though I'm shivering.

He gives a stiff shrug.

I steel myself, then reach over and rest my hand on his chest, partially to see if he's warming up and partially because I want to. The scars are little valleys in his skin.

He takes my fingers and traces them over the scars. "This one, I rested a mug on my stomach that was too hot." Moves it again. "A kid at my old school bet me a hundred dollars he could make me scream. I made a lot of money that day." Moves it again. "In middle school I'd just draw lines on myself with a knife, out of curiosity, I guess, and to remind people they couldn't hurt me." Moves it again. "That one's from Gabriel."

I whip my hand away. "Gabriel?"

"He wasn't a happy teenager. Hard to be when you have the misfortune of being him, true, but we were also moving constantly, making faraway trips to new doctors and hospitals. Our mom had been used to things being easy, and I made things very not easy." He draws smiley faces nonchalantly on the fogged-up window. "We fought a lot as kids. Once he hit me, and for a second, I remember he had this look of release, like he was finally getting rid of the million reasons he had to be angry with me." He stares at the faces, then wipes the window clean. "It didn't hurt me, and it helped him. So I told him to go ahead. It was our bargain— he could hit me when he needed to let off steam, and he'd forgive me for driving Mom farther and farther away. It ended when he accidentally sent me to the hospital."

I make a sound in my throat. He immediately forces his expression into a smirk. "I told him that he had the muscle mass of a ferret, so it wouldn't have hurt even if I could feel pain, but he still acts like he slaughtered a litter of kittens whenever it comes up. If I'd known he was going to feel so guilty that he'd helicopter over me for the rest of my life, I'd have bought him a punching bag."

"Eliot, I'm so sorry."

"Why?" he demands. "I don't have to feel pain. The scars, the hospital visits, my parents—if I think of them as a trade-off, it's fair, isn't it? You can't get something without sacrificing something."

I think of Mom, and my leg. Sometimes you don't even get anything for your sacrifices.

He points at the window. "I went to a drive-in with my parents when I was little, before Dad left, and the windows fogged up just like this. Stupid idea, to watch a movie in your car."

I clench my fists. "They shouldn't have left you."

"Of course they should have. It's logical. Human nature is fight or flight, and you can't fight my condition. When you're faced with something unbearable, you leave. It's what people do."

"You're not unbearable, Eliot." I'm still quivering, even though the car is now full of so much hot air it's like a sauna.

"Years of evidence to the contrary."

"I'm here, aren't I?" My voice sounds like begging. I press my arm against his so he can feel me being here.

"We'll see for how long," he says offhandedly.

It'd be ridiculous if he was afraid of me tiring of him just like I'm scared of him tiring of me. I'm the normal one, the boring one. Before I can figure out how to explain this, he lights a cigarette and rolls down the window, so that the steam escapes into the night and the night creeps back inside.

★ ★ ★

After I'm satisfied that Eliot isn't dying of hypothermia, he drops me off at home, where I spend the night unable to sleep, overwhelmed with sadness about this random weird boy's life.

The next day, I have family therapy. It's usually on Saturdays, but we rescheduled because Lena apparently had too much work to do yesterday. The blankness is always at its worst during family therapy. It transforms reality into a crackly TV screen with the volume low, and I'm perfectly content with it, because when depressing things happen on TV, it means they're not happening to me.

Before Eliot, the TV filter was on all the time.

On the TV show, my family files into the room, minus Lena, who's stuck in "traffic." We take our usual spots—Rex in the squashy yellow armchair by the Legos, Dad on the couch next to me. They each have a resigned look. None of us really thinks that Dr. Brown is helping.

After she checks to see if there's any accomplishments we should be proud of, Dr. Brown sits back and folds her hands in her lap. "What if today we explore something we haven't discussed much yet? The driver of the other car—I'm interested in hearing all your feelings about this person."

Dad exhales long and slow, and Rex resorts to his usual strategy of combining his cells with the chair by osmosis. My leg starts aching. Why this topic? She couldn't possibly

124

know what I remembered.

"The fucker should be dead in the ground. There's not a whole lot to explore," Rex mutters.

"So you have feelings of anger." Dr. Brown's eyes are calm, even though Dad and I are obviously in agony. "Given the chance to talk to this person, what would you say?"

"I'd be too busy murdering their ass to talk," he says gruffly, but there's a thickness in it. "I'd run them down with my truck, see how they like it."

"You wouldn't do that," I blurt.

"I fucking would." He scowls at me, then fixes his gaze on the Legos and adds abruptly, "Sometimes I play this game where I pick a random dude crossing the street and pretend it's him, because you never know, right? It could be. And I have to stop myself from slamming the gas pedal. Do you guys, uh . . . ever do stuff like that?"

"Anger is a natural response to tragedy," Dr. Brown says quietly.

Rex fidgets. What he wanted to hear was probably more along the lines of "It's okay, you're not crazy."

"Also, every time something shitty happens to me, I imagine I can psychically make it happen to them, like I'm a voodoo doll. Stubbed my toe? Fuck their toe, too."

"Rex . . ." Dad's face is heavy.

"Or I picture them eating breakfast. Maybe today they had toast and eggs; maybe yesterday they had oatmeal. And no one will ever bust in and stop them from enjoying a delicious goddamn breakfast every day for the rest of their life."

He'd never say any of this in front of Lena. I can't believe he's saying it in front of Dad, who he's very carefully not looking at.

"Grief often—" Dr. Brown starts.

Something clearly occurs to Rex, because his back straightens so fast it's like he was shot full of mercury. "Why did you bring this up? Did the police find him?"

There's so much weight to the hope in his voice, the rage and relief and desperation. It's so heavy it's pressing me into the ground.

Can you remember the type of car? Any detail will help us catch them.

"I'm afraid not," says Dr. Brown.

Dad glances at me uneasily. "That's nobody's fault. It happened so fast, it's not like Sam could have seen . . . she can't be expected to—she tried her best."

Rex stares determinedly into his lap, away from me.

I see it as clearly as if the words had scrolled across the bottom of the screen: *THEY BLAME YOU.*

And they should. Because I did try my best—to keep it buried.

"Let's talk about something else," says Dad with sudden firmness.

Dr. Brown nods, thin eyebrows arching. Dad's never taken charge here before. "Anger is a draining emotion, but positivity is energizing. Why don't we share some memories you have of your mother. Rex?"

She's capitalizing on Lena's absence to pry Rex open.

I fold my knees against my chest, the heaviness still suffocating. I picture Eliot in the passenger seat last night, the water trickling down his face probably the closest I'll ever get to seeing him cry, and for some reason it helps me breathe easier.

"Yeah, okay. So this one time she bought this giant toaster oven off craigslist." Rex is agitated, swinging his legs like a kid. "It stuck out over the edge of our tiny-ass kitchen counter, and the guy overcharged her for it, and I kept teasing her: 'You'll have to chuck it. You dragged it all the way in here,' blah blah. . . . She was always giving me these heartfelt talks about responsibility and it was, like, *she* wasn't responsible. She was always bringing home junk. Anyway, I kept going and going, and eventually she just started crying. I stressed her out so much, man."

And then Rex is the one crying. He takes stilted shuddering breaths, and suddenly I realize what I would have noticed if I'd been paying attention to the TV screen—his eyes have been red-rimmed since we got here. He came high to *therapy*.

But I'm the one who gave him the pills, and I'm the reason he hasn't gotten the closure he needs, because the person who hit our car is still free. Because nobody ever looked for a silver Jeep.

I cross the room and wrap my arms around him, bracing my good leg against his chair. All hugs have been awkward since the accident. His broad chest catches. Hugs aren't part of his life anymore. Other than Tito, he has no one—his friends had abandoned him even BMD, and he was born at war with our family.

Maybe he doesn't need someone to love but someone to hate. If I could give him the driver, maybe he'd flush the pills and get off the couch.

It was all Mom wanted.

Dad stares at us hugging with a frozen look, like he wants to join but doesn't know how. And that's how we are when Lena walks in. Her eyes widen, but it only takes a quarter second for Rex to wrench away and dry his eyes.

"I'm sorry I'm late," she stammers, looking at Rex in a way that's almost tender. "Traffic . . . I was hoping I'd catch the end of the session."

"Understandable," says Dr. Brown. "Unfortunately we're nearly out of—"

"I just wanted to make an announcement really fast, while everyone's here."

My heart sinks. What announcement would she only make in front of Dr. Brown?

She tears her eyes from Rex and adopts a big smile. "I was reading your book that you lent me, Dr. Brown. It's so *enlightening*. It brought me to some realizations."

"You wrote a book, Dr. Brown?" inquires Dad, grasping for small talk.

"Lena spotted it on my bottom shelf." Dr. Brown fiddles with the buttons on her blouse. "It's out of print, and apparently she couldn't find it at the library or online, so finally I agreed to lend her a copy. But I'm working on a new book that will sell much better, so . . ."

"A new book?" Lena lights up. "Do you need any help? I could organize your notes—"

"God, you were like this in high school, too," Rex moans, then adds in a nasal imitation, "'Oh, Ms. Robbins, let me carry that for you—Ms. Carol, if you need me to print out the syllabus—'"

"I like being of assistance to women I respect," Lena snarls, any tenderness gone. "It gives me an opportunity to follow a good example. You should consider doing that sometime."

"I mean, you sucking up to Mom didn't help you follow her example of not being a—"

"Anyway," she bellows, ignoring Rex. "Her book is called *The Best Thing About Pain: How Pain Makes Us Human*, and there's a section about getting a fresh start both emotionally *and* physically, and it made me realize—we need to redecorate! Our house is so cluttered with old things."

"Redecorate?" repeats Rex like he just threw up in his mouth.

Dad's brow furrows. Then he smiles painfully. "You know, Lena, maybe it is time to make some changes. Sam?"

Even though the word *redecorate* nauseates me, it's impossible to shut down Dad's rare moments of hope. I turn it up to a hundred watts. "That's a great idea!"

Rex gapes at me with fury and betrayal. "And who's going to do all the work?"

"I am!" Lena is beaming. "That was the second part of

my announcement. I asked to change my internship to a remote position where I only have to commute one day a week."

Rex stares at her, uncomprehending. "Why?"

"Oh, for goodness' sakes," she sighs. "Because I'm moving back in!"

She looks at all of us with a bright, expectant grin. Then it starts to fade. I can't tell who's most horrified, Dad or Rex or me. I'd say me, but Rex's face is hard to beat.

"That's wonderful, honey!" Dad croaks, too late.

Dr. Brown stands up. "I'm happy for you, Lena. Looks like we'll have lots to talk about next week."

In other words, scram.

Lena, Rex, and Dad go into the hallway, bickering, and Dr. Brown shuts the door behind them. I can hear Rex's voice get louder as he recovers from shock. "What the *fuck*, Lena?"

Dr. Brown turns to me. "How are we feeling about this development?"

If my home life sucked before, it'll truly be hell from now on. Rex and Lena will drop bombs on each other until we all burn down. BMD, my one important job was to stand between them, a human Berlin Wall, but that's the nice thing about tragedy—you can let all your important jobs slide and no one will say a word.

"Fine," I lie. "She's my sister."

"That's a big sacrifice, to take time off from her life because she believes you all need her," says Dr. Brown.

When I don't reply, she adds, "People need to feel needed. It gives them a purpose."

What if that's why I've been spending so much time with Eliot? Gabriel thought I just wanted a project.

"It'd be one thing if we did need her, but she just wants to think that," I blurt. Eliot does need me, though. Someone to take his condition seriously, to remind him to eat, to be his friend when no one will tolerate the attitude. Maybe I'm the only one who understands him enough to do that.

"Some people convince themselves they can handle their own problems by trying to tackle other people's. Be patient with your sister." She opens her notebook. "By the way, did you try the exercise I suggested last time we met?"

I almost lie, but then I hear Rex asking about the police, and Dad claiming I tried my best. "Yeah."

"Was it helpful?"

"I remembered some of the accident, if that's what you mean." My leg throbs, and I dig my fingers into my jeans. "Just a flash of the other car. It was a silver Jeep."

She leans forward, looking genuinely interested for the first time. "Really."

"It doesn't matter. It's been so long, the police couldn't—"

"Could you recall more if you did the exercise again?"

"I don't know. Maybe."

"You seem reluctant," she notes.

"It's just that I don't see the point in dragging all this stuff back up after six months."

"You might remember what the other driver looked like. Information like that could certainly help the police."

"I don't know. It's been six months," I repeat quickly, my mouth full of sand.

"Does the idea of meeting this person frighten you?"

"I'm not like Rex. I don't think about them as a person. Just . . . a force, like a tsunami, or an earthquake." Something insentient and all-powerful, shredding our lives without knowing or caring.

"It's understandable to be frightened by something like that." She pauses. "But it's not about who or what this person is. It's about you processing what happened. If it also ultimately helps the police catch them, that closure would just be an added benefit for you and your family."

In the weeks after the accident, people kept prescribing time. There were stages to grief, they said. Complete the steps, and you'll be okay again. But my family and I must have skipped something crucial, because we're stuck spiraling apart.

Confronting the driver is what we missed. We're in stasis because I'm afraid to remember.

Dr. Brown is muttering to herself. "Fascinating that pain jogged the memory. Senses often trigger recall, certain scents, sounds . . . makes sense that trauma would be associated with pain. I wonder if . . . criminal investigations . . ."

My leg pulses in time with my heart, and I see broken glass every time I close my eyes. My stomach is a hard ball of panic. I can't do it. I can't write it down again and relive it, even if it'd fix my family, even if that makes me selfish and weak.

"That exercise didn't really change my anxiety." I try to smile. "Is there anything else I could do when I'm stressed?" Like now.

She returns her focus to me. "Alarming images can be combated with positive images. The next time you're anxious, picture something that relaxes you, or makes you happy."

My mind automatically switches to Eliot. I paint a picture of him inside my head, detailing his dark eyelashes and the clean curve of his jaw. He wouldn't feel one bit of this pain. My chest starts to untangle.

"All right, Sam. I'll see you next week." Dr. Brown is writing in her notebook, bent over it so that her shoulder blades stick out under the fabric of her button-down. "And don't forget to give that writing assignment another shot."

My chest tangles back up.

That night, I try again, alone in my room. I decide to replicate the conditions of the first time it worked. Once it's almost midnight, I turn off the lights, leaving my crutches propped against the wall. One step and I'll be on the carpet, the memory silver in my bloodstream.

I'm going to do it for Rex and Lena, I'm going to do it for Dad, I'm going to do it for M—

I curl my fingers so tight into the edge of my mattress

that they go numb. Tito watches me from the floor, his worried eyes shining in the dark. I imagine Eliot walking painlessly in front of me, offering his hand. Maybe if he was really here . . . but he's not, and if I do this it will hurt.

Sometimes no matter how much you need to do something, no matter how important it is to you and the people you love, you just can't, and it's that simple. This Can't is mountains tall and oceans deep and a fucking fact of the universe.

Tito jumps into my lap, and I wrap my arms around my stupid dog and drown his patchy fur in tears.

Chapter Eight

AT SCHOOL, THE BATTLE OF ANTHONY VER-
sus Eliot is a one-sided massacre, an army marching against
a rebel coalition that can't be bothered to pick up a gun.
Eliot's disinterest pisses them off even more. Someone
pours cafeteria milk through the slots in his locker, warp-
ing the covers of his books. Anthony's friends hiss insults
at him in the hallway. There are ominous references to a
Facebook group.

As for Anthony himself, he pretends Eliot doesn't
exist. Like a true mafia boss, he's delegating, setting up
claims of innocence in case Eliot ever reports it to Principal Chase.

"Just tell her." I'm near tears when we head to the parking lot after school to discover that his tires have been

slashed. "Someone will get suspended, and everyone else will back off."

"You want me to narc, to cure my reputation as a narc."

"You don't care about your reputation."

"I don't care about any of this. Why report it when I don't care about it?"

"*I* care about it," I bark.

"Have you considered not doing that?"

I storm off, and then storm back because I'm afraid of what will happen if I leave him on his own. It's been a while since I've been this stressed about something other than my leg. Going to school has never been great, and SMD it's just been a place to exist during the long hours of blankness; but now it makes me tense and hypervigilant, like there are enemies on all sides.

And the harassment isn't even directed at me. Yet somehow Eliot's not afraid. I don't know how he survived this, at school and after school. Maybe physical pain isn't the only kind he can't feel.

Eliot calls AAA, but I need a ride home, and unfortunately Lena is the only one who answers her phone.

"So do you think you're making progress in therapy?" she asks in a horrifyingly chipper voice on the drive, which is supposed to be ten minutes, but she manages to extend it to a trillion years by slowing to a crawl behind a bicyclist instead of passing him.

"Yeah. Sure."

"Now that I'm here, you and I have got to team up. We're

the girls in the family." She glances painfully at my oversize jeans, my short haircut, and makeupless face. "Maybe we can do a shopping day!"

I stretch my lips horizontally in a rough approximation of a smile.

Mom never complained about the way I dressed. It's not that I hate girly clothes—they look nice on other people, but they'd look stupid on me.

"Are the people at your internship really okay with you working remotely?" I ask. "It's not bad for, like, networking?" Hint.

"Obviously I'd form stronger connections if I was there every day, but my place is here with all of you. I was thinking about Rex's outburst at our session before last, and I figured out it's his way of telling me how much I'm needed here!" She hums with cheerful determination. Rex calls her delusional, but I'm jealous of her ability to interpret everything in whatever way makes her feel the best.

"And since Dad is obviously depressed, I should step in as the head of the household," she adds.

"Dad's depressed?" The gummy dinosaurs and the forgetfulness definitely aren't normal, but my depression was a black, black hole, and Dad just wanders around looking confused.

"Of course he's depressed. He has no idea what to do with you two. He's stuck. We—you're all stuck. That's why it's time for a change."

My stomach fills with doom as the bicyclist's butt waves

in front of us. "Hey, why didn't Dad answer his phone? He doesn't have work today."

"Dad," she says proudly, "is at an estate sale. When an elderly person is transitioning to assisted living, or when they've passed away and some of their belongings need to be sold, it's called an estate sale. I gave him a newspaper clipping."

"I know what an estate sale is. It's a depressing yard sale."

"*Estate* sale," she corrects.

Drinking game: take a shot every time Lena says *estate sale*. Alcoholism would be a fair coping mechanism at this point. "It's a step up from craigslist, but not that many steps."

She wrinkles her nose just like Mom would whenever Rex left a mess on the couch. She probably practiced in the mirror. "It's all in Dr. Brown's book—domestic entombment can cause emotional stagnation. *Excuse me!*" she shrieks out the window at the bicyclist as she inches around him into our driveway. "So I took the initiative and cleared out some of Mom's old things while you were at school."

The doom worsens. "What things?"

"Oh, some of that awful stuff Mom found on craigslist. Like that smelly couch . . ."

She keeps talking, but I'm already wrenching the car door open, swinging out before it's fully stopped.

"Samantha, wait, let me help you!"

She couldn't have unglued Rex from the couch long enough to chuck it. And if she tries, we'll set up a barricade and take turns marinating on the polyester, bringing each other rations of gummy dinosaurs. But I can't rush to the living room, due to the fact that half our furniture has been relocated outside.

All the weird junk Mom had accumulated over the years, things so ugly only she could love them—the coffee table that some kid painted to look like a globe, the egg-shaped clock that runs seventeen minutes fast and is the only reason I'm good at math—are discarded on the grass.

"You're probably wondering how I got it all out myself. One word: *Pilates*." Lena stands triumphantly beside me, surveying her destruction.

"Are you having a yard sale? I'll give you ten bucks for that coffee table!" our neighbor screams over her fence like she's miles away instead of several feet.

"We're not selling it!" I scream back.

"Hang on, Samantha," Lena says, then howls at the neighbor: "How about twenty?"

"*Lena!*"

"Oh, come on, it'll save us having to drag one more thing to the dump."

"The WHAT?"

"Dr. Brown's book said that you may be reluctant to let go of old possessions." She gives me a look of bottomless pity.

My world is disintegrating, and pieces of it are on the grass. "Why don't we just burn the house down, since phoenixes rise from the ashes or whatever?"

"What a beautiful metaphor, Samantha! I'm glad you

understand where I'm coming from."

I fly past the boxes blocking the steps and go inside. The best thing about crutches is that nobody expects me to hold the door open for them anymore, and the worst thing is that nobody takes offense when I let the door slam in their face.

In the living room, the couch is gone.

It's GONE.

A horrible empty coffin-shaped rectangle is in the carpet, studded with candy wrappers and pennies and pairs of lost earbuds because nobody ever moved that couch. There's a soda stain on the wall that Rex probably didn't bother to clean up because nobody in a million years would ever move that couch.

Lena follows me. "I'll have this cleaned up in no time; you know how tidy I am—"

"Where is it?" I whisper, ready to wrap my hands around her stupid pencil neck. She abandoned us when Mom died, and now she thinks she can show up and start replacing everything Mom loved?

"You hated that couch. Be reasonable." She steps away from Tito, who's hopping around her feet, and actually snaps at him. "Bad dog. Down."

I scoop him up and tell him he's not, in fact, a bad dog before whirling on her. "Where *is* it?"

"I . . . paid the kid down the street to take it to the dump," she says, wide-eyed. "I figured nobody would buy it, so there was no point leaving it on the lawn. . . ."

"Where's Rex?"

"Upstairs. Don't bother him. He's—"

I climb the stairs faster than I thought I still could and murder Rex's door with my crutches. Mom used to joke that she was lucky she had me to stick between Rex and Lena in the backseat when we were little. I'm supposed to be the buffer, the neutral party. But right now Rex and I have a common enemy, and I've never been happier to have a grumpy bulldog of a brother.

The door cracks open. Rex's headphones are falling off his neck, still blasting the music that must have drowned out the sound of Lena disemboweling the living room.

"I don't *care*, she can do what she *wants*, I don't *care*," he says miserably, and slams the door again.

Apparently the battle was fought and lost while I was at school.

Lena lurks uncertainly at the foot of the stairs. "Samantha, please tell Reginald that I'm sorry if I was a little harsh earlier."

The only other time I've ever heard her apologize to Rex was when she shut the window on his fingers when he was six. She must have really laid it on.

I keep bashing the door with my crutches. It's therapeutic. Eventually it opens again, and Tito nips between Rex's legs into the room.

"What can I do?" He's wild-eyed and wobbling. "She's a nightmare."

"Reginald, I can hear you."

He leans in close. "I'm too high for this, Sam."

Why is it that the only time I want to cry is when I'm faced with my mess of a brother? He's not just too high for this, he's too high for work applications, college applications—too high for everything, every day, and it's my fault because I give him the pills.

"We have to get everything back to normal before Dad comes home," I croak.

"Normal?" He begins to laugh, doubling over, and he's right to, because normal died with Mom.

I have to stand up to Lena. I have to fight, too, not just break fights up. This is my life, not a TV show.

I inhale as if I can swallow Mom's ability to handle Lena, like some part of her still hangs in the air that she used to breathe. But she hasn't breathed this air in a long time. How long does it take for all the oxygen in a house to be replaced?

"You're not really mad, are you?" asks Lena in a small voice at the bottom of the stairs, tapping her foot on the steps, tapping her finger on her elbow, all nervous energy.

Eliot would be able to say it. *Of course I fucking am.* But she's shrinking back, like she genuinely didn't realize how I'd react.

It's always been a fair fight between Rex and Lena, one versus one, and I'm scared of what will happen to the losing party if I finally decide to tip the scales.

"I . . . I have to go out."

I speed-hobble downstairs, past the scalped section of

carpet, and go outside, where I shoo away the neighbor vul-
turing over our yard. My stomach burns. I close my eyes
and try to calm down by envisioning myself sitting next to
Eliot in his car, his arm draped out the window.

But I can just have the real thing, and so I text him.

When he arrives, he's in an unfamiliar green car, his arm
out the window exactly as I pictured it. "Rental while my
tires are replaced," he explains as I careen into the passenger seat. "Are you having a yard sale? How much for the
hideous coffee table? I'll put it in Gabriel's room."

"Can you drive me to the dump?" I manage.

His eyebrow lifts, but for once, he doesn't ask. He ditches
his cigarette in my driveway and peels off, nowhere near as
carefully as he did the first time he gave me a ride. He's not
actually a cautious driver, I realize—he was being consid-
erate because of the accident.

"Are we going Dumpster diving?" he inquires.

I slump against the window and breathe out my nose.
"No. Couch rescue operation."

"Sounds dangerous. I'm in."

Fifteen minutes later:

"WHAT DO YOU MEAN IT'S NOT HERE?" I politely
ask the dump owner, an old man with a beard the length
of my arm.

"Big striped couch, ugly as sin? Some fellow in a Ravens
shirt picked it up half an hour ago. Dunno what in hell he
wanted it for; looked like one of them with a rat nest in it."

My leg gives an enormous throb. I limp to a discarded

tire and beat it to death with my crutches.

"Anger issues," I hear the dump owner say in an aside to Eliot. "You want to watch that."

The couch is gone. Like Mom, like lacrosse, like my old friends and my old life, and I have to accept it because I don't get another option. I'm tired of things I love being gone forever. I didn't think there was room in me for any more holes, but that's all I am now, a collection of empty spaces where things were ripped away.

Eliot stands beside me, smoking a cigarette. Then he smokes another. I can practically feel all the things he's struggling not to say.

Finally he breaks. "ISFJs often project their emotions onto representational objects. It makes sense that you'd hit the tire, since a tire is a component of a car—"

"Not now," I pant.

A pause. "If you need a couch, you can have my white one. Gabriel spent lots of money on it, so I was planning on putting it in the driveway before the next big rainstorm anyway."

"I don't want that couch. I want *my* couch."

"By virtue of grammar, once I give it to you it will become *your* couch—"

"It was my mom's, okay?" I fight back tears. "She found it on craigslist, and we've had it forever, and my sister just threw it out."

"I see. So it's the couch you have an emotional connection to, not the tire."

I didn't expect Eliot to have flawless comforting skills, but this is ridiculous.

"The couch represents your mother—" he starts.

"Are you seriously psychoanalyzing me right now?"

"Which is nonsense," he finishes loudly. "Your mother wasn't a piece of furniture. The presence or absence of furniture has no effect on your love for her."

I gulp a protesting breath, but he's right. I can't compare losing a couch to losing Mom or my ability to walk unassisted.

And maybe redecorating really will help Dad and Rex. If I can't help them by remembering the driver, I should at least let Lena try.

"Fine, Eliot. But I have to warn you that I'm going to cry in about thirty seconds."

He practically catapults away from me, holding up his hands like I'm about to open fire on him. "If you agree with me that this couch thing is stupid, why do you insist on crying?"

"I'm not *insisting* on it; that's just how emotions work. And it's not stupid." I haven't cried since the funeral, but now I'm too revved up not to. It's actually a relief to feel the tears coming, like I've been dying of thirst and I've just taken my first step toward a desert oasis.

"Oh, no—wait, Sam, this is really not my area."

This is the first time I've seen him show weakness, and it's kind of adorable. I have to force myself to ignore it so I don't lose the need to cry now that I've built it up.

"Ten seconds," I sniffle threateningly. "Five . . . four . . . three . . ."

"Should I get you a tissue? I don't have any tissues. Maybe the old man has tissues?" His tortured expression is so cute that all I manage to squeeze out is a single tear. I point at it wickedly as it wiggles down my nose.

"Look! I'm crying."

"Please don't— Ahhh, shit," he yelps. A few feet away, the old man is snickering.

I'm fully cracking up now, my eyes still wet. I might be losing my mind. Dr. Brown will be excited.

Eliot flings out his arms belligerently like he's presenting me to an audience. "And now she's laughing! Laughing isn't supposed to come after crying! The specimen is clearly deranged."

For once, he's lost and I'm the one who understands: when it comes to people, Eliot's confused and mistrustful, like a little kid who's been hurt. He has no experience with relationships, and books and wikiHow can't prepare a logical person for the silly moments and nonsense that are part of human closeness.

It makes me want to treat him gently.

"That's because you only see stuff like this if you're friends with somebody," I gasp, breathless.

"You're saying there's a lexicon of behavior I haven't observed because you only find out about it by being in relationships?"

"Yes," I choke out. "Duh."

He looks devastated.

Once he takes me home and drops me off, still sulking, I wander up to Lena's room. It seems like there should be an apology, though I don't know which of us it's supposed to come from. But her purse is gone. She must have fled, too.

When she moved out, we didn't touch her room, just like we didn't move Mom's stuff from all over the house. But with Lena, there was nothing left to touch. She took her clothes, desk, file organizer, and makeup, and threw away almost everything else: old toys, old photos, anything that could be construed as sentimental. Even now that she's back and her empty suitcase sits on the floor, it could still be a guest room.

Dr. Brown's book is on her bedside table, heavily bookmarked. I'm tempted to hurl it out the window, but I pick it up instead. Dr. Brown's author photo is on the inside cover. She's younger, with the face of someone who thinks she's smart and wants you to think so, too.

I page through it, stopping when one passage catches my eye.

Part 3: The Relationship between Pain and Empathy

Originally, pain evolved as a way to alert us to danger and injury. Pain is humanity's common denominator: we all know what it means when someone says "Ouch," and we instinctively reach out to help. Our shared experience of pain connects people with nothing else in common— different ages, languages, religions. In this way, pain is the root of human empathy.

This drive to assist our community in times of need likely ensured the survival of many tribes and, by extension, our collective survival as a species. Is it hard to imagine that even in the modern day, pain remains key to our ability to understand each other, to forge meaningful relationships, to view others as kin rather than as predators or prey?

I let go of the book, and it thunks to the floor. I kick it under Lena's bed.

My pain doesn't make me more understanding or empathetic—it makes me miserable, and I'm better off taking pills to get rid of it. Eliot just doesn't need pills, that's all. He's not inhuman because he can't feel pain. If not for the downsides, any normal person would leap at the opportunity to have his condition. Even with the downsides, I still can't stave off the jealousy whenever my leg aches. Just picturing him and his imperviousness makes me feel better.

Eliot would be so hurt if he read this.

Or would he? He's Eliot. He probably wouldn't care.

I have to sit down on the bed as I realize that kind of proves her point.

But he panicked at my single tear. Even if he acts like an alien, even if he told me about his parents leaving him and his brother hitting him and his classmates bullying him without a trace of sadness in his voice, I know he cares. It's just easier to go numb.

I understand that.

I take out my phone and find the book on Goodreads. It only has four reviews, all under three stars.

Interesting ideas, but mostly conjecture.

Would benefit greatly from real-world case studies.

The internet has spoken. Dr. Brown doesn't know what she's talking about.

Chapter Nine

THE NEXT MORNING, LENA WAKES ME UP. "I'm making acai bowls for breakfast! Come on down!" she sings through my door.

Since I know from past experience that my choice is to go of my own volition or be dragged downstairs by my pajama pants, I get dressed and find her in the kitchen. The sight of her is like an electric shock.

"What's wrong with your hair?" I blurt.

"Do you like it?" she asks brightly, even though I didn't ask what was right with her hair. "I did highlights in the bathroom last night with a kit from CVS. Salons are *so* expensive, and Mom was a strong supporter of DIY."

It looks like random chunks of her hair were dipped in bleach, but I guess that's technically what highlights are.

With her hair changed on top of her new eye color, she's becoming less like Mom on the outside while simultaneously aiming to become more like her on the inside.

Even Eliot wouldn't be able to explain my sister.

"They're . . . nice," I attempt.

"I love them, too! They're so fun!"

She's clearly trying to drown out yesterday by reaching a new pitch of cheeriness. She hands me her version of an apology, a bowl of what appears to be granola mixed with deer poop.

"Eat. The mind can only be as healthy as the body."

Seconds later, Rex finally slouches into the kitchen. He jerks back. "Holy fuck, who pissed on your hair while you were sleeping?"

Her smile weathers this. "Samantha likes it," she informs him.

"Just because you're making our house hideous doesn't mean you have to match." Rex dumps his acai bowl into the trash and loudly pours himself some Lucky Charms.

Tito says good morning by head butting each of our ankles in turn. Lena's the only one who dodges, fake sneezing like she's suddenly allergic to the dog who's lived with us for ten years.

"Let's you and me have a girls' day this weekend, Samantha," she announces, pointedly ignoring Rex. "They're having a sale at Kohl's on Saturday, and you would be the cutest in a T-shirt dress with a statement necklace. It'd still fit with your casual style!"

"Actually I thought Sam and I could walk Tito across Hensley Field that day." Rex mashes his cereal with a spoon. "Since we both love Tito. Since he's fucking awesome and too good for you and all."

"She can't walk all the way across that field anymore! You need to put thought into *accessibility*."

She says *accessibility* in a perfectly audible whisper. I pour sugar onto my breakfast while she's distracted, hoping it'll revive my appetite.

Rex sloshes his half-full bowl into the sink. "Come on, Sam, I'll drive you to school today."

I can tell by his eyes that he's not high. I gamble on a nod, and we run for it as Lena flutters after us, protesting.

Every time I ride in Rex's truck, it's gotten filthier. I raise my good leg to avoid the crumpled McDonald's bags beneath my seat as he drives, blasting Drake.

"So this fucking sucks," he says over the music.

"We can survive until she leaves. It won't be long—she hates it here."

She can't stand people who are sad and stuck when she's so desperate to move, move, move.

"Dad's being a pussy—" he begins.

"Don't say *pussy*."

"Dad's being a *vagina* and letting her boss him around. He didn't say anything about the couch—he just stared at the empty space and went all quiet. . . . He needs something to snap him out of it, and she needs something to focus her energy on, other than ruining our house."

He waited to bring this up until we were alone, and

people don't wait to say good things.

"So, since it's been a while . . ." His knuckles redden and whiten as he tightens, relaxes his grip on the wheel. "I thought maybe you just needed time. You know."

"I obviously don't know."

"Well, I was just wondering . . ." Tighten, relax. "I was wondering if you'd remembered anything else about the guy who hit you."

My leg aches hard and fast, and I flinch away from the windshield like it's about to shatter. The pain fills me with sudden and irrational rage, a need to attack what's hurting me in order to survive. "Maybe I was too busy having my leg crushed to be memorizing license plates and finger-printing people."

The car fills with tension and Drake.

"Sorry," he whispers.

When he's sober, the lines under his eyes are deeper, his voice sadder. This is what the pills hold back.

The one time I suggested he start antidepressants like me, he pointed out that we probably couldn't afford another co-pay.

"No, *I'm* sorry," I grit out. *I'm sorry I haven't tried harder to remember.*

I think I could, if I tried.

And that scares me.

I *will* try again. I memorize the bags under Rex's eyes. I will.

"I don't deserve to ask, but . . ." His voice breaks.

"I'll give you more after school," I say quietly.

He falls silent, his head drooping.

I force myself to think about anything else, and my mind lands on school, where I'll be the only one standing between Eliot and everyone else—until Gabriel finds out and transfers him somewhere far away from me.

Apparently the only way to distract myself from stress is with other stress.

"Rex?" I ask, and he seems relieved that my tone isn't accusatory. "This is random, but could I ask you something about Anthony?"

His head shoots back up. "I swear to God, if he's hitting on you—"

"He's not! Jesus! He's just pissed at my friend, and I need advice on getting him to lay off."

"What friend? Are you talking about the random kid you told me he jumped last month?"

"Well, now he's a friend."

"What kind of friend?"

"Not the kind that's hitting on me."

"He better not be, because—"

"Can you shut up and tell me what to do?"

"There's nothing to do." He slurps from a week-old soda, gags, and spits the flat syrup back into the cup. "Let Anthony flush it out of his system, and he'll back off once he feels like he's won."

Which will be when Eliot is dead, because he refuses to let people feel like they've won. "I need something faster."

"You need to stay away from him is what you need to do.

How do I say this so you listen? You, Anthony, stay away from."

He sighs. Even though Anthony and I shared a grade, it was Rex he latched on to, trailing after him in our house and carrying Tito from room to room. "If there's anyone who shouldn't be scared of him, it's you."

"I don't know, man. It doesn't matter."

"If it doesn't matter, tell me what happened, because something obviously did."

Suddenly he's the most attentive driver ever. He fixates on the road until I poke him.

"Don't repeat this, okay, because it's probably not even true," he mutters finally. "I smoked too much weed senior year and had a paranoid phase. By the way, don't you fucking ever do drugs. Or drink, for that matter. Or have se—ergh—*relations*. Or watch *Game of Thrones*. That shit is not appropriate for—"

"Fact one, I'm already on drugs; they're just legal. Fact two, I'll become a nun right now if you get to the point."

"You know what I mean. . . ."

We're almost at school. "The point!"

"Ahh." He rubs his head hard. "Remember when I got expelled? I don't remember putting weed in my laptop case, okay? I don't remember a lot of things from that year, but there it is."

It dawns on me. "You think it was Anthony."

He groans. "It sounds dumb as shit."

"But you had weed on you all the time back then. . . ."
I scratch my ear, confused. "What makes you think that?

Did you piss him off?"

"Nah, man, it's more of a feeling." He reaches unconsciously for the flat soda again, but I swat his hand away. He lets it fall. "We were cool, or I thought we were, but there were times he'd get weird."

"Weird how?"

"I'd tease him about the old days, and he'd laugh like normal, but his eyes would go *cold*. Gave me the chills when we'd hang, like he secretly hated me. It was probably just paranoia. I also thought Mr. Tennyson was batting his eyes at me in English."

I've gotten that same feeling around Anthony, the sensation divers probably get when they brush up against a shark.

But it's ridiculous—he's No-Moore; he's not capable of subterfuge or psychopathy. At worst, he's a bully. Not to mention what he owes our family. He was part of it, for a while. Rex was probably too high to remember he'd put his weed in his laptop case. It's his style: hide it in the charger compartment, unzip it in class, drop it on the floor. Anyway, it'd be too ironic, Anthony *and* his ex-girlfriend pulling the same trick.

And didn't Eliot say that people with Anthony's personality type were deliberate? He wouldn't gain anything by getting his old friend kicked out of school.

"I don't know," I murmur as he rolls up to the building.

"It's cool. I wouldn't believe me either. I'm not the definition of a reliable dude."

And he laughs this sad, awkward laugh that stays with me long after he drives off.

After first period, I text Anthony, telling him to meet me in the stairwell before gym. The surprising part is that he shows up. He's already in his gym clothes, his backpack slung over one cleanly muscled arm, his eyes the lightest blue in the world.

"What can I do for you, Samantha?" he asks.

I don't waste time. "When are you going to be done with Eliot?"

"If it was anyone else, I would have been done ages ago."

That wasn't what I was expecting. "Why is Eliot different?"

"Oh, it's not him I care about. It's you." The light, light blue eyes are icy. "Yelling at me in the hallway, talking shit about me behind my back, all for this random asshole? Did *he* grow up with you? Did he name every stuffed animal he ever had after your dog?"

He always manages to edge in sideways with a guilt trip. But I rally.

"If you care about me, you'll leave him alone." I square my shoulders. "He's the reason I'm not lonely now."

"Why the *fuck* did you ever have to be lonely? All those months after the accident, I was right here, but you never even spoke to me." His voice wavers, and he clenches his fists. "I always wished your mom was mine, too, that I could trade and be one of your sibs. After the accident, I could have used a shoulder, but you were obviously only interested in solitude—until this guy shows up, screws me over, and suddenly he's the one and only person you'll talk to."

Mom was always extra nice to Anthony, the poor rich kid with the empty house—buying him McDonald's when we weren't allowed to have it, passing him endless treats for Tito so our dog would love him as fiercely as any of us. Now that I think of it, I remember hearing he stayed home from school for a week after the accident. My sadness was so big at the time, there wasn't room in my field of vision for anyone else's.

"I'm sorry," I tell him. "I never realized you were grieving for her, too."

He lowers his eyes.

Even jerks are capable of struggling. And ironically, now that he's tormenting Eliot, I've tasted what it must have felt like to be Anthony Moore in middle school.

Maybe he's just trying, in the most obnoxious way possible, to keep himself safe. "I'm sorry we grew apart, too," I say. "Maybe we can catch up sometime. But only if you leave Eliot alone."

"Oh, no." He points at me. "That's not the ultimatum—this is. *You* leave Eliot alone. As in, stop speaking to him. Then I'll end it. He's not good for you, okay? It's for your sake that I'm doing this."

The most douchebaggy, asshole-teenage-boy way possible.

"That's not happening."

He looks at me coldly. "Then we'll have to see how long it takes him to break."

That's the stupidest thing I've ever heard, I want to yell.

Instead I say, "He honestly doesn't give a shit about anything you've been doing."

"I guess I'll have to try something new."

He strides around me and goes downstairs before I can shrug off my bag and hurl it at his head.

Gym class, a modern-day hell. The worst part is that I used to like gym.

It's ridiculous that I have to go, but my doctor has stopped writing notes and started saying things like "There are some activities you can still do, Samantha" and "I want you to stay involved with your peers, Samantha" in a poorly veiled attempt to bully me into going back to physical therapy.

"Today we will be playing basketball." Mr. Englewood announces it like a military drill, marching back and forth in front of the bleachers. "Anthony, Trez, you're team captains. Let's take this game seriously."

Everyone watches in wordless fascination as Anthony and Trez face each other.

"Therese," Anthony says with a warm smile, pronouncing the two syllables distinctly. She ignores his outstretched hand, her expression black ice, though I spot her jam her fingers into her pockets so nobody sees them shaking. Anthony throws a what-can-you-do glance at the audience. The message is clear: she's a bitch, and he's trying his best.

They pick teams until there's only Eliot left, sitting next to me. I can't tell which one is more irritated when Trez calls his name.

"What?" he snaps.

I nudge him. "You're on her team."

"Teams for what?"

Trez grabs him and drags him toward her half of the gym floor. "Just stand somewhere and be tall."

She must not be too guilt ridden about the bullets he's been taking for her, but then, she doesn't seem like the type of person who lets herself feel guilty.

"Help me keep score, and pay attention. You could still be a sports analyst," Mr. Englewood tells me.

I give him the finger when he turns to blow his whistle.

Both teams are afraid of their captains, and the breakup is common knowledge. The game gets brutal fast, but even after the third kid is elbowed, Mr. Englewood doesn't call foul. "Love the enthusiasm!" he shouts, a bloodthirsty gleam in his eye.

Eliot loiters in a corner. I know who he's texting before my phone buzzes—there's only one person he messages.

What is the point of requiring that we constantly bounce the ball instead of carrying it like sane bipeds? This sport was likely invented during a contest to find the stupidest way of transporting an object.

I'm giggling when Anthony rams him.

The phone flies out of his hand. I lurch upright, and Mr. Englewood reaches for his whistle, but Anthony is already whipping around. "It was an accident! He was just standing there on his phone. I'm so sorry."

He yanks Eliot upright with a fake smile.

"He deliberately assaulted my teammate!" shouts Trez.

"I don't hurt easy." Eliot scoops up his phone. I notice I'm rubbing my leg and make myself stop.

Just show some weakness, Eliot. Let him think he's won.

The game restarts. At Englewood's frantic gesturing, Eliot wanders vaguely toward the ball, feigning elaborate distress when someone steals it from in front of him. The next time someone passes to him, he stands there making a face.

"Dribble or pass!" moans Mr. Englewood.

Across the gym, Anthony takes advantage of the moment to whisper something in Trez's ear. She turns pale, jerking away.

Anthony is grinning when the ball hurtles at him. It literally knocks the smile off his face.

"It was an accident, et cetera et cetera," says Eliot, yawning.

"I want the rest of the game *accident free*," Mr. Englewood thunders. "Now go, go, go!"

I'm imagining all the different ways Anthony could separate Eliot's head from his body, but Anthony spends the rest of the game loping around the gym and scoring points with his easy smile, getting nowhere near Eliot.

It ends in a tie just as the bell rings. Englewood retreats to his office, dabbing sweat off his forehead. Trez storms out into the hall, and everyone else follows, except for Anthony.

He walks right up the bleachers past Eliot, bends down, and pushes his mouth against mine.

I don't think the word *kiss*. I think *get off*. *Get off*, *GET OFF*. But I can't say it, can't push him away. I'm frozen. Anthony doesn't move his mouth, just holds it against mine, hot and revolting. Only when one of my crutches clatters to the bench below does he break away to hand it to me.

"She might give you attention," he remarks to Eliot, who is paralyzed near the doors, "but you'll never be able to do *that* with her. I can tell just by looking at you. You're not brave enough, and even if you were, you'd never get it right."

I barely hear his words. I'm scrubbing my lips repeatedly with my sleeve, so raw with fury and humiliation that I can't string a sentence together.

Anthony hops to the floor, winks at Eliot, and leaves the gym.

Eliot just stands there staring at me.

I don't want to hear whatever sarcastic comment he has cooking in his stupid brain because he can't comprehend that now isn't the time, and I don't want his laser eyes on me when I'm already on fire.

"What?" I bite out. "Go!"

And he does.

I waste gallons of scalding water showering the disgustingness off. Even though I take forever, I still kind of expect him to be waiting in the hall when I come out.

But no one is there. And he doesn't answer my apology text, or the second or third.

It's not just that Anthony stole my first kiss. It's that he did it in front of Eliot, which shouldn't matter, except that it does.

My leg hurts, so I go to the nurse's office and lie down until school is over and I have to call Lena for a ride home.

After school, I visit Mom's grave.

I never got the point of going to a graveyard and talking to a rock, so I've come zero times since Mom's funeral. It's extra terrible, because the graveyard is down the block from our house, short enough for me to walk if I take half a Vicodin first.

Tito whines at my feet as I wrap my fingers around the gate. The sky is so blue. Every time I consider coming here, it ends up being a sunny day, and everyone knows you're only supposed to go to a cemetery when it's pouring rain.

Mom's grave is partway down the third row, neighbors with a man who died in 1943. Not living next to her, but not dying next to her either. Just there.

Tito doesn't curl up on her grave like a movie dog, but he does mush his tiny body against me, transferring whatever comfort he can to my ankle.

There's fresh roses from Dad and a packet of Mom's favorite sugar-free green tea gum from Rex. It doesn't look like Lena's been here, unless she's the one who brought those dramatic white-and-pink flowers with the huge petals—but they're not her style. There's piles of them, the stems uneven, like someone cut them from their own garden.

"Hi, Mom," I say to the stone. No answer. Leave a message. *I need advice.*

"Hello, shiny rock," I correct myself. "From a quarry in Minnesota, according to the sales guy."

Stupid, stupid. Across the graveyard, someone's baby is crying. It feels rude to be so blatantly alive here.

"I met this guy," I say to the stone.

I would achieve just as much informing the fence.

"He's, um. Cool." Digging deep into the emotions now. Dr. Brown would be proud.

Okay, if I'm doing this, I'm doing it.

"His name's Eliot. He's like . . . five inches taller than me? But I don't know, I stand weird now. He's super into personality types—or he used to be; he's not into anything for more than a month. I think he's into me now, actually, but we're coming up on more than a month."

The gravestone expresses little surprise at this.

"Oh, and he doesn't feel pain. I guess Eliot and you have that in common." I clear my throat. "Probably the nicest thing about being dead. Eliot figured it out while he's still alive."

I'm so glad she can't hear me.

"I don't know, like. What a crush is." I clear my throat again. These dead people will think I have pneumonia and that I'll be joining them soon. "He doesn't like anyone else but me—he thinks everyone else is stupid. And that makes me feel special, and I've been sort of looking for a new way to feel special."

Did you feel special when you met Dad?

Were you scared he'd get bored of you?

"This isn't really helping, but I never talked to you about my problems when you were alive, so I don't know if it would have been different. I mean, hopefully it would have."

I want to ask Mom if she saw who hit us. It's not fair that she left me with the responsibility of figuring it out. But asking questions is different from just talking—it makes it obvious that no one is going to answer you.

So I say something pointless instead.

"I got my first kiss today."

And then I'm crying so suddenly I'm startled. My mouth opens, and the tears get inside. It's stupid and I hate it and it makes Tito upset.

Even though it's only four, I head home and go to bed.

Chapter Ten

ELIOT'S NOT AT SCHOOL THE NEXT DAY, SO I
have to sit through lunch by myself. Then I have to sit
through Social Studies by myself as everyone else pairs up
to grade each other's quizzes.

I watch them do it like they're in another dimension. It's
so messed up to make us choose teams in gym, or partner
up in class, just in case anyone was wondering who has no
friends.

It wouldn't kill you to text me back, I message him. If
it would kill you, you should see someone about that.

I can't shake the feeling that something's wrong.

I mean, something's probably wrong. Eliot lives crisis to
crisis. I bet his house was swallowed up by a giant crack in
the ground.

I google that under my desk to find out if it's something that actually happens, and it is, and it happened to a family in New Mexico.

If you don't text me back in the next hour I'm going to assume you've been swallowed by a giant crack in the ground like that family from New Mexico, I text him.

What family from New Mexico?

I nearly knock over my crutches.

Why aren't you in school? Are you mad at me

Come over, he finally responds.

I'm in the middle of class, I can't just waltz out.

Buzz. Don't waltz, then. Walk.

What's the matter? My fingers are sweaty on the screen.

May be dying. Need you to deny or confirm. Don't call 911.

He has to be joking, some bizarre prank to break the ice from yesterday.

You're not serious right

Eliot???

Oh, God.

How do I get to your house I don't have a car. Fuck fuck fuck

I leap out of my chair as much as I can leap and basically scream, "I have to go to the nurse's office."

Everyone looks up from their partner's quiz to silently judge me.

Mr. Parish frowns. "Samantha, did you know you've excused yourself from class six times this semester?"

He had to choose number seven to be a dick about. "I really don't feel good."

"You look fine to me."

Eliot better be drawing his last breath.

I lean over and fake retch like I'm going to puke. Someone says, *"Ew."*

"Very well." Mr. Parish sighs. "Would someone please escort—"

I'm out of the room before he can finish.

At the end of the hall, I stop. Am I going to walk all the way to Eliot's?

If he said not to call 911, I should probably call 911.

But he also said he hates hospitals.

After an hour of walking in the abnormally hot April sun, I'm soaked with sweat. The Vicodin staves off the pain, but I'll be feeling it tonight.

When I finally reach Eliot's, I want to fall on his front porch and die. Instead I shoulder his door open, my hand so moist it slips on the knob.

"Eliot?" I wheeze.

The house is roasting, and all the windows are shut. Luckily Gabriel's shoes aren't by the front door.

Eliot isn't in the living room, so I check the kitchen. The oven's on, which explains why the house is a furnace. A limp bag of frozen french fries, which I bought him at the grocery store, is melting by the sink.

I'm about to search upstairs when I trip over his foot, sticking out from behind the kitchen counter.

"Eliot!" He's lying in a heap on the floor, his phone inches from his hand. I'm hit with a wave of pain from my leg, and my chest splinters, but there's no blood on the white tiles.

I kneel beside him, fumbling for my phone, and his crystal eyes flash open. "You got here fast."

"You're alive," I croak.

"Not sure. I was hoping for a second opinion."

He doesn't lift his cheek from the tiles. He's as pale as he was the night we went swimming, apart from the two red spots of color that burn in the hollows of his cheeks.

My heart is pounding. "How long have you been like this?"

"Five years. No, three. Ask someone who was paying attention." His pinpointed pupils swing up toward my face. "You're sweating."

"It's hot; I walked here."

"Impossible. I texted you, and in a second you were in my kitchen."

"I think you fainted," I say, trying to stay calm.

He nods, his hair scraping against the floor. "That would explain the headache."

I move two fingers along his temple to find a slight bump. He's hotter than any human being should be. "Do you have a thermometer?"

"Yes, but it's covered in substances I don't want in or around my mouth. Or wherever you were planning to put it."

"Then I'm taking you to the hospital, because I don't know what's wrong with you."

"I do, if it's hot out," he says. "Heat exhaustion. Happens every so often, nothing to worry about. I can't sense heat any more than I sense cold. But I know the difference between heat exhaustion and heatstroke, and I only have to go to the hospital if it's the latter."

That definitely seems like something to worry about. But a girl on my lacrosse team almost passed out once during a summer practice, and I remember what the coach said to do.

I roll him onto his back. "Have you had any water lately?"

"Define lately."

"Eliot, I'm calling an ambulance."

He waves his other hand weakly. "I just wanted your professional opinion as to whether or not I was dying. You're free to go."

"I haven't given it yet." I fill a glass of water and mix equal parts salt and sugar in it to hydrate him faster, my fingers trembling. I can't believe I was jealous of his condition. He's lying on the floor.

"Well, hurry up," he says. "You'd make an awful mortician."

"I think," I say, dragging him into a half-sitting position, "you need to go to the hospital."

"If you take me there, I'll die on purpose and haunt you."

"Shut up and drink this."

"Not unless you promise not to take me to the hospital."

I have to physically stop myself from bashing my head

into the refrigerator. "Are you five years old?"

"No hospital."

"JESUS CHRIST, *fine*. Just drink. Slowly."

Eliot achieves a smirk as he swallows, water spilling down his chin. His shoulder presses into my chest, so angular it hurts.

"Now up," I tell him.

His legs shake as he hauls himself upright, gripping the countertop for support. He takes two steps and promptly throws up into the trash can.

"You said the water would help," he says accusingly.

"I said to drink slowly!"

In the living room, he tosses himself facedown on the couch, and I have to make him turn over so he won't suffocate. He always looks a little undead, but now even his lips are white. And I was jealous.

He deserves someone better than me.

To avoid meeting his eyes, I open every window in the house, place an ice pack on his forehead, and make him drink cold water until he's a more normal color.

"Just rest, okay?" I say. "I'll be right here."

"You can go home."

"I don't have anywhere to be." I perch on the edge of the couch. The sunlight trickling through the window is a lazy kind of bright.

"Does this happen a lot?" I whisper.

"Only when I'm distracted. I was pacing." He's drowsy, less Eliot-sharp.

"What were you distracted by?"

He doesn't answer. His eyes drift half closed.

"Have you ever kissed anyone before?" he murmurs.

The worst thing about crutches is how easy they are to knock over, and the other worst thing is how much noise they make crashing to the floor.

Eliot watches me scramble for them. "Before Anthony, I mean."

"No," I hiss. "And that one doesn't count."

"I'm sorry." His voice is thin. "I was useless when he did that. You've been standing up for me, and I just . . ."

He trails off. Guilt isn't prickly or sarcastic enough to be an Eliot emotion, and it's new and shifting in his voice.

"Forget about it," I say determinedly. "I'm sorry, too, if I ever acted like congenital insensitivity to pain with anhidrosis was something to be jealous of."

"It's okay." He's almost completely asleep now. "It's just . . . part of my life."

"You're not bitter about it?" I should let him sleep, but I'm leaning forward. "It's not fair that it's part of your life. It shouldn't have to be."

Rex pretends that my leg isn't a part of my life, that I can do everything I did before. Lena acts like it's my entire life. Dad is convinced that a miracle awaits me in physical therapy. But to say to myself *It's just a part of my life* feels like defeat. It sucks, and I want to let it suck.

"There's nothing to be done about it," he says quietly. "It just is."

There's a long silence, and I'm starting to feel sleepy, too, but then his eyes fly open.

"Sam!"

I have a heart attack. *"What?"*

"You walked here." He's breathing hard. "All the way here. Are you okay?"

"I . . . yeah." My heart plummets to my stomach. "Of course."

"Good," he murmurs.

Gradually he dozes off again, the rise and fall of his chest slowing, softening.

That was the weirdest part of Mom's funeral, her chest not moving. I couldn't remember ever paying particular attention to her chest moving, but it's not something you notice, because it's constantly happening. You only notice when it's gone. That's when the world turns dizzy and unsafe, when you lose something you had no interest in because it was always there.

Eliot's chest goes down, and for a millisecond I'm completely convinced it won't ever come up again, but then it does, and I'm hit with such raw relief that I almost cry.

I slide off the edge of the couch onto the cushion next to him and tilt sideways, letting my shoulder fall into his hip, my head into the curve of his waist.

Either he doesn't wake up or he pretends not to. I listen to his heartbeat. An unbelievably frail, thready noise is all that's keeping him alive.

I suddenly feel incredibly protective, like my heart is

swelling to cover him. It's the most intense emotion, and the saddest; but it's a full kind of sad, so it's okay.

Over the next few days, the shootout between Rex and Lena morphs into a cold war, with both sides employing couriers and spies. And since Dad is working overtime to avoid the situation, I'm everyone's courier and everyone's spy.

"Samantha, can you please tell Reginald that drinking straight from the juice carton shows disrespect for the other human beings with whom he shares a house?" Lena says over Girls' Breakfast, a new thing before school where she gives me a flaxseed smoothie and teaches me about feminism. "There are glasses in the cupboard."

After deciding I'm more afraid of Lena, I go upstairs to Rex's room and deliver the message.

He throws his covers off his head and snaps, "Can you *please* tell Lena that if she has a fucking problem with the way I drink my fucking orange juice, she's welcome to go fuck herself?"

"I'll tell her that when I want to die."

He squints at me, then sighs. "Fair enough."

I linger in the doorway. "Couldn't you at least try—"

"No."

"But—"

"*No*," he says. "She's never tried."

"All she does is try."

"She tries to be my overlord, my—my mom. Give me a call if she ever decides to try to be my goddamn sister."

He rolls over until he's not facing me anymore.

"Can't you at least try?" I ask Lena later in the kitchen. She's teaching me how to cook a vegan casserole, because taking on traditional feminine responsibilities isn't anti-feminist if you do it by choice, apparently. I don't point out that she didn't give me a choice.

"He needs tough love." She tucks a strand of hair behind her ear, leaving a streak of tomato paste that makes her look like she has a head injury. "Mom never told him what he has to hear, so now it's my job."

I stir the pasty vegetable glop. "Don't you think maybe you're hurting his feelings?"

For a second she looks so shell-shocked that the head injury seems more realistic. "Not that I'm on his side," I say quickly.

"I know that Rex is sensitive. . . ." She washes her spoon, her expression lost, but then she shakes her head. "But I'd rather hurt his feelings than his future. I'm putting *my* future on hold because I'm the only one who's willing to push him hard enough to do anything with his. I refuse to let him be the waste of space he thinks he is."

"It's Rex. He'd probably throw away his future just to annoy you."

She laughs, and her anxiety lines disappear, and for a second she looks like Mom again. "Which goes to show that he can achieve whatever he sets his mind to. And so can you. A lot of colleges are still accepting applications for spring enrollment, Samantha."

I stir harder. "I have to repeat next fall semester because I missed so much school, remember? I told you I'm probably going to take spring off."

"Then you have to do something with your time. You're a valuable person, and it'd be a shame to waste it. You can't just sit around being sad—you, Dad, Reginald, all of you stagnate." She makes a frustrated sound. "The best way to move on is to *move*, Samantha."

"Right."

"To make changes and discover new things and live your life instead of letting it drain into the sink. I tried to do that on my own, but you all refused to do it, too, so I'm going to drag you with me if it kills me."

I don't answer, because she's talking mostly to herself.

It turns out that our conversation must have energized her. When I get home from school the next day, she has skinned our house.

"That wallpaper was old-fashioned. I thought we could repaint." Lena steps away from the front door, where she was waiting to ambush the first family member to come through it, which unfortunately was me. The walls are hemorrhaging swans, strips of wallpaper torn and dangling half attached.

I picture my sister mutating into a werewolf, claws sliding out, *shick-shick*, slashing through the paper in a predatorial frenzy.

"I was thinking cerise," she twitters while Tito writhes

in piles of shredded paper. "Nice and happy."

I can't speak. Now I'll never finish counting the swans.

And Lena knew the story behind that wallpaper. She knew.

When Dad gets home, I expect him to finally break, but all he does is stare. Maybe that's just how he breaks.

Rex shows up behind him with a McDonald's bag in hand. "Fuck," he roars when he sees the walls.

"Eloquent," says Lena. She's twisting and untwisting her hands.

Rex rounds on Dad, who is still gazing at the eviscerated walls. Rex-Dad interactions are rare and tense, since Rex doesn't bother with the everything-is-fine smile like me.

"Are you going to let this slide, too? Next time we leave for five seconds she'll probably tear up the floorboards because it'll remind us how Mom walked on them, or some other pseudopsychology bullshit—"

"It's not pseudo anything; it's Dr. Brown's *book*," Lena protests.

"Which she agreed was bullshit, so shut up about it."

"We agreed to redecorate. It's not like anyone else has tried to help." Her face is red. "Call me crazy, but—"

"All right. You're crazy."

She glowers. "*Call me crazy*, but I truly believe it'll be more pleasant for you all to live here if you aren't surrounded by constant reminders!"

"*You all?* So what, you're going to run for the hills again as soon as you've finished ruining everything?"

I want to stand beside Rex and snarl, too: *Does it make you feel better to pretend you're like Dr. Brown, someone whose job it is to help us with our feelings without having to feel them, too?*

But taking sides is forbidden, so I shovel the anger down deep until it burns in my stomach like pain.

Dad coughs, and I pray. It's not forbidden for *him* to take sides. He can tell her off, ask how dare she start fires when she doesn't have to breathe the smoke.

"Maybe we could use some fresh paint," he says quietly.

Damn it.

Lena sags, relieved. "Samantha and I will pick out the colors! Not because girls are inherently better at domesticity, you understand. I just know she'll want to be involved even if the painting itself is too much for her."

She gives me a look that says *Please.*

I throw up inside my head and say, "Sure."

Rex drops his uneaten McDonald's on the floor and storms out of the house.

Lena stays behind in the living room, glancing around at the carnage like even she isn't sure how it got there.

That night, my leg keeps me awake. I while away the hours sorting all the things I'm mad about, arranging them like little candles.

I'm mad at Lena for being pushy, and Rex for taking pills, and Dad for being passive. I'm mad that Mom had nothing to offer me in the graveyard, at Anthony for kissing me without permission, that my and Eliot's bodies don't work right when everyone else's does.

Then I'm mad about everything at once, and for a second I'm so overwhelmingly unbelievably angry that I could go downstairs and tear down not just the wallpaper but the walls themselves.

My heart beats a mantra: *It's not fair. It's not fair. It's not fair.* But then a different part of me replays Eliot saying, "It just is. It just is. It just is."

That's what I'm thinking, over and over again, when I sit at my desk and open my notebook, letting my leg twist underneath me just enough.

In order to get to the school, her mom has to drive past the community art college where she met the daughter's father.

"There it is." She says it every time like she's unveiling something.

The daughter knows the story of how her parents met—not because she asked, but because her sister told her.

Back then, her mom was a pretty, young student who made sculptures out of trash, and her dad was ten years older and had a job cleaning up trash. The only thing they had in common was that they both liked to eat lunch alone. One day, they happened to eat lunch alone together at the pond next to the school, which had a legendarily unfriendly swan that had been raised on a diet of college students' sandwiches.

Her mom went to pick up a discarded bottle for her newest sculpture, the swan made a break for her tuna sub, and her dad valiantly rushed to defend it. Her mom turned and suddenly had to save a surprisingly cute janitor from being beaten up by a swan.

Fifteen years later, once they saved enough to put a down payment on a cramped house, the Realtor told them they could change the wallpaper when they moved in.

Her mom said, "It stays. It's a good omen. I met this man because of a swan, so if this house is marked by swans, it's the house for me."

The daughter props her feet on the dashboard. She's not doing it to be annoying—she wants to stretch her legs before the game. She thinks that her legs look okay, stuck out like that without the fat squished against anything. She's always had strong negative opinions on the other parts of her body, but she's pretty neutral about her legs.

The mother glances at her, away from the road. "Feet off the dash."

She takes one leg down but leaves the other up. Sometimes when she's away from her brother and sister, she acts like the baby in front of her mom and only feels a little bit guilty.

She likes when her mom drives her places, likes the feeling of being carried through the world with all responsibility handed over to someone else.

Beyond the windshield, the silver Jeep is still coming fast.

And then, suddenly, it turns into their lane. Not the wild swerve of a drunk driver, but a sharp, neat turn

Don't stop. Don't stop.

I picture Eliot on his couch with the afternoon sunlight slanting into the room, but I can't get his chest to move in my mental image, and it just makes me panic more.

I close my eyes to block out the other images, but they stay crisp on the insides of my eyelids. The Jeep turns again and again, tires not squealing, brakes not grinding.

It turns on purpose.

I grip my head to squeeze out this thought, but it seeps through me like acid. My leg is searing. I fumble with my pain pills and drop them all on the floor.

I try to remember how to go blank, but it's been too long; I've lost the trick. I've been letting myself feel the good things, and now I have to feel the bad things, too, and I'm too small for them.

It's not fair.

It just is.

My phone screen lights up on my desk, and my brain processes a message from Eliot.

Look out your window. I'd throw rocks at the glass, but modern technology renders such romantic gestures obsolete.

Also I might break it.

I look out my window. There's a shape on the lawn, and as my eyes adjust to the moonlight, I realize it's Eliot Rowe, perched atop our ginormous, ugly, striped couch that is supposed to be gone forever. He's waving.

I attempt to break it into bite-size pieces of information to fit into my brain: Eliot. Couch.

Crutches, Vicodin, bra, sweatshirt, shoes, in that order.

I sneak downstairs as much as I can sneak, but Rex passes out high every night, Lena wears earplugs and a face mask, and Dad takes sleeping pills. In the living room, Tito wakes up from his vigil on the empty rectangle in the carpet, following me into the backyard.

Eliot hops off the couch as I approach him wonderingly, half afraid the whole scene will vanish if I get too close. He lands softly in the grass like some nocturnal forest creature, no coat as always, the moonlight lining his hair with silver.

"Hello, animal," he greets my dog.

He never knows the right thing to say, but somehow he knew to come tonight.

I fling myself at him in a hug, knocking us both back into the couch. The jolt hurts my leg, but I don't care.

"Sam—" he stammers.

He's stiff but he's warm. This is the person I picture to lessen my pain.

"Thank you, thank you, thank you," I manage, and then I make myself stop. Beside me, Tito yips when he recognizes the couch and leaps onto his favorite cushion. I run my hand over the coarse fabric. All its familiar lumps and crevices are in the same places.

"How?" is all I can say.

He straightens, recovering his smirk. "The old man at the dump said the person who took it was wearing a Ravens shirt. So all I had to do was ask around until I found somebody with a new neighbor from Baltimore. I went door-to-door. For a while. Probably why I overheated the other day, actually, but if I'm going to die for a cause, I'd like it to be furniture."

"*All* you had to do?" I imagine every citizen of Forest Hills opening their door to find Eliot, holding a cigarette and demanding intel about their neighbors. I start laughing.

"The Ravens guy didn't even charge me for it," he adds casually, like he's talking about something normal and not a miracle. "Said it was stinking up his house."

I trail my fingers over the divot that Rex's body has carved into the cushions, the one comfortable spot in an uncomfortable object, made to fit only him and Tito. "How'd you lug it here?"

"I paid the dump owner to borrow his truck. He loaded it up and everything. Apparently decrepit people can still be useful—who knew."

I'd burst into happy tears if that wouldn't be an awful thing to do to Eliot Rowe specifically.

"You said it was stupid that I cared about the couch," I point out.

"It is stupid." He looks away and coughs awkwardly.

"Should we throw out our backs maneuvering it inside?"

"Let's leave it here. My brother will see it in the morning and pee himself."

I sink into the cushions. With Eliot as a protective layer between me and the panic of what I wrote in my room, I can breathe again. The memory sat wrong in my brain for so long it got scrambled, that's all. Just because I can't recall tires squealing doesn't mean the Jeep turned on purpose.

More importantly, I came so close to remembering the accident. It's terrifying but thrilling, too, like a fifty-foot fall with a safety net at the bottom.

Eliot lounges back and gives the couch a fond pat, as if they've bonded. "I was going to bring it during the day, but then you'd have had to explain the couch *and* me to your family. One bizarre thing at a time."

"You're not bizarre, Eliot. You can meet my family anytime."

"Tomorrow at five, then?"

Shit. "Um—"

"You didn't think I'd actually say yes." He's grinning. "Don't worry. My quota of lunatic family members is already filled."

I'm ashamed of my own relief. Who cares what my family thinks of him?

He shifts and grimaces. "It's like sitting on sledgehammers covered in packing peanuts. Now that you have it back, can we ceremonially burn it?"

"No."

"Well, if you ever have a bout of temporary insanity and do decide to introduce me to your family, I'm sitting somewhere else."

I'm giggling. He smiles. His arm fits snugly against mine, a line of heat on my skin, and I imagine us fused there, our veins opening into each other like a network of rivers leading into the sea.

"You know what's really weird?" I ask.

"Too many things in my life lately."

"It's the fact that it's one a.m., and I'm sitting in my backyard on my ugly couch with Eliot freaking Rowe." I shake my head slowly. "But it's also really good. I don't know what random events in my life led to this weird situation, but I'm glad they happened that way."

He's silent, which usually means he's generating a sardonic comment, but I can tell by his dumbfounded expression that this time he's not.

He looks at me. His eyes are the exact color of the crater shadows on the moon.

This is a bizarre twilight zone where couches come back from the dead, and I'm capable of facing my fears, and it's okay, right now, if he kisses me.

He glances away, looking twice as confused as before.

Tito jumps in my lap and then his, bringing us back to earth the way he does when he's afraid the humans are drifting away. Dreamily Eliot strokes his back.

"This animal isn't so bad," he says softly.

A flood of affection for him slams the breath out of me.

I normalize my voice. "He's getting fat because I was always the one who walked him."

I can't even walk my own dog anymore. For a jarring second, that ruins everything, but then I let it pass, because my leg isn't stopping the rest of me from being happy tonight. I may not be good at dog walking anymore, or lacrosse, but at least I'm good at Eliot.

"I could walk him. I mean, if you want." He gives an exaggerated shrug like he doesn't care either way. "I go for walks at night when I can't sleep, which is always. I could stop by and pick him up."

I stare at him.

He squirms. "It's safer to walk with a dog at night, that's all. Scares off the bears and murderers and whatnot."

Tito drools on Eliot's elbow and then licks off his own drool, as if to say *I love you and walks and bears and murderers.*

"That'd be great," I stammer. "I'll start leaving him in the doghouse for you."

He rubs one of Tito's ears between his fingers like a coin.

"I had a dog when I was little," he says distantly.

I hesitate, and then I put my arm around his shoulders. I squeeze him briefly. He's too tall, too rigid and angular, but I'm glad I did it.

"Hey, Eliot? Next time Anthony does something, don't act like it doesn't bother you."

He slips away. "But it doesn't bother me."

"It's okay to be bothered."

"It doesn't bother me," he repeats. It fits his voice easily, like he's spent years reciting it, which I guess he has.

Even now, he won't let me in.

But there are so many things he doesn't know about me either, so many parts of my life I have yet to share. It would take years to give him all that. It'd be worth it, though, to get some of him back. We could trade ourselves back and forth until we had enough pieces of the other to become more than just ourselves.

I refocus on him. "Anthony will leave you alone if he thinks he's successfully bothered you. Even if it doesn't, pretend it does. Your safety's more important than your pride, okay?"

"If you really believe that showing weakness makes you safer, that it convinces people to leave you alone, you haven't met any people." He says it lightly, but he folds his hands together in his lap with a kind of resigned sadness he probably thinks is secret. "They only leave you alone once you prove with finality that they can't hurt you."

I shut my eyes. "Just—please? Eventually it'll blow up, and someone will do something bad."

"Like hit me?" He laughs.

I punch the couch cushions. "It's not funny!"

His laugh fades. "It really bothers you that much."

"*Yes.*" It bothers me even more that he's still pretending it doesn't bother him.

He opens his mouth, then closes it, then opens it again. I watch him struggle to phrase the question in his eyes.

At last, he just says, "Fine. I'll end it."

But he doesn't tell me how or when, only leans back and closes his eyes like he's too exhausted to do anything but fall asleep right there in my backyard.

I breathe in the cool air like it's cleansing me. People have such different perspectives on humanity, just based on how much kindness or cruelty they've experienced. I want to be nice to Eliot until his perspective changes.

People have been pretty nice to me. Maybe I shouldn't waste the opportunity to be someone who thinks humans are all right, even if sometimes they say they're sorry for my loss when they haven't felt its depth, or they don't realize that their shouting and arguing harms me even if it's not directed at me, or they persist with obvious lies because they're scared of the truth.

After a while, the sky starts getting lighter, and I have no choice but to poke Eliot awake and send him back to his lonely house.

Chapter Eleven

THE NEXT MORNING, REX GOES OUTSIDE IN his boxers, sits down on the couch, and drinks his coffee right there in the yard like he always expected the couch to find its way home.

Lena demands an explanation, but when her interrogations don't yield anything, she stomps into the kitchen and furiously chops fruit, running the blender on the loudest setting. During breakfast, though, I catch her sneaking peeks into the living room with something like relief.

At school, I sleep through all my classes, through lunch, and through the bell. When I wake up, the classroom's deserted, chairs shoved back wildly everywhere like there was a sudden evacuation.

The problem with having no friends is that nobody wakes you up to ensure you don't miss the bus. But now I have Eliot to bring me home.

I peel my cheek off the dried drool cementing me to the desk. A note falls to the floor.

I HAD NOTHING.TO DO WITH IT.
-trez

My leg starts throbbing.

The hallways are abandoned, too, even though they're usually peppered with people waiting for rides. Did the zombie apocalypse happen while I was unconscious?

I pop an ibuprofen and walk faster.

Eliot's not waiting by my locker as usual. Or reading in the library. Or smoking in the bathroom.

Finally I go outside, where the sun gleams off the glass doors, blinding me like it did on the day we met. I loiter helplessly on the steps. He's not answering my texts, which has never led to anything good.

Then Kendra appears behind me, her ancient floral backpack dangling from one shoulder.

"Hi, Sam," she says politely, and maybe a little coldly.

"Hey." I try to sound calm. "Where is everyone?"

She shrugs. "I was making up the Calc test."

"Have you seen Eliot?"

"Isn't he always with you now?"

Definitely a little coldly.

"Is there something going on?" I ask.

I'm talking generally, but she must think I'm referring to the situation between her and me, because she sighs a particular sigh that means she's upset.

"It's no big deal, Sam. I swear I'm happy for you. It's just that I tried to reach out to you for months, and you kept shutting me down—which is fine, if being alone was all you needed. But suddenly you have a boyfriend, and you've made it very clear that you didn't *need* to be alone; you just didn't want to be with me or the team."

I stand there with my mouth hanging open like an idiot.

"We worked our asses off, is all. We signed that giant card for you and had that benefit bake sale." It keeps spilling out of her like blood that won't stop pumping now that the wound is open. "Erin thought you didn't really like us, that you were only hanging out with us because of lacrosse, but—I thought you were cool, Sam. I wanted you to like me for more than lacrosse. But you dropped us as soon as you couldn't play anymore."

She turns bright red and looks as if she might cry.

I'm speechless. I hadn't imagined that losing me could hurt these girls, because I thought that they only hung out with me because of lacrosse, too. That we were all under the same impression that I didn't quite fit.

After a moment, Kendra covers her mouth and lets a muffled "Oh, God" escape into her fingertips. Then she drops them and blurts, "Anyway, it's fine. Let me try to find out what's going on."

Her shoulders hunched, she starts texting frantically.

"Ahh . . ." I'm strangled. "Kendra . . . I'm sor—"

Her phone buzzes.

"Oh, shit," she says suddenly, staring at the screen.

"What?"

Her forehead knots up, and she shoots me a frightened glance.

"Erin says that Eliot challenged Anthony to a fight. Everyone's over behind the gear shack by the senior lot."

I'll end it, he'd said.

I start swinging toward the senior lot, fast enough that my leg stabs at me, my mouth sharp and dry with broken glass.

Anthony's finally so fed up with Eliot's lack of reaction that he himself is going to attack until he gets one. What neither of them understands is that no reaction doesn't mean Eliot isn't hurt.

Dr. Brown was right in her book—people only help someone when they show pain, which means no one has ever tried to help Eliot.

The senior lot is all the way across campus, half-hidden behind the sports equipment shack. It's so far that the faculty rarely police it, so it's the second-best place for drug exchanges and the best one for fights.

Half the school's population is clustered on the pavement—not just Anthony's friends, but people from groups who never got involved in their war. Anthony must have marshaled as many witnesses as possible to make a final example out of Eliot.

I wedge apart the crowd with my crutches until I spot them.

In the middle of the circle, Anthony is calmly shedding his jacket, handing it to a girl who looks like prebreakup Trez. Eliot yawns and checks his phone, his brow furrowing slightly as he reads the texts I'd sent.

I'm about to tackle him when a hand grasps one of my crutches. It's that asshole who tailed us to the parking lot, Anthony's friend Jaden. His breath smells like Cheetos.

"Eliot gave me fifty bucks to stop you from getting involved," he says simply.

"*Eliot* did?"

He shrugs. "He didn't pay me to lie."

They only leave you alone once you prove with finality that they can't hurt you.

I hate him.

In front of us, Anthony winds up and breaks Eliot's nose.

I should probably be used to it by now.

Jaden grabs my other crutch, to steady or trap me, I don't know. "Get off," I scream in his ear, but he's busy yelling his head off in support of Anthony.

Eliot wipes his nose, smearing the blood across his cheekbone like a comet, and waits.

Either Anthony's too focused to question why Eliot's not defending himself, or he's just used to everything being easy. There's a scary confidence in his eyes, like he's done this before and doesn't mind at all that he has to do it again. He drives his fist into Eliot's stomach. I flinch more violently than Eliot does. Eliot cocks his head as if to ask what, exactly, Anthony's trying to accomplish.

I know what Eliot's trying to accomplish.

I inhale deeply, about to make so much noise they'll have to register me, but Jaden covers my mouth with Cheetos-dust fingers right as Anthony hits Eliot again, this time in the jaw. Eliot's head snaps to the side. He faces front again immediately, blood streaking upward from the side of his mouth.

"Did the fight start yet?" he asks loudly, nasal from the broken nose.

A few people laugh, but most are frozen, in horror or fascination. Some have their phones out. Anthony's grinning, like this is all part of the performance he planned, but it's a tight grin. I stare at him desperately, but he doesn't look back.

He's just No-Moore, isn't he? Just an insecure jerk acting big. But I know how small he used to be. He won't really hurt Eliot.

Two more punches to the face, knocking Eliot down. Anthony kicks him in the chest so hard he's thrown onto his back, but Eliot just crosses his arms under his head like he's napping in the sun.

No one's laughing now.

"What's wrong with him?" someone mutters near me.

"Let me go or he's going to die," I rasp into Jaden's palm, but he has a rigor mortis grip on my crutches. Even though he's not yelling anymore, this time I think he legitimately doesn't hear me.

Anthony's confidence is gone, and now his eyes are just scary, his fury whole and radiating. Eliot isn't sobbing like he anticipated, not begging or embarrassing himself. He's embarrassing Anthony. In front of everyone. He glances furtively over his shoulder at us, like he's afraid I won't be the only one who remembers how small he was.

Eliot checks an imaginary watch. "Does anyone want to hold my arms behind my back?"

His voice slices through me. Nobody answers him.

"No?" He crosses his wrists behind his back and sneers at Anthony. "Will it help if I keep them like this?"

Anthony flexes his bloodied, shaking knuckles.

"Everyone's looking at you," Eliot says quietly, but loud enough for us all to hear. "What do you think they see?"

The break happens in Anthony's face, in the whites of his eyes.

He punches Eliot again and again, until the pavement is splattered with blood and broken glass.

No. No broken glass.

But Eliot will smirk until the moment he dies, because he literally won't fake a reaction to save his life.

Then Anthony gets his hands around Eliot's throat.

I thrash against Jaden, but he's glued to my crutches like he needs them to defend himself.

Even as Anthony's biceps rope with how hard he's squeezing, his expression melts from rage to nothing-ness. But Eliot's lips are white beneath the blood, his face stricken. Pain or no pain, he still needs to breathe.

No matter how much he jokes that he won't make it to thirty, he's obviously never believed for one second that he could die.

I'm losing him, just like I lost Mom, my mobility, my friends, my sport. I'm going to lose everyone who defines me and everything that makes me special until I dissolve into nothingness.

I can't save the person I picture to lessen my pain, and it's a Can't, mountains tall, oceans deep, a fact of the universe.

It just is. It just is—

But Jaden's not holding on to me. He's only holding on to my crutches.

I lunge forward *pain* another step *pain* three steps *PAIN* and my knees buckle, but I'm falling right. I crash into Anthony and Eliot. The three of us tangle, and it's strangely intimate, the sweat on Anthony's cheek marking my shoulder, my elbow scraping Eliot's ribs, all our staccato heartbeats.

I seize Anthony's wrists, and for a second it's like both of us are strangling Eliot. Life drains by centimeters from his half-closed eyes, and some faraway part of me wonders if that was what Mom looked like as she died.

But I've broken the seal over the crowd. Two guys help me haul Anthony off and push him to the ground, where he lies gasping and motionless. Eliot regains consciousness almost immediately, rolling over and hacking so deeply it's like it's coming from underground.

The second they're apart, everyone backs away. I swim through panic and pain, focusing on Eliot's chest, moving up and down with all the life still in him.

He staggers to his feet. The bruises on his neck are already blackening.

"See?" he shouts hoarsely at all of us, not seeing me, just the enemy. "None of you can hurt me! None of you can fucking do anything to me anymore!"

Chapter Twelve

Dear Gabriel,
I think it's time to move Eliot to a different school.
He's so good at convincing the world he can't be hurt
that even I fell for it, but

Dear Gabriel,
Eliot's doing well! I've been looking out for him at
school, and

Dear Gabriel,
Most of the time I feel like a stranger inside myself. I
couldn't tell you who I am, because I don't know.
But Eliot gave me a personality type. He acts like
he's above everything, but he's not above me. They

say you have to love yourself before someone else
can, but Eliot liking me makes me wonder if maybe
there's something to like—he's a logical guy, and
that's the logical conclusion. But I'm not sure what
that thing is, and I'm not brave enough to ask.

You'd take him away if I told you what happened.
But what's the point of moving him from place to
place when his problem isn't a place? People are,
and they're everywhere, so he'll have to learn to deal
with them eventually.

He's starting to get the hang of dealing with me.
So keeping him here might be better for his safety in
the long run, right?

Dear Gabriel,
You suck. Your stupid long-distance methods of
caretaking suck. You say it's for his sake, but I think
it's so you can relieve your guilt by looking after him
without actually having to look at him. Have you
considered that your guilt isn't the most important
thing in this situation?

Deleted messages: 4

Eliot doesn't come to school for three days.

He ignores my texts, except to say Yes when I ask Are
you alive? If you don't answer I'm calling an ambulance.

I add: You better text me every hour while you're refusing

to see me, so I know you're alive and not passed out on the kitchen floor again, or I'm calling an ambulance.

Alive. (1:02 p.m.)

Alive. (2:02 p.m.)

Alive. (3:04 p.m.) . . .

Every night I steal Rex's truck, drive to Eliot's house, and whack on his door with my crutches until my arm goes numb.

"He just needs time," I tell Tito once I get home and he trots out of his doghouse to greet me.

Because he's a good dog, he doesn't point out that when I'd needed time before, it had turned into forever, which I now realize must have sucked a lot for Kendra if it felt like this.

Which it might not have, because I wasn't her only person like Eliot is my only person.

If you're hiding from me because you think I'm mad, I am mad, and this is making me madder.

Alive. (11:04 a.m.)

At school, everyone avoids me, like Eliot's problem is contagious. Nobody mentions an obscure congenital condition that I hear of. The general consensus is that Eliot was psychopathically high on six different drugs—so not only is he a narc, he's a crazy addict.

"Which explains how weird his eyes always look, right, like he's freezing the inside of your brain. . . ."

Anthony's version is that he was doing a good deed, trying to teach the dangerous nut job a lesson. He acts like he's the most Anthony he's ever been, flirting with teachers in class and swaggering around with his tiger smile, but people still talk.

"Did you see him lose it? I was scared. . . ."

Maybe that's why no one reports the fight to the principal.

I don't reward Anthony by acknowledging him, but when he leans against my locker on Tuesday with a sigh and an "Are we still not talking?" I do spit in his face.

Alive. (4:06 p.m.)

Alive. (5:09 p.m.)

How does one put out a medium-to-large kitchen fire? (6:36 p.m.)

For the first time since the accident, I speed on the road, Rex's truck bouncing over potholes. My leg aches with each jolt, and I hear the tinkle-explosion of breaking glass; but I keep going, because it figures that I leave Eliot alone for less than a week and he sets himself on fire.

The front door of his house is unlocked, and the hallway is thick with smoke. I open windows as I go.

"Where are you?" I call.

"Kitchen," he calls back. "And you were going fifty in a thirty-five, judging by how fast you got here. Very illegal."

It doesn't sound like he's on fire, and that means I get to be pissed at him.

I stick my head into the kitchen. Black smoke billows from the microwave as Eliot ineffectually flaps a pot holder. He nods at me like absolutely nothing horrible has happened recently.

"The microwave's smoking, and I know how you love

to tell things not to smoke."

His face is a mask of bruises, his neck a nightmare. I force myself to speak. "Are you okay?"

He takes out his phone and types. Mine buzzes with a text.

Alive.

I want to hug him, or hit him. "This is my second-least-favorite way I've found you in this kitchen."

"I was cooking, which is supposedly what you're supposed to do in a kitchen."

"It smells like death." And he looks like it. "Go stand by the window so you don't suffocate."

I squint into the microwave, my eyes watering. An evil-colored lump smolders behind the glass.

"What was that before you killed it?" I ask.

"Cake," he says briskly.

". . . Cake."

"I mixed the things in the cupboard together and put them in a bowl and heated the bowl up." He flourishes his pot holder. "Cake."

It's hard to know if this is strange behavior or just Eliot.

Miraculously I find a pair of salad tongs in a drawer. I carry the cake and melted plastic bowl outside, depositing them both on the gravel, where they should ward off any neighborhood demons.

Then I go back inside and inform Eliot, "If you set your house on fire, you in fact die. Smoke inhalation also exists."

"Obviously. I was inhaling it earlier."

In the living room, there's a mountain of cigarette butts on the table, and the once-white couch is gray. Eliot lolls on top of it. Something about the sight bothers me, but I shrug it off and confiscate his cigarettes.

"Smoking in the house is a fire hazard *and* a lung cancer hazard. You're going to kill yourself."

"I'd be lucky to live long enough to have the option of killing myself," he quips. "It's kill or be killed, isn't it? In this case, my body is my nemesis. At least by committing suicide my brain gets to participate in my fate."

I refuse to let him wring shock from me.

"Are you *okay*?" I ask. "And I'm not asking if you're alive—I know you're alive. I'm talking to you."

"You are. Highly unusual—typically people avoid that."

"Are. You. Okay."

He sighs. "I both love and hate that question."

"Great answer! I especially like how helpful it is, and how it's a totally adequate response to what I asked!"

"Do you think grocery stores deliver cake?" he inquires at the ceiling.

"Why did you even text me? You didn't need me; all you had to do was open a window." I slam my hands on the coffee table. "You ignore me for *days*, and then for some reason you pick this random moment to call me over and play weird mind games?"

"Isn't this what you're supposed to do today?" he mumbles. "Invite your friends over?"

"I don't know if you're aware of this, but since you like

to be aware of things—*you're not making sense.*"

He gives himself a little shake. "I wasn't ignoring you. I texted you hourly. I've never done anything hourly in my life."

Now that I have visual confirmation he's alive, my desire to kill him has returned. If he was acting at all like a human being who'd gone through what he had . . . instead he's acting high.

"You *paid* that asshole to hold me back," I spit. "That's what pisses me off the most, that you knew I'd want to stop it, and you made sure I couldn't. Why the hell did you think fighting Anthony was a good idea? What's wrong with you?"

"Ahhh." He lies back and steeples his fingers. "*What's wrong with me.* The eternal question. The answer depends on who you ask, you see. My doctors say congenital insensitivity to pain with anhidrosis; everyone else says it's the fact that I was born."

"I'm not indulging you right now," I snarl. "You could've been seriously hurt. You *were.*"

"Breaking news—" He pinches his wrist hard. "*I don't feel pain!* So by definition, he could not have, and did not, hurt me."

"When are you going to stop believing that not feeling pain makes you invincible?"

"When you do."

"I don't think that!" I'm yelling now. Good—he deserves it.

"Sometimes I wonder why I was born like this." He's not listening. "Maybe someone up there saw that I was special, that there was something about me that would make other people want to hurt me more than normal, and making it impossible to hurt me was God's way of giving humanity the middle finger. Like, 'Ha-ha, you can't do anything to him, no matter how hard and how often you try.'"

I swallow. "What have you even been doing for the last few days?"

"Pills, mostly."

My rant dies in my throat as some submerged part of my brain recognizes what bothered me about him sprawled on the couch, covered in bruises.

It's that he looks like Rex.

"What do you mean, pills?" I ask, even though I know exactly what he means, pills.

"Adderall, specifically. It's been sitting in a drawer, because I haven't needed the distraction since I met you."

He twists toward me like he expects me to be impressed.

Adderall, like Anthony sells. If I was boiling over before, now the water's gone and I'm choked with steam. "You were *buying pills* from Anthony that day behind the Dumpster. That's why you warned him about Trez, and why you went to that house. You didn't want to lose your *supplier*."

"You're not as good at hiding when you're hurt as you think you are." He sits up. "No one is, except me. Prey animals have evolved to show fewer outer signs of sickness and injury so predators are less likely to target them. Did you know that? It's only a problem when people try to keep them as pets and don't know it's time to take them to the vet until it's too late. You can demand I fake weakness all you like, but I should teach you how to conceal yours."

Now that I know, the signs are obvious, but it's a high high, not a low high like Rex gets. The otherworldly energy, the flashing eyes. He really is an alien now, his mind spinning faster than planets and asteroids, faster than mine ever could.

"It's not . . . *weakness*," I say. "It's being human."

"Then I choose not to be. It's not worth the trade-off."

"I hate to tell you, but you don't get to choose."

"A scientist learns by watching mice; he doesn't crawl on the floor and try to *be* a mouse. Because you're wrong—I can never be a mouse. I'm different. Fundamentally."

"Eliot—"

"I prefer watching to being anyway. Why bother getting messy with relationships when I can learn that people are stupid and shallow and selfish just by watching from a distance?" He attempts a smirk. "And yet watching you didn't explain the mystery, so here I am, trying to be a mouse. I probably look ridiculous."

"What mystery?" I ask faintly.

"You're so normal! You're so amazingly normal. There must be something distinctive about you I haven't figured out, though, because I don't *like* normal. . . ." The smirk shivers and falls apart. "But I like you."

He wouldn't be saying this if he wasn't high. I close my

eyes. "If you knew everything about everyone like you think, you'd know I don't want to talk to you when you're like this."

"*Exactly*," he shouts. "Because this is unfiltered me. You think I don't have a filter? You have no idea. If I was a hundred percent myself all the time, you'd hate me, because I'm not designed for you or anyone else. I'm alone on an entirely other plane of existence where you wouldn't last five minutes."

"You—"

"Every day you see more pieces of the real me because you're around me constantly and they slip out; I can't hide them all forever. The longer you know me, the closer you get to hating me, like everyone who's ever been around me constantly. Do you know what it's like to be inherently hate-worthy? To listen to the tick of people's timers counting down until they reach the built-in limit they have for your yourself-ness? It's kinder not to waste their time and to show them who you are from the start, so you don't lose track of the timer and get caught off guard when it suddenly goes off. I'm afraid I've wasted your time, Sam. I was selfish for once and tried to act like one of you, but the truth was always going to come out eventually. And I think I just heard your timer go off."

His voice is simultaneously despairing and prideful. I can tell he's fascinated by how intellectual and tragic he's made his own loneliness sound, but he's not the great dark enigma he wants to be. He's just a sick teenager who was left behind by the people he loved because he was too much work.

I say the only thing I can think of:

"That is so *stupid*."

Then I shoot out of the living room and outside, where I devour purifying gulps of fresh air. The sky is a waterfall of gold fire as the burned cake offers the last of its smoke to the sunset. Several houses down, someone is mowing the lawn.

I walk. It hurts, but I don't stop. Soon I'm whispering to my leg with each step, "Fuck you, fuck you, fuck you. . . ."

Everything Eliot's dealt with at school, that we've dealt with, is because he wanted to get high. I can feel sorry for him while recognizing that he's a rich, entitled, pill-abusing asshole, and that even the other rich, entitled, pill-abusing assholes hate him because he's also a pretentious, elitist, self-absorbed *dick*.

I only sniffle a little bit. Lena would be proud.

It's not until the sunset washes out into a dark pink-blue that I sink to the curb, throwing down my crutches. My leg throbs predictably. I don't want to think about Eliot, so I imagine Tito and his soft ears, and it helps until the Vicodin kicks in.

I'm in an unfamiliar section of Eliot's neighborhood, the doors of each house closed. Even though they're just other people's houses, it feels like they're specifically shutting me out.

I'm about to call Lena when I remember she's in Northton

today. Dad's at work, and Rex is probably high, because getting high is the most important thing in the world to the people I love, and anyway I left his truck at Eliot's.

So I don't move. The sky doesn't care and continues to darken.

After a while, a sleek car pulls up alongside me. Eliot rolls down his window, and here I am with my head in my hands like I was just widowed by war.

"Go away," I say.

"Please let me drive you home. You'll hurt yourself." His eyes are mostly normal now, except for the guilt. "I promise I'm fine. It was already wearing off when you came over."

"You shouldn't worry about a mouse like me from your higher plane of existence," I snap, and then I hobble off, because I want him to feel bad.

He follows me slowly. A minivan rumbles up behind him and honks.

"Fuck off!" I scream at it.

"I do need you," Eliot says from his window. "For my experiment."

"What is it with you and experiments?" I whack his car with my crutches before remembering it's a nice car. "What are you doing, spiking my food with hydrochloric something-or-other to see if it turns my hair blue?"

"No," he says in a voice that could only be called small.

"Then what? Measuring how long it takes my timer to go off? Because when you average me in with everyone else, I'm pretty sure you've got a one-point-one-second time frame before you make everyone want to get as far away from you as possible—"

I bite off the rest.

His eyes are so sad.

"That's a fair assessment," he says. "My experiment. It . . . ah. I was seeing if it was possible. For me."

The sound of him failing to string a sentence together is inherently bizarre. "For you to what?"

"To have a person," he mutters, looking down. "To be fair, I did predict this. So that does strengthen my hypothesis that I'm right most of the time."

God damn it.

"Get out of the car," I say.

He does, right away. I get in the driver's seat, and he climbs back in next to me.

"I'll take you to your truck," he says haltingly. "Then I won't ever bother you again."

I lean over and hug him. Because he's not a rich, entitled, pill-abusing asshole, or a pretentious, elitist, self-absorbed dick.

Well, he's a couple of those things, but not the worst of them. And most important, more than them.

Still not used to my touch, he's rigid, his pulse light as a breeze against my skin. Again I can't believe a little fluttering like that keeps him going despite Anthony beating him, his parents abandoning him, and all his scars.

"I was mad because I was scared, Eliot. I don't want to lose you. I don't think I could find someone else like you."

"I don't want your timer to go off," he whispers.

"There's no timer." I guide his head gently to my chest. "Just my heartbeat."

He pulls back. "That is a timer."

"It's not counting down to me hating you." I'm wiped, but I also feel soft and spread out and protective. The kind of feeling that could make someone love themselves as well as someone else.

"I know enough about you to know that I like you, and that's not going to go away for no reason," I tell him.

"You say you know enough, but you don't know everything. Not even close." His shoulders are tucked as if there's a blow coming. His body language says, *Don't get my hopes up.* "Unless you have all the information, you like a version of me that isn't real."

"When we met, you said I couldn't give myself a fair assessment, because I'd be judging myself about stuff that doesn't matter. Right?" I grip his arm. "There will always be a million things I don't know about you. There were a million things I didn't know about even my mom. But I know the important stuff, namely that you're the right kind of person for me, and slowly finding out more little things is the fun part, because I know it won't change how I feel. Maybe I won't be crazy about everything I find out, but the important stuff is worth that. There's no hidden bomb in you that I'll eventually find and set off."

I catch my breath. I don't think I've ever done that before, just barfed out words in a coherent stream.

"*And*," I burst out when he opens his mouth, "I'm already not crazy about some things. Like the smoking, and the Adderall—which you are *never doing again*—and being mean to people off the bat because you're scared they'll ditch you later when they find out you have mean thoughts. Everyone has mean thoughts, okay? *Everyone* is making judgments about other people *all the time*. You just treat it like scientific data when everyone else mostly recognizes that they're first impressions, unreliable. You don't know someone until you . . . get to know them. Duh. But you find that out by doing it, and letting people surprise you, and you haven't, until now."

For a minute, our breathing is the only sound.

"I'm glad it was you," he says in the oddest voice. "That I got to know first."

Instead of thinking *It's because there's something special about me* like a smug jerk, I say, "I'm glad I was the first person you took a chance on."

"Imagine if it was some asshole. I'd have scrapped the rest of humanity and called it a loss."

I giggle. And then I leap up, banging my head on the ceiling, because the minivan behind us is laying on its horn.

"Holy shit, they're still there!"

"Drive, drive!" Eliot shouts as I twist the key the wrong way twice and then drop it. The earsplitting honk keeps going until finally my brain remembers how to start a car, and we fly down the road.

The minivan sets off at a crawl, like they want to keep their distance.

"Why didn't they just go *around*?" I shriek, and Eliot is crying laughing, and then I am, too.

When we get back to his house, I ask him to give me every pill he has left.

It's not a ton, but it's not a small amount either. I hold them over his toilet, tiny pink circles in my palm. I'm glad that meeting me meant he stopped needing the distraction, because meeting him helped me stop needing the blankness.

"How often did you take these before you met me?" I ask.

"Not as often as I smoke."

"Nobody does anything as often as you smoke," I point out. "*Why* do you take them?"

I'm hoping he doesn't have a reason that will make me feel too guilty to throw them away, like Rex.

He stands there staring at himself in the bathroom mirror.

"Sometimes I think I don't feel enough," he says to his reflection. "Most of the time I don't want to feel anyway, because that's what people like Anthony want, so I get in the habit of not doing it. But then I worry I'm forgetting how. The pills remind me I still can."

It sounds like the blankness.

I close my fingers over the pills. "If you really need—"

He flips my hand so that they fall to a watery grave. "Now you remind me."

It's like I become aware of a new organ, near my lungs

but lower than my heart, pumping faster and spreading something better than blood through my body.

Before I can blush, he blushes. He's so pale that his face flames spectacularly scarlet. When he's too cold or too hot, he gets paler, so maybe this means he's at exactly the right temperature.

"Let's watch a movie," I mumble, flushing the toilet.

In the living room, we play a game where I close my eyes and pick something on Netflix at random. I played it a lot during my Major Depressive Episode, except then it wasn't fun, just a listless inability to make decisions. This time it's fun. We watch a terrible eighties movie about cowboys in outer space. Eliot analyzes the personality types of each character, and for once, he does it jokingly.

Once the credits roll, I point at him and announce, "INTJ."

"I just told you the captain was an INTP."

"No, you're the INTJ. You wanted me to guess, remember? I was bored when you were ignoring me and so I read through more type summaries."

I'd spent six hours combing articles, but he doesn't need to know that.

He smiles. "I thought you gave up."

"INTJ. The System Builder." I open my notes on my phone and read aloud: "'People often see INTJs as arrogant, when in reality they're just confident in their opinions, having honed their mental database of specialized knowledge.' *Totally you.* 'Obsessed with improving their methods, they will study aberrations until they unravel them.' I googled *aberration*, and it means 'a weird thing.'"

"I know what *aberration* means."

"'INTJs' interpretation of their own opinions as facts can mislead them in personal relationships. However, INTJs have a deep capacity for love, and the select few to whom they devote their time and effort are fortunate indeed. INTJs want others to make sense—they are frustrated and, at worst, condescending when confronted with seemingly illogical emotional impulses.' Ha! You!" I thump the couch. "'INTJs do not easily grasp social rituals, due to their naturally private nature and impatience with small talk and flirtation—'"

He pushes my phone down.

I sulk. "But it was just getting into how much you suck at romance."

"So tragic that we don't get to hear that part."

"Tell me if I guessed right."

He slings his arm over the back of the couch. "All that personality-type stuff sort of seems like bullshit now."

I hit him with the pillow.

"That hurts," he says solemnly.

"No it doesn't!" I hit him several more times until he's forced to disarm me. The pillow knocks Eliot's backpack off the coffee table, where it spills papers all over the floor.

"It hurts emotionally," he clarifies. "Did you think I was invincible just because I don't feel physical pain? Please, Samantha."

"That was such an INTJ thing to say."

"Tell me that's not as obnoxious when I do it."

"It's twice as obnoxious because you're twice as smug about it."

He winces. After a few minutes, he adds thoughtfully, "It really is bullshit, though. It's just a list of traits on the internet, and your selection bias makes you pick out the ones that happen to apply to me. Though I am obsessed with improving my methods, now that it turns out my categories aren't accurate. Apparently the only way to learn anything about people is by getting to know as many of them as possible. It's very inefficient."

"Then you better get started." I like the idea of Eliot surrounded by friends—until I imagine all the friends as girls. Luckily the internet says he sucks at romance.

To avoid acknowledging the implications of this chain of thoughts, I get up and gather the fallen papers. Homework, and a piece of blank notebook paper titled GOALS.

I don imaginary reading glasses. "First goal: stop being such a nerd."

He leans forward and plucks the paper out of my hands. "My therapist calls her idiotic activities 'homework assignments' because she thinks I'll take them more seriously. So I do what I do with regular homework, which is hand it back with nothing but the title."

There's no way.

A lot of therapists probably do that.

"Your therapist?" I say fake casually. "What's their name?"

"Dr. Brown. So named due to her close relationship with bullshit."

I force a laugh, too late.

I guess it's not that weird, that we have the same therapist. There can't be that many therapists around here. I should tell him—we could make fun of her together.

But then I remember the passage from her book.

I sit cross-legged on the floor. "Do you like her?"

He shrugs. "I've seen her since middle school."

"How? Didn't you move a lot?"

But Dr. Brown mentioned that she moved to the area right before she started seeing us.

"We usually just go one or two school districts out—makes Gabriel's taxes easier. Far enough where I won't bump into anyone, but I wouldn't have to switch any of my doctors. But this time we skipped a whole county—and she relocated, too. I think Gabriel paid her to do it. He probably figured it was less effort than finding a new one who'd tolerate me."

"I'm surprised you tolerate therapy." Specifically that therapist.

"It was one of the things Gabriel made me agree to in exchange for a certain level of independence once I turned seventeen. Being annoyed one hour a week is better than being annoyed always."

"Is she a good therapist?"

I'm being sneaky, but I don't want to bring up her book.

If he's been seeing her for years, though, he's probably already read her book and the passage that argues he's not human.

"Therapy is predicated on the notion that you can fix

what's fundamentally wrong with a person. There are no *good* therapists, just people wasting your time."

"Well . . . do you feel good after talking to her?"

"No," he says after a moment. "She always seems very interested in me, but not in a way that makes me feel good. More like I'm a specimen. I think I tried to become more complicated to stump her."

Then he stops and shakes his head. "It doesn't feel normal, telling you that. Surely normal people don't run around telling everyone about their own private lives."

"We don't, until someone earns it. I'm sorry to tell you this, Eliot, but I think you might be a normal person."

I just earned a piece of him, which he gave to me not because he was inebriated but because he trusts me.

But I still feel prickly, like how my hackles have been rising at school whenever Anthony's friends approach Eliot. *Go away, I don't trust your intentions!*

"Which makes you not normal, as the only one to earn it." Eliot is smiling. "An aberration."

And even though all he did was call me a weird thing, it feels like he said something nicer.

Chapter Thirteen

DR. BROWN'S OFFICE IS THE SAME AS ALWAYS, with its Legos and banana-colored walls. But now I'm seeing it through Eliot's eyes, imagining his scathing Eliot thoughts about the strategically positioned tissues and the subliminally quiet classical music.

"So, Sam," says Dr. Brown.

Maybe she starts sessions with him like that. *So, Eliot.*

"I'm not scheduled to see your family until next week, but you requested an appointment. Is everything okay?"

Dad asked, too, when I'd said I wanted to see her. I'm probably being crazy, but I had to find out if she's okay for Eliot, even if I'm not sure how. She's not an amazing therapist, but I don't think she'd break patient confidentiality laws.

It'd be easier to ask Eliot again, but I'm learning that he's terrible at recognizing when someone is bad for him—he assumes everyone is, so he accepts shitty behavior because it's normal for him.

"Everything's fine," I say.

"Have you made progress with your streams of consciousness?"

I squeeze my leg. "Just waiting for the right moment."

"Remember what I said about closure." She scratches her nose. "It's important to let ourselves *feel* pain."

"Why?" My heart beats faster. "I mean, I take painkillers so I don't have to feel pain, because a bunch of doctors agreed I shouldn't have to suffer for no reason. Isn't that what my antidepressants are, just for emotional pain?"

"Emotional pain and physical pain are alarms that alert you when something's wrong with your body or your mind and environment. Sometimes you can't fix what's wrong with your body, so there's no harm in muting that alarm—"

"Sometimes you can't fix what's wrong with your life," I interrupt.

"It's true that you can't bring your mother back. But with emotional pain, there's rarely one obvious culprit, so you need to stay tuned in to what it's telling you. Antidepressants don't *block* your emotions; they make them manageable. Say you take a pill to get rid of hunger because it's an unpleasant sensation. Eventually you'd starve to death."

Her voice is tranquil. It's strange that she has a whole

life outside of this, that she's a person I don't know anything about.

"Pain alerts us to the needs of others as well as to our own," she says. "It makes us human."

"But, hypothetically, what if someone couldn't feel it? Everyone feels emotional pain, so say they've never felt physical pain." I swallow. "They'd still be *human*."

She smiles slightly. "I'm actually writing my next book about this, Sam."

I'm silent.

"When you're a therapist, you notice patterns in how people describe their emotions. 'Like a punch to the face . . .' et cetera. Physical pain is our introduction to both kinds, and not feeling it means you'd lack a basic understanding of what pain is—the alarm systems are connected. You'd never be able to empathize with others."

"But if I stub my toe, I don't know how it feels when someone *else* stubs their toe. Maybe their toe was already broken. At some point I'm using my imagination a bit." I speed up. "So if someone had to rely entirely on their imagination, and knew they couldn't assume anything, wouldn't they be less likely to make mistakes?"

"I have a case study close to what you're describing, funnily enough. A person who can't feel pain."

I tense up.

"As you can imagine, I've done my research," she adds, a little drily.

She doesn't have to worry about patient confidentiality,

because she doesn't realize I know she's talking about one of her patients.

"I'm afraid he disproves your point. Due to his lack of empathy, this subject repeatedly failed to connect to peers, despite various social environments."

"Lots of people are awkward," I mutter.

"He himself had no need for human connection. At best he isolated himself; at worst he'd provoke people. He relied on strange categorization systems to compensate for his absence of natural insight into others."

She was studying him like he was literally a lab mouse.

"Was he unhappy?" I ask quietly.

"That's not what the study was about."

"Oh," I say.

"I'll send you a copy when it's published since you're so interested." She leans back like a smug cat. "But let's get back to your life."

She's still smiling, but it's resigned. I'm not the patient proving any of her theories. She's just not getting paid to brag about her book.

I stand up. "I think I'm all set now, actually."

"I'm sorry?" She's frowning.

"Like, as your patient," I elaborate. "I made a new friend, see. And he's super smart, and he tries hard to understand me. So I don't have to pay you to try to do that anymore."

She puts down her notebook. "Sam, a friend is not a replacement—"

But I'm already out the door.

The lobby is populated by a white-haired woman next to a man in a wheelchair, and a father whispering sternly to a toddler. They stare at me as I pant in the doorway. I pour myself a cup of water from the cooler and chug it until my mouth is no longer dry.

I take out my phone to text Eliot that he needs to stop seeing Dr. Brown, but he'd want to know why, and I don't ever want him to know why.

So I'll have to figure something else out.

> Dear Gabriel,
> You said to email if there were any issues with Eliot.
> It's not about him per se, but his therapist. Someone
> I know sees the same one, and apparently she
> mentioned that she's writing a book about Eliot and
> his condition.
>   I thought I'd let you know, since Eliot told me you
> like to sue people.
> Sincerely yours,
> Sam Herring

I like to err on the side of formality when I write emails to adults. By the time I've phrased everything the way I want, it's past ten.

He replies within two minutes.

> agree that this is concerning. will investigate.
> glad to know eliot says such wonderful things about
> me.

did he get my birthday present?
(Sent from iPhone)

I only process one word: *birthday.*

I text Eliot immediately:

Were you trying to bake a cake the other day because it was your birthday?

Yes, he answers.

Why didn't you tell me??? I text frantically.

For some reason I thought you knew.

That reason may or may not have to do with an altered state of mind.

Oh, my God. I rest my forehead on my knees.

This explains why you were so confused about the cake.

HAPPY (LATE) BIRTHDAY! I'll give you your present at lunch tomorrow!

I groan, so loud Tito barks downstairs.

Why did I send that? There's no time before school to get him a present.

I consider going back to sleep, and then I realize why he texted me randomly that day about a fire he didn't need me to put out.

I'm not big on birthdays. They're like tests for how much your friends like you, and it always felt like I failed. Before I joined lacrosse, people would RSVP to my halfhearted Facebook events but cancel because too many things in their lives were higher on the echelon than my birthday parties.

Even when you rebel and plan nothing, it's still failing the test, because if someone *really* cared, they would have thrown you a surprise party.

I must have a present for Eliot tomorrow, and it must be perfect.

I climb out of bed.

All my possessions that I use are on my floor, and everything else is in the closet. I yank the doors open, and everything falls everywhere: Girl Scout sash, stained towels, old My Little Pony figurines. . . .

Mom had said a present measures how well you understand someone, but it also needs to have a piece of you in it. A Girl Scout sash won't work for Eliot, but there are plenty of other pieces of me lying around.

I dig holes with my crutches, accidentally unearthing the cardboard box that Rex and I have been using to hide framed pictures of Mom from Lena when she's on her trash bag rampages.

I want to go through them, but the pain is too intense, collected in one place like this.

Maybe if I wrote down the rest of the accident and processed that pain like Dr. Brown wanted, I'd be able to do things like open this box.

Instead I shove it to the back of my closet.

My old jacket topples onto my head. It belonged to Mom's grandfather when he was in the army, and she passed it down to Rex when he was depressed after being expelled from school, and he gave it to me after the accident. It was comforting, so I wore it all winter.

I press it to my cheek. It smells like family.

Eliot never wears a jacket.

Another thing Mom had said about presents: that finding the right one feels like a puzzle piece sliding into place.

Students aren't allowed to eat lunch in the library, but the cafeteria is full of people pretending not to stare, so Eliot and I do anyway.

I poke at my cold lasagna I brought from home. Another one was dropped off at our door last night, even though neighbors aren't supposed to keep giving you baked dishes after half a year.

"I have it . . . your present," I blurt.

I'm wearing the jacket, because the idea of taking it off and handing it to him seemed poignant at the time.

A faint pink tinge appears in his cheeks, and he casts around for a different topic.

"Where did you get that coat? Did someone win a who-can-design-the-ugliest-item-of-clothing contest?"

My expression must plummet as much as it feels, because right away he winces.

"You get me a present, and I insult your clothes. I've never gotten a birthday present from a friend before, but I'm assuming that's not the correct procedure."

I should have bought him a gift card. A gift card doesn't have your whole family history tangled in it, and their skin cells on it, which I now realize is gross.

After school, I'll get the gift card.

Except I already told him I had his present, and now he's

looking at me expectantly, and I can't say, *Sorry, I know this is your first birthday present but I was actually kidding.*

I shed the jacket. Even though I've done it a thousand times, number one thousand and one is when I manage to get stuck.

"You don't have to keep it," I say, muffled by the fabric over my head. "But I thought you should have a coat, since you don't feel cold. We sort of pass this one around in my family to whoever's having a hard time—and my mom thought presents should have a piece of you in them—"

Light floods me, interrupting my rambling. Eliot has freed me from the coat and is putting it on.

"I've been wanting to augment my—what did you call it?—*slutty-vampire* aesthetic." He inspects the sleeves. "This jacket screams down-on-his-luck, ex-army, drives-an-Impala vampire hunter. The ideal ironic contrast."

"Really, I'll get you something else."

"Do I *have* to give it back?"

He clutches the jacket around him.

I cover my face. "No."

"Excellent," he says. "Because I'm never taking it off."

I sink into my plastic library chair and peek between my fingers. The rough-but-exotic vibe actually works for him.

"You have to, when it's hot," I croak. "You'll get heat exhaustion."

"I'll take that trade-off." He looks at me seriously. "This is the best present I've ever gotten."

"Better than your ukulele?"

I guess I hate that ukulele. Eliot probably has to think

227

about his stupid parents every time he plays it.

"A good present doesn't force a self-respecting individual to learn an instrument championed by hipster tweens." He removes a pack of cigarettes from his backpack and tucks them happily in a jacket pocket. "When's your birthday? It'll be hard to outdo this, but I have a competitive streak."

"It was four months ago."

"Before I met you." He swears under his breath. "I'll get you a late one. The jacket was late. Fair's fair."

I have an idea. "Only if I can pick what it is."

"I'm not above bullying Gabriel into giving me large amounts of money, so your price range is—"

"I want you to stop smoking," I cut in.

"Sam." He recoils. "I'll tell him I need a new car. I'll give it to you."

"A car won't save you from lung cancer."

"I'll die from my condition way before lung cancer has time to start in on me," he scoffs.

"Oh, no you don't." I point at him. "That's not an excuse not to take care of your health. I've researched it; plenty of people with your condition live long and happy lives. Why did you even start smoking?"

"Same reason for everything I do."

"Stupidity?"

"Boredom." He hesitates. "But I'll stop if you're truly so personally offended by lung cancer. Also because I want to get you a present."

He toys with the jacket zipper, looking away.

I almost tell him about how our family gets attached to objects because Mom taught us that things retain the magic of the person who owned them. That I'm glad the jacket will have his. But then my leg twinges, and opening my mouth feels like opening the box in my closet.

But if I'm going to know everything about Eliot's life before he met me, about the seventeen birthdays I've missed, I have to be prepared to offer secrets to trade.

"This is unrelated," I start.

"Hm?"

I bite my lip. What if he thinks I'm damaged? But I'm locked into the follow-up now.

"I don't remember my accident," I tell him, and he sits up, because I've never talked about the accident before. "But when my leg hurts, I get flashes of it. If I write what I'm seeing, I remember more. Only usually I'm too afraid."

As I say it, though, I realize I want to remember. Not because of what Dr. Brown said about closure, but because it was something that happened to my mom and me, and it should be remembered. I've been acting like Mom died alone.

"Fascinating," he murmurs, then smacks his own arm. "I mean, I'm sorry you have to go through that."

"It's okay." I steel myself. "Actually I think you might be able to help."

"How?" He's too surprised for sarcasm.

"Sometimes, when my leg hurts and it reminds me of the accident, I . . ." It's so hot in this damn library. "I picture you. Not doing anything in particular, just being. It helps."

He stops playing with the zipper.

"As in, just by existing, I'm making you feel better? As in, the concept of me as a person causes you positive emotions?"

Maybe he's teasing me. But no, I'm finally learning how to tell when he's joking or not, and right now his eyes are wide and startled. For some reason it makes me shy.

"Well, that's how it is with people you're close to. If I think about my family, I feel happy."

At a basic level, I'm not unhappy they exist, anyway.

"I didn't know I could do that," he says almost inaudibly, like he's discovered a superpower much better than invulnerability to pain. Then he fake coughs. "Of course I'll help. Tell me when you're ready to try writing down your memories again. We can do it at my house or yours."

"I'm ready," I blurt before I can overthink it. "Let's do it soon."

I'll never be ready if *ready* means that I'm not scared. Sometimes it has to mean I don't want to, I am scared, but I'm going to do it anyway because it needs to be done.

Which means *ready* is whenever I decide.

Chapter Fourteen

ON SATURDAY, I FACE OFF AGAINST DAD across the kitchen counter to tell him I'm not going to our family session with Dr. Brown and I'm never going again.

"I don't understand. You wanted to see her last week." He rubs his balding spot. It's our first argument SMD, possibly ever. "If you don't like her, why are you just saying so now?"

This is admittedly hard to explain.

"I'm not sure she's helping," I try.

"Give it more time, Sam."

My least-favorite phrase. Time did nothing to help me, even when everyone promised it would.

"I know your brother and sister draw a lot of Dr. Brown's attention," Dad says, softening. "We can focus more on your problems next time. As a family. You're allowed to talk outside your private sessions."

I rarely spoke at Dr. Brown's because Dad couldn't think I still had problems that need focusing on.

"I'm pretty sure I don't need therapy anymore."

Unexpectedly his expression tautens.

"How can you say that when you just had to schedule an emergency appointment? Without your medication . . ."

He's breaking two of our cardinal rules: pretend the antidepressants don't exist, and never bring up the Major Depressive Episode.

"Just because they're helping doesn't mean they're solving whatever made you need them in the first place," he continues, echoing Dr. Brown. "You're controlling the symptoms, not addressing the cause."

I overheard Lena telling him this yesterday, about his junk food addiction. I can't believe he's recycling her self-help sayings to replace actual parenting.

"You're going. I'm not letting this slide like the physical therapy," he says, adopting a wobbly authority that apparently only applies to me, because it would have come in handy any of the million times Rex and Lena tore at each other's throats.

"How can you pretend you know what's right for my mental health *when I have literally never talked to you about it*—"

Then, in the living room, we both hear Lena scream.

I assume it's something Rex did until I follow Dad to find Tito on the carpet in front of the TV, having a seizure.

I cry out. Every part of his body strains as he twitches, his lips curled back from his teeth in a frozen snarl, froth spiking the fur on his muzzle. He looks like a wild animal.

I can never drag my gaze from Tito's seizures.

Dad runs to the kitchen, filling a bowl of water for him when he wakes up. Rex sprints to the bathroom for a towel. Usually Lena times the seizure, but this time she just stares with her eyes wet and mouth open.

The seizures always end with the four of us hovering in rare silent unity, each of us counting Tito's ragged breaths as his thrashing quiets. We're all remembering what the vet said, about how Tito is old and a bad seizure could kill him.

I get a drowned feeling.

It takes five minutes for him to wake up. Dad strokes him so he knows he's with family as he struggles blindly to stand, making hurt, bewildered sounds. We can't explain to him what's happening, that he's okay.

Dad collapses on the couch and heaves a sigh. "I don't know what happened. We increased his dosage just like the vet said. He hasn't had a seizure in months."

"I know what happened." Rex is shaking with black fury. "Lena forgot to give him his meds. I asked her to do it yesterday morning while I was out."

If she'd let him see her with her eyes wet and round like they were, I'm sure he'd go easy on her, but she's already straightening defiantly. "It was just a seizure."

Dad crosses his arms. "The medication really is important, Lena."

She stiffens.

Rex takes Dad's unexpected involvement like a shot. "Wrapping a goddamn pill in some goddamn cheese, how hard is that? She probably forgot on purpose. She hates him now; he reminds her of Mom, and she can't deal with anything that reminds her of Mom—"

Her face whitens beneath the makeup. "Every day you come up with more ways to demonize me for trying to help this family. Now I'm a maniacal dog murderer! No wonder you're so creative; you have the free time to sit around brainstorming."

"At least I have a brain—"

Tito whimpers. Normally we lavish him with love after a seizure, but Lena and Rex are busy bickering, unloading new resentments they've stored in their arsenals. Dad holds up his hands but doesn't stop them because he's mastered the art of looking like he's just about to do something until it blows over on its own, and who could blame him when he was *just about* to intervene?

Then Rex, who is flinging his arms around the way he does when he's mad, whacks me in the shoulder, knocking over one of my crutches. He starts to apologize, but Lena dives like a hawk.

"Samantha, are you *okay*?" She repositions my crutch under my arm like I'm a doll before rounding triumphantly on Rex. "I don't know why you think it's appropriate to react so *violently* that you imperil your sister—"

"SHUT UP!" I explode. Everything in front of my eyes

flashes white. "Both of you *shut up!*"

They look automatically at Dad, because those words couldn't have come from their sister, who only ever steps in gently, who has a list of strategic conversation topics to distract them, whose muscles lock up in these situations because what if, eventually, they turn on her?

Tito whines again and nudges Rex, who ignores him because he's glaring at Lena, like *See what you did?*

I want to take out every weapon I've saved and detonate them all in their faces.

"Why is it that you two getting your daily chance to scream at each other *is so fucking important* that you don't realize there are people and a dog in this room who *don't want to hear it?*"

Lena frowns sideways at Dad and Rex as if to say *Be quiet, I'll handle this. I am the one who handles.* "I understand that things have been hard for you, Samantha," she says in a cajoling, tantrum-in-the-grocery-store kind of way.

"Right!" I cackle at the ceiling. "I'm only complaining because things have been hard for me! *Obviously* it's unrelated to anything *you* did wrong!"

If I have one get-out-of-jail-free card left from the accident, I'm going to cash it in with the worst crimes I'm capable of.

She blinks several times. "Samantha, I want you to know that—"

"I want *you* to know that I'm tired of hearing what you want me to know! If you listened for once instead of lecturing, you'd realize that most of your advice isn't right for me at all!"

"I want you to know that I forgive you for this outburst—"

"Don't you dare forgive me! You freak out at Rex when *he* talks to you like this."

"She does freak out at me," says Rex delightedly.

Dad's palms are fully open and all the way up to his shoulders.

"Well, you need more patience." She's determined not to let her therapist facade crack. "You should understand that *I* understand how *hard*—"

"How could you understand when I haven't told you anything? And why would I tell you anything when you don't listen?"

"Listen to what? You've never even tried to talk to me!" She's finally getting pissed, too, and it energizes me. "You never talk to me! When I ask how you are, you just say, 'Fine'!"

"We *were* fine before you came back—well, maybe not *fine*, but not getting worse! Then you show up and rip apart *our* house and *our* memories even though you're the only one who needed them gone, because Rex is right and you can't handle anything that reminds you of Mom! You act like you're a saint for coming back when you probably just couldn't deal with living on your own."

The words come out like I'm punching something blindly.

"You can resent me if you want, but you need me." Her chin is quivering but she doesn't cry, and the monster in me is glad, because her tears would kill it and it likes being alive.

"You need me to need you, but I don't," I snarl. "I don't need you behaving like I'm some helpless infant."

"I told you not to treat her like she's disabled," says Rex, jumping in gleefully.

I whirl on him. *"I am disabled!"*

His mouth snaps shut, but I'm not done.

"You need to grow up and deal with the fact that just because I can do some stuff doesn't mean I can do everything we used to, even if it makes you feel bad, because pretending it didn't happen doesn't stop it from being a thing. It just is."

He shrinks back, but why should it be sugarcoated for him when it can never be sugarcoated for me?

"But with physical therapy . . ." Dad is almost inaudible. "People can heal up better than the doctors expect. I read about this boy in the *New York Times*. . . ."

"No! Amazing! The *New York Times*?"

Tito flees to the kitchen, which is so devastating that I start yelling louder.

"The doctors *said* I'd never walk without assistance. It's ridiculous that I had to accept that there's no miracle fix before you could. You can't make me go back because you haven't acted like a parent since Mom died, and you can't start out of nowhere. Those two walk all over you, so don't complain when I do, too."

I scowl fiercely at all of them, but they don't say a word. They're watching me in terror. I pant into the silence while a slow sickness settles in my stomach.

The problem with screaming everything on your mind is that it feels *really good* when you're saying it, but it's like being drunk. Afterward you have to deal with the hangover and the people you pissed off. I'd shut off the entire world if it meant I didn't have to, but I haven't been able to do that since I met Eliot.

So instead I run outside and text him to please pick me up as fast as he can.

He doesn't press me for details when I tell him I fought with my family, though Eliot loves the details.

He doesn't even argue when I tell him what I want to do. All he says when we get to his house is "Are you sure now is the right time?"

"Yes," I bark.

Anger is the extra shove I need.

And I'm 5 percent less scared with Eliot here, which will have to be enough.

We walk inside and go directly to the living room. I set my notebook down on the coffee table, empty page open next to my pen, except my leg isn't hurting bad enough to shatter glass.

"I think I have to walk without the crutches. That's what I did the first time."

"Why hurt yourself? Just wait until the next time it gets sore by itself."

It melts me a little that he doesn't want me to hurt when he has no idea what *hurt* means.

"It has to be now," I say. "When I'm already in pain, I'm too afraid."

I have to make it inevitable. If I keep putting it off, *ready* will never come.

Eliot goes upstairs and carries down armfuls of blankets and pillows, spreading them on the floor in front of me. "In case you fall," he explains. "I stripped Gabriel's bed."

I stare at the cushioned floor. The question I ask myself now before I do anything, my barometer for life, is *Will this hurt?* And everything does. Getting up in the morning, or talking to Kendra, or lying to Dad that school is fine.

But I can't not do anything because it might hurt. It will hurt. And I have to do it anyway.

Eliot clears his throat at the moment the silence reaches maximum pressure. "You said my presence would help, but surely I have to *do* something."

"You don't."

There's a struggle in his expression. "I don't want to let you down," he explains, rubbing his brow like the right words are written there in Braille. "I don't want you to be wrong about . . . my existence being a good thing."

I melt more. "Just—say nice things, even if you privately think it's bullshit. Don't be honest. You're saying it for me, not you."

"How could that possibly help?" he snorts, but then he shuts his eyes briefly and stands up straighter. "What sort of thing should I say?"

"You can do it," I suggest.

"You can do it."

"You'll be okay."

"You'll be okay. . . ."

"It's just pain, nobody's—" Nobody's about to get hit by a car. Nobody's dying. This pain won't be permanent like the other pain was permanent.

"You seem pretty capable of saying it yourself. Are you sure you need me?"

I nod. "I also privately think it's bullshit, but it's easier to believe if I think someone else does."

"Okay," he says, his voice steely. "Then you should know that I don't, in fact, privately think it's bullshit. I've spent more time thinking about who you are than anything else recently, and you're someone who always does the right thing, even if it's hard. If you know it's the right thing, you can do this."

I still privately think that's bullshit, but if he believes it, maybe I'm wrong. Or maybe he's just giving me the chance to make it true.

"I'm sorry I'm not better at this," he says steadily.

"You are really good at this," I tell him.

I've taken thousands of steps in my life, the ease of which I never appreciated, but all that matters are the steps I need to take next. Two is all I need. I can do two steps. Hopefully where I'm going is worth how bad they feel.

I pitch forward. My leg's the wrong length, but my body remembers the habit, and my other leg swings forward to match it. I take a whole unnecessary extra step before I fall, and it turns out we didn't need the cushions, because Eliot catches me.

I am feeling this pain because my ancestors needed a warning that walking into the campfire was a bad idea. But there's no way to walk out of this fire, no matter how loudly the pain screams *Get away!*

The anxiety is the same, a shrill alarm ordering me to escape from the car, but there's no car. Nothing there. Nothing.

"Sam? Are you okay?"

"No, but that's the point."

"I hate this," he says with sudden passion. He helps me to the couch, where my notebook is waiting.

I stop telling myself there's nothing there. I let it be there.

The car ride was full of lasts I didn't realize were lasts until later. Last time I'd see her alive, last time my leg would be smooth. When you don't know something is happening for the last time, you don't savor it.

"Mom!" I cry, and it's the last time I'll ever call anyone that name.

The other car passes through the invisible threshold of time when there's no longer enough. It's called the event horizon, when it's too late to escape the pull of a black hole. But even after the event horizon, your body is still demanding with every cell to get away, an earthquake-tsunami-hurricane-wildfire RUN, but you can't, and it's a Can't. This is what it means to be alive and about to die, to have God himself bellowing that you do the impossible.

Except I don't die. And neither does that voice. I hear doom in my bones even when I'm safe, because my body has learned that any pain means death, and I must be warned. But I can't escape an imaginary death, so I can't escape the warning. The only way to block it out is to block out everything.

At the last second, the other driver finally seems to realize what's happening. I get a clear view of them frantically twisting the wheel, and I recognize them.

But then there's an incredible tearing apart of everything, a noise so loud I swallow it more than hear it.

That can't be my leg, opened up, red and pink and white instead of the color of my skin. That can't be Mom, those raw unraveled shapes.

Mom, did you get out of the way when God told you to?

The colors and shapes are starting to tell a story now, and it's the story of the end, and how I won't be winning any more points in lacrosse, and how Rex won't be getting a present for his birthday.

The shimmering glass throws sunlight into my eyes, and with it comes the pain.

242

I can't get away from it, can't not see it, can't not feel it, can't process it, can't take it apart and figure out what's going on. All I can do is hyperfocus on the blinding light until it blurs the world into white blankness, where everything is still torn to pieces but the edges aren't making me bleed.

"Sam?" Eliot is begging.

There's something slicing inside me. There's no room around it for my lungs. *Sadness* is too soft a word for this storm of knives.

"Can you hear me?" Eliot reaches out but stops with his hand inches away, like it met a force field. But it's his force field, not mine. I want him to wrap his arms around me and hold me together so I don't come apart from all these cuts.

I'm crying with my whole body. "This is the trade-off for being alive when she died."

His fingers shake in midair, and he closes his hand into a fist.

What Dr. Brown didn't get is that understanding your pain doesn't fix it. Knowing who hit us doesn't change the fact that they did, and I can't think about that knowledge right now; I have to bury it even if I'm aware it's unhealthy, because it's still the only option that helps.

"I feel terrible." Eliot's voice breaks. "Why do *I* feel terrible?"

That's how it is when you care about someone, Eliot. You get to feel all their pain.

He battles the agonized thing in his expression until finally he wins. He pulls me into him with a single jagged movement, his heart pounding over my heart, and I press my forehead into his collarbone until it hurts.

"I can't do this. I can't feel this. I can't. I can't. I can't."

His hands ball against my spine. "Remember that you're physically fine. Biologically speaking, this won't kill you."

Then that must mean there's more than one way to die. "It's the—most horrible—"

I want Mom back so I can get to know her. I was supposed to have enough time.

"It's just a feeling. You're bigger than a feeling."

"I'm not." My voice twists into a howl, and he holds me tighter. "I can't."

But I don't have a choice.

I leave Dad a voice mail telling him I'm sleeping over at Kendra's. Our fight seems so far away now, but I'm still relieved when he doesn't pick up.

Eliot brings the blankets and pillows back upstairs and remakes Gabriel's bed. I lie exhausted on the couch, exploring the edges of the gulf inside me, seeing how far down it goes.

It feels like I'm carrying something heavy and warm, but not warm like Eliot's skin on mine. Warm like blood.

The blankness wasn't really nothingness—it was this. Everythingness. I just wasn't looking at it.

I didn't know I could cry for so long and still be able to stop. Or that someone could hug me so hard I could feel his indents in my skin after he lets go, new grooves in me made for him, waiting for us to be fitted back together.

That night, he lingers for a long time in Gabriel's doorway even after he turns off the lights. He's fighting his own force field again. But now that he's gotten past it once, I know eventually he'll be able to do it again, even if tonight all he manages is closing the door.

Gabriel's room is clean and white, like the inside of an egg, empty except for the bed. I could easily detach myself again, let it all fade back into blankness. But I've been hauling this around with me like an unused lump of coal. Now I'm going to let it smolder until the last ashes cool. I curl in the glow of it, tears slipping steadily out of the corners of my eyes and pooling in the curves of my ears.

It's burning, but it's not burning me up. I'm feeling it, but it's not killing me.

I think about how powerful it is, and how strong that must mean that I am.

When I wake up the next morning, the first thing I remember is the face of the other driver.

It's too much to sort through, everything contained in this piece of information. I almost go back to sleep. But I don't want it to weigh me down any longer than it has to, so I climb out of bed, grab my crutches, and swing into the hall, where I trip over Eliot.

He was slumped against the wall, asleep, with my notebook on his lap.

"Were you out here all night?" I ask.

"No," he lies.

"Did you read it?"

"I was going to." His voice is tired and nervous. "But I figured you'd want me to ask."

I nod. Once. Then I ask where his shower is.

At first I turn the knob as hot as it will go, and then the other way, until the searing cold makes me aware of every inch of my skin.

I know who was driving.

I handle it carefully. It's so large. There are so many places the fallout could land once I set it off.

When I go downstairs, flushed from being scalded then frozen, Eliot is dumping the charred pieces of an attempt at pancakes in the trash. I sit down, and he slides unbuttered toast onto the table instead, next to my notebook.

He stares at it with a heavy expression.

"You really remembered who it was?" he asks after a second.

Saying the name is the key that will set it off. Whatever the fallout touches is my responsibility.

As soon as I say it, his face changes, taking on the rage I should be feeling, but it's like I'm teetering at the precipice of the same torrential river that's ground Rex down like driftwood, and I'm afraid to get in.

The river sweeps Eliot upright. He says in a genuinely frightening voice, "I'll handle this."

He slams his pan in the sink and leaves the house.

I chase him, my leg throbbing, but he's already so far

ahead of me on the sidewalk, and I can't stop long enough to take a pill. This time, though, the broken glass is so dull it barely cuts me.

At first he doesn't realize I'm following. I shout his name until finally he stops. "Where are you going?" I pant when I reach him.

His eyes are lightning, not the kind that strikes at random but the type Zeus smites with. "To her house."

"I was . . ." I don't say *going to call the police*, because I wasn't, not until I had a chance to look at her. Maybe I made a mistake.

"She's been at school this whole time, passing you in the hall, listening to the sound your crutches make on the floor like she had nothing to do with it."

He's pale, trembling.

"I don't want you to go in there and yell—"

"I don't yell." He turns and starts walking again.

Her house is only a few blocks down from his, but it's much smaller. There's a brilliant spray of familiar pink and white flowers by the front porch. I almost don't remember where I saw them before.

"Eliot," I say, but he's already knocking.

Trez answers, and immediately I think, This is who killed Mom, but it still doesn't become real. She's not a tsunami or an earthquake, just a scared-looking girl in slippers and pilled fleece pajama pants.

"What are you doing here?" she asks, and adds like she's a little kid, "My parents aren't home."

I focus on her feet. The slippers are patterned with faded snowflakes.

If it had to be a human being, not an insentient, all-powerful force of nature, it was supposed to be a stranger.

"We're coming in," says Eliot.

I expect her to tell him to fuck off, but she just stands aside.

Despite the fact that her house is in a wealthy neighborhood, the inside is dusty and dark, the kitchen table propped on one side with a dictionary. At my house, the fridge door is thick with report cards and photographs, but hers is dominated by an unfriendly chart covered in things like *Vacuum*, *Rake the yard* and a column labeled *Consequences*.

"Do you want water, or . . ."

Her voice dies. There are deep circles under her eyes from yesterday's mascara. The blond of her hair shows through at the scalp.

"You were driving that car," I say out loud.

She makes a little choking sound, and then she meets my eyes for the first time, I realize, since the accident.

Which is also when she and Anthony broke up, when she stopped coming to school, when she turned unrecognizable. Wearing black all the time like she was in mourning.

I fall into the river so suddenly it's like I was pushed.

Eliot moves closer, cornering her. "As soon as we're done here, we're calling the police, and you're going to jail. That's what's happening to you now."

She's still looking at me, not him. "I don't care what happens to me now."

"You don't know what isolation is, everyone thinking you're inhuman. From now on, your entire existence is a punishment. You don't *think* you care. Maybe you hate yourself, maybe you believe you deserve it. You should, and you do—you know you're wrong inside."

I can tell that he's saying the cruelest things that occur to him, but she just hugs herself and fixates on me, straining like she's staring into the sun.

"Stop it." I want her unable to face me; I want to see her tears and horror so I can know if her pain is as bad as mine. "Why aren't you crying?"

"I don't get to cry," she explains. "I'm the one who . . ."

But then a tear does roll down her cheek, and she grits her teeth so hard her jaw cracks.

"What do you think she owes you?" Eliot asks softly. "You'll never be able to give back what you owe her."

"Please be quiet." His words are poison gas, clouding my brain.

He scowls, confused and hurt. "Don't you want her to hear what she's done?"

There's a threshold of viciousness where you're no longer supposed to say your thoughts out loud.

I remember everything I said to my family.

"Wait for me outside, okay?" I ask.

His eyes flicker, but he leaves the kitchen. I hear the front door shut.

"You have a guy who'll do anything for you." Trez wipes her face over and over, until it's raw. "That's good."

"Tell me why it had to happen," I whisper. "Why?"

"First, remember that it was my fault. Don't feel sorry for me once I'm done."

I can't make sense of that, so I ignore it.

"I wasn't supposed to hit you so hard," she says hoarsely. "All I was trying to do was sideswipe your mirror."

This makes no sense either.

"Supposed to?" I echo numbly.

"He . . . he's had a thing about you and Rex since we first started dating. You tease him about the old days, call him No-Moore. . . ."

I can't breathe.

"He was afraid that if you kept reminding everyone of how he used to be, they'd treat him like before. He was obsessed with not going back to that. . . . That's why he got your brother expelled, when we were freshmen."

Rex was right.

But his teasing was affectionate, an attempt to remind Anthony that he'd *liked* the old version.

"Why are we even talking about Anthony? This is about the accident."

"He left you alone because you were quieter, until you joined lacrosse and started telling the girls stories. But you didn't have a reputation like Rex. You'd have said any drugs weren't yours, and they might've cut you slack. He was right to worry—when I put that weed in his locker . . .

he gets straight As. He's going to Yale. They didn't care what was in his locker."

Dimly I remember giggling with Kendra about Anthony sneaking Tito home in his backpack, pretending he was a dog so they could be brothers. Sweet memories, not mocking ones, but I was still cashing them in. And maybe I was tired of people believing his stupid act.

But to want me expelled?

Her words spin out faster, a whirlpool I'm drowning in. "He decided a cop had to find it. Not a lot, nothing serious, but the school couldn't ignore it if cops were involved. So he hid it in your sports bag before your game when your family was out. He knew where you kept your spare key—he said not even the dog would bark at him."

I'm underwater, everything distant and warped.

"I'd wait for a red light and tap your bumper. I'd say my parents told me to call the cops if I was *ever* in an accident, and once they came, I'd whisper that I'd smelled marijuana. Anthony said I had to be the one since your parents knew him, but it was just a little bump. . . . He asked . . . what I'd be without him, who I'd have. There wasn't someone better, not for me. I thought it wasn't a bad trade-off, having a life and friends in exchange for staying with him and doing what he wanted. . . ."

He made me feel guilty for not being there for him.

How could he have hidden hate like this?

"He gave me something for bravery, but it slowed me down. I couldn't cut in behind you, but he'd said I *had* to do it before you got to the school, so I looped in front at the last minute. I thought I'd sideswipe your mirror, but I wasn't used to the wheel—it was Anthony's friend's car, a big one that wouldn't dent. I lost control."

She talks the same way that I'd written in my notebook yesterday, sobbing like I sobbed, reliving it, too.

"I think I blacked out. The car was more than dented, but I guess it drove, because somehow I got to Anthony's, and he made sure I wouldn't tell. He has anger he never shows at school. . . ."

This can't be all Mom died for—a boy scared of losing his image, a girl scared of a boy.

I know how it feels to be trapped in the worst day of your life, to accept unfair trade-offs, to believe a boy is the only reason you're special. But I don't want her to know how she feels when she needs to be a monster.

But the way she picks pilled fabric off her pajamas until she's standing in a cloud is human. The way she's squeezing one wrist like she wants to stop her own pulse is human.

For a second, I can't remember her name or why I'm standing here. All I remember is fifth-grade Anthony stuffing Tito in his sweatshirt. Eleventh-grade Rex giving him a noogie. Eighth-grade Trez, a silent shadow. The Trez on her kitchen floor feels like just another ghost.

"You deserved to know sooner," she chokes. "Call the police, I'll confess, I'm ready now. Anthony won't, and he's had a long time to figure out his alibi, but you'll know one of us suffered."

That was what I thought after the funeral, that someone should suffer, and it seemed safer to do it myself than to trust it to someone else. Suffering was the only way to tell the universe I wouldn't accept the new world.

I imagine the police and their questions storming back into my life, the wound reopened right when it was starting to close.

"I have to think. I'm going to go," I say, even though I can't think and there's nowhere to go.

I stagger out of the kitchen and outside, past the exotic flowers. Rays of sunlight are lancing off mailboxes and car fenders like arrows shooting in all directions. There's air everywhere but inside my lungs.

Eliot pushes off the fence and chases me down the sidewalk.

"You need to take out your anger on her," he says decisively. "Make it hers so it doesn't have to be yours. That's why it's called taking it *out*."

But I can't surgically extract it from my body and implant it in hers, or even split it between us. I've been suffering, and Rex, and Lena, and Dad, all of us lashing out at each other, trying to off-load something that can't be off-loaded, only reproduced.

Maybe Trez's mom will hit somebody because her daughter went to prison. And that person will hit their dog because someone hit them. And since people usually cope with pain badly before they cope well, the suffering will spread until everyone is miserable. If there's a cosmic debt to be paid, the interest is too high.

"She's not invulnerable to pain like you," I gasp.

"Good," he says. "Now what are you going to do?"

You're someone who always does the right thing.

I don't know what the right thing is.

My family deserves a say, but their say would be calling the police, which only hurts Trez, because Anthony will have made sure she can't prove he was involved. He'll always be golden, untouchable. He's going to Yale on the pass that the universe writes for people like him, for his smile or his money or his maleness or his whiteness.

I count Eliot's chest rising and falling, proof that there is some steadiness left in the world, until we get back to his house and he can drive me home. He keeps looking at me in the car, but this time I don't know if it's his force field or mine holding us apart.

If he says good-bye, I don't hear it, because I close the door too fast.

Chapter Fifteen

I PLAN ON APOLOGIZING TO MY FAMILY THE next morning, but I don't. Then the following day, but I don't. And that just sort of keeps happening.

I can't go to school, because I'd have to ask Anthony why he indirectly killed my mom, and he'd just tell me Trez is crazy. But he already proved she's not by trying to convince the whole school she was. Eliot's first assessment of her seemed like it was genius, but he'd just bought the subtle story, Anthony's extra layer of protection: a psycho ex-girlfriend seeking revenge.

I'll never really know why, because the only one who knows is Anthony, and he will never tell me the truth.

So I decide I have the flu.

Obviously I should stay in my room and banish my

family whenever they knock, because it's contagious, the flu. It's for the best, now that they handle me like a ticking bomb. This way I'll be the only one blown up.

Finals are coming, and school is all review for things I can study from home anyway. I already missed the fall semester—what's a few more days?

It's okay if I don't text Eliot back, because we should both be studying. At first he accepts that I'm sick, but when I stop responding altogether, so does he. He doesn't try like Kendra did.

It's like he expected me to drop off the face of the earth and never speak to him again.

I don't *mean* to never speak to him again. I'm going to reply in an hour, or that night, or the next day.

The worst part about falling back into old habits is that you've learned what you're doing is bad, but here you are again anyway, and the reason must be that you are either very stupid or very weak.

Staying in my room does strange things to time. Even though the sun rises and sets outside my window, it's like being in a cell with no night or day.

Suddenly it's been a week. Then two weeks.

And that just sort of keeps happening.

On one of the uncountable nights, I dream about my phone ringing, but then it wakes me up.

I grope for it in the dark, knocking over empty Coke cans and bags of Famous Amos I've been stockpiling so I won't have to go downstairs.

As soon as I pick up, Rex begs, "Help me, Sam."

It's past two. "What's wrong? Are you okay?"

"I need a ride, I can't drive, I'm at Anthony's friend's place."

Drive. I sit up. "Dad's at his night shift, and if you took the truck, the only car here is Lena's, and she sleeps with her keys under her pillow—"

The line goes dead. He either dropped his phone or hung up.

Anthony's friend's place, where Anthony might be.

But Rex is my brother. Since I flipped out at my family in the living room, Rex has knocked on my door more than once, and I've ignored him every time.

I throw on jeans and rush downstairs in case Lena forgot her keys in her coat pocket, but her hypervigilance hasn't faded. I could wake her up, except then everything would be hell forever.

I go outside to clear my head. I'm struck by that reverence for nature you get when you've been inside for too long, the world twice as crisp as you remember. The neighborhood trees rustle, gently moving shadows. I want to clasp the breeze to my cheek.

I scroll through my phone for someone to call, but the only contact I've added in months is Eliot.

Flu symptoms typically last for around a week, according to the internet, but it's deceived me before. (11:52 a.m.)

Gabriel's here, so if you want to come over, let me know so I can poison him in advance. (5:35 p.m.)

I hope it's okay that I've still been walking the animal. You haven't stopped leaving him in the doghouse. (9:02 p.m.)

We've developed a form of nonverbal communication for late-night conversations about existentialism. (2:00 a.m.)

Did I do something wrong? (1:55 p.m.)

The last one is more than a week old.

I'd be such an asshole to text him now, but I'd be even more of an asshole if I abandoned Rex.

I know this is weird, and that I suck and haven't replied, but could you give me a ride somewhere? I don't have anyone else to ask. (2:32 a.m.)

I delete the last part, then put it back because it's true.

Minutes stretch out. All my message probably did was remind him of how mad he must be at me. I'm ashamed of how relieved I am that I won't have to face him.

But then his car pulls into my driveway, the lights off.

I buckle myself in, my sweaty fingers slipping on the belt. "Thank you so much. My brother's stranded at that house where Anthony's friends hang out."

He doesn't say hello or tell me how pissed he is. He just nods and drives off, his profile glowing in the streetlights. He's paler, the circles under his eyes deeper. He cut his hair. I suddenly comprehend the gravity of three weeks.

Then Tito licks my elbow, scaring the shit out of me.

"I was bringing him back when you texted me," says Eliot, breaking the silence.

I rub Tito's ears gratefully. His presence makes this less excruciating in the way dogs somehow manage to do. "Thanks for walking him, despite . . ."

"No problem."

He's not cold, just careful, and all at once I'm positive that after tonight ends, he'll let me go right back to ignoring him without bringing it up once.

This makes me want to puke, but my only excuse is, *It just sort of kept happening*, and I don't have a lie to replace it with.

We reach the house where Eliot's shoulder was dislocated. All the windows are dimly lit, low voices punctuating the night.

"Stay here with Tito," I tell Eliot, but he follows me out of the car anyway.

I text Rex and wait on the porch, but he doesn't show up. Finally I have to knock. If Anthony answers . . . but it's one of his friends who all look the same, white guys in their twenties trying out beards.

"I'm here for Rex," I say bravely.

He turns and yells into the house, and a minute later Rex comes staggering out, crashing into me so hard I nearly topple over on my crutches. I do my best to guide him to the ground rather than straight up drop him.

"Sam! You came," he says, and immediately starts crying.

"You're Rex's sister?" asks the guy at the door with

interest. Realization dawns in his expression as he glances at Eliot, who's observing Rex's tears from a safe distance. "And you're Eliot Rowe. I've heard about you."

This is exactly why I wanted him to stay in the car.

I move to propel both him and Rex to safety, but the guy's voice floats out behind me. "You're the stupid asshole who narced on Anthony."

Adrenaline surges into my throat, and suddenly my hand whips up and across his face. The slap almost drowns out Eliot's startled noise.

The guy trips backward and falls into the house, and the only way I convince Rex to mobilize in time to flee is by hissing, "Tito's in the car waiting for you!"

Once we're all inside, Eliot speeds down the road, a giggling Rex sprawled in the backseat as Tito takes advantage of his incapacitation to lick every available inch of his body.

"What did you take?" I snap, but the smell on his clothes answers me. I try to make my sigh sound irritated and not relieved.

"I'm sorry, Sam." Rex struggles to sit, but the twelve or so pounds of Tito is too much for him. "I was out, and I couldn't ask you for more, not when you were too nice to yell at me about the Vicodin in front of Lena and Dad, even though I could tell you wanted to. Lena's right. I'm a bad example. A bad big brother."

He starts blubbering again.

"Rex, it's okay," I begin, before electing not to waste a pep talk on a stoned fool.

Eliot pretends he wasn't listening. "Am I delivering him to your place?"

Rex hears the voice of a human male and shoots upright, launching Tito across the car. "Where the hell did you find *this* guy?"

I open my mouth, but Eliot cuts me off. "Sam and I met when she stopped Anthony from beating me up, which was unnecessary since I have congenital insensitivity to pain with anhidrosis; but she has a habit of hitting people who aren't nice to me, which, confusingly, has persisted even though we aren't friends anymore."

What?

I figured he'd be mad, but—not *friends* anymore?

Rex interprets this pretty much how I expect him to. "I said to tell me if you got a fucking boyfriend so I could fucking check up on him. You, boyfriend! How many girls have you been with?"

"Touching people and being touched are not in my skill set, or list of interests, for that matter," Eliot says.

I can't believe this is happening.

"So you don't play?" Rex demands.

"Only mind games, reportedly."

"And that weird-ass disease, that isn't like an STD?"

"If it could be passed on that way, I'd be fending off a lot more attention than I currently am."

"All right." Rex sinks back out of sight, dazed. "It's what I've always said, Sam. You can date a pussy, just don't date a dick."

"So you wanted Sam to be a lesbian," says Eliot politely. This is the end of my life.

"You've never said that, Rex," I grit out. "Please keep not saying it."

"Dude, it's my only wise saying. Shit, I should copyright it. What if Drake steals it?"

When we arrive at my blessed house, I drag Rex and Tito out of the car but hesitate before closing the door.

"Don't go yet," I tell Eliot.

Rex slumps into my shoulder. "Take her out to dinner three hundred times before you kiss her."

It takes a while to sneak Rex upstairs, and I pray Eliot doesn't leave. Finally I dump him on his bed. He bobs right back up and wraps me in a damp bear hug.

"Are you depressed again?" he asks miserably. "We've all been way worried—me and Lena hardly even fight now, and Dad's been on the phone with the insurance company, finding a new therapist."

Somehow I still haven't learned that time passes for others even when it stops for me. Turns out people mind when you take a weeks-long break from their world. I took a six-month break from the lacrosse team, and they had the perfectly reasonable reaction of moving on, and I resented them for it anyway. Even Eliot is ready to cut his losses. But my family just worries and waits, every time.

Rex is sniffling. "Is it my fault because I'm a bad big brother?"

"You are not a bad big brother," I say fiercely. "I love you, you ass."

"I . . . I thought I was being cool about your leg. Not like Lena."

I sigh. "My leg doesn't define me, but it doesn't not exist either. That's all."

"Stop being so much cooler than me," he mumbles.

"Yeah, it was so cool how I yelled at you all and then ignored you for three weeks." I'm hot with shame. "Rex, I'm sorry."

"Just warn me in advance next time you're going into zombie mode. Just so I know." He topples back into bed. "Thanks for the ride. . . . Tell your boyfriend thanks, too."

I cover him with a blanket and stick Tito on his chest so he can alert the house if Rex starts dying in his sleep.

I'm terrified that Eliot is gone and we'll be Not Friends Anymore forever, but when I race to the driveway, his car is still there. I dive into the passenger seat like he's going to start accelerating.

"I am so sorry," I practically yell. "Please don't hate me forever. That would suck so much, you don't even know."

He's frozen.

Okay, starting over. "Sometimes when I'm dealing with too much, I stop dealing with anything. That's no excuse. But last time I assumed I couldn't get back any of the life I lost, so I didn't try, but I'm going to try really hard not to lose you."

I can't tell what kind of silence his is.

I take a long breath. "I know it's three in the morning, but I have the most ridiculous craving for McDonald's right now."

More quiet. And then he says, "I've never been to McDonald's."

Inside the restaurant, which is deserted apart from the exhausted-looking cashier girl, Eliot orders us both Big Macs, fries, and sodas, plus one of those mini-apple pies, which he hands to the girl without a word.

I like that that's the only impression of him she'll ever have, a kind guy who bought her a snack and didn't expect anything back.

We take a corner booth. Eliot sets his bag down unopened. "So it wasn't something I did wrong? I thought it must have been either when you spent the night, or during the next day, with Trez. I thought you came across one of those little bombs."

I shake my head. His voice is casual, but his eyes aren't. Of course he's ready to cut his losses—he's been prepared with scissors since the start. He didn't try because he thought what I was doing was fair.

I lean forward. "You can be mad at me, Eliot."

"That would be unreasonable." He tears open his bag mechanically. "I don't resent people for taking the rational step of walking out when they can't deal with something. You said it: when you're dealing with too much, you stop."

I'll have to hack his own stupid logic to get through to him.

"You're new to friendship, and I'm not, so my information is technically more reliable, right?" I say. "So you have to trust me, scientifically, when I say it was shitty of me to close you out and not explain. Again, I am sorry."

"Apologies are a waste of time."

"I'm still sorry."

"You don't—"

"Just let me be sorry, okay?"

He blinks a few times. "I refuse to cry. I haven't cried since I was six and our dog died."

I wince. "I'm sorry about your dog."

"He was hypoallergenic, and he had to wear a muzzle and claw caps whenever I played with him. We robbed him of his natural defenses. Although I guess they wouldn't have mattered against a car anyway." He takes a bite of his burger. "This is delicious."

I let my head flop against the booth. "God, I missed you."

"I missed you, too," he says quietly.

And then, suddenly, more businesslike: "You need to figure out what you're going to do about Trez, or you'll stay stuck in this rut."

Right. "It's like . . . a big ball of stress in my brain, and if I go near it, I feel like I'm freaking out."

"So I'll go near it. It's not a ball of stress for me."

I shred a fry so I don't do something stupid with my hands like cover my face. "I thought if I remembered, we'd have closure. But what if involving the police is the opposite of closure?"

"Maybe it's not about closure," he says. "Maybe it's

about what Trez deserves."

"It wasn't just her fault. She told me—"

"I know about Anthony. I talked to her at school. Wanted to see if she had anything to do with you being out."

Thank God. I really wasn't ready to explain it. I don't even understand it. "It's wrong, her being the only one who gets punished."

"Isn't one better than neither?"

"Anthony made her do it."

I don't know why the idea of ruining Trez's life makes me feel worse, not better. Maybe there's something wrong with me.

"She still did it," he says.

It's simple for him. But it needs to be simple for me, too. "Anthony acted this whole time like he didn't do anything wrong."

"He doesn't think he did. The best liars aren't really lying—they believe themselves. No one will take Trez's version over Anthony's because she blames herself, and he blames her."

"I'm just lost," I say numbly. "We grew up together. We were his friends. I wish I understood."

"It takes a messed-up brain to understand a messed-up brain. Luckily you have one at your disposal." He taps his forehead. "When you're a smart little kid who gets bullied, you tend to decide that the bullies are just stupid, shallow, jealous. And maybe they are—they're kids. But you internalize this when your brain is programming the section on dealing with people forever, so even when you're older, you still operate under the assumption that everyone is a middle school bully."

"I won't feel sorry for him."

"Don't. It's his own fault. If you refuse to give people the chance to be something different, you're the one who stays stupid and shallow, stunted forever, unable to comprehend the depth of anyone else." His voice is hard. "He never hated you. He probably likes you. He just didn't think it mattered if he hurt you, because you're lesser than him."

"That's worse," I rasp. "I don't think I can come back to school with him there."

"We'll get him kicked out, see how he likes it."

"It's literally impossible to get Anthony Moore kicked out."

"No, it's literally impossible to prove he's at fault for the accident. But we can prove he's dangerous and violent, and we can show that proof to the world."

The smug mysteriousness is unbearable.

"This time, can you not do the stupid thing without telling me first?" I ask.

"I've already done it." He has the decency to look a little abashed. "Except it's not stupid, it's brilliant, obviously. It's a surprise for you. You'll see."

And however much I plead, he won't explain any further, until finally I just have to eat my cold fries and wonder about it until I'm so tired I have to ask him to take me home.

Chapter Sixteen

THE NEXT MORNING, REX IS APPARENTLY feeling better, because he wakes me up early by pummeling my door.

"Sam! Let me in!"

"It's unlocked," I moan into my pillow.

He barrels inside in jalapeño-patterned boxers and jumps onto my bed like he's ten, waving his phone in my face. "You need to see this."

I roll over. "I'm not using my eyes for anything until you put on pants."

"Isn't this your boyfriend?"

I roll back immediately.

It's a video of a crowd, tinny shouting, and then it zooms in. "Shit." The video's titled "High School Kid Doesn't Feel

Pain!" And there's . . . "Oh, *shit*."

"Yeah, it's a lot of views. That *is* your boyfriend?"

I scroll through comments:

new superhero origin story!

Is he faking? I literally cry whenever I stub my toe!!!

Did he survive to press charges tho blondie needs to fricking chill

And the reply: His name is Anthony Moore, he goes to my friend's school :(

"It's on BuzzFeed." Rex opens the page and reads the title. "'15 Annoyingly Common Injuries that Make Us Envy This Guy Who Can't Feel Pain.' And look at this other article."

This High School Student Has Real-Life Superpowers

You might have seen that video of a teenager surviving a beatdown that would bring a pro wrestler to tears—without showing an ounce of pain. (Seriously, he's like a jack-in-the-box—he just keeps getting up.) But there's a name for his condition, and it would make a superhero jealous.

We contacted the uploader of the video to learn that the secret identity of this Wolverine is Eliot Rowe, a senior at Forest Hills High School in Vermont. Rowe suffers from congenital insensitivity to pain with anhidrosis—which, in medical terms, means he can't feel pain.

"We had no idea about that. We just thought he was high or crazy," said the student who filmed the fight. "We were pretty freaked out by them both."

The incident had not been reported to the school or police prior to its online presence. When contacted, the school's administration shared this statement: "FHHS has a zero-tolerance policy. The consequence for seriously harming another student is immediate expulsion. It will absolutely apply in this case."

The attacker's name is Anthony Moore, a straight-A senior on track to attend Yale (UPDATE: as of this morning, Yale has reportedly rescinded their acceptance). He was arrested early this morning for assault and battery.

The words spin. *Immediate expulsion . . . rescinded acceptance . . . arrested . . .*

It's the most I could have hoped for.

This is Eliot's surprise. While I was ignoring him, he was orchestrating this.

"I can't believe I called your boyfriend a pussy." Rex replays the video, shaking his head. "This is what I was talking about when I told you to stay away from Anthony. Too bad. He used to be an okay kid."

I hug him, which confuses him. Then I kick him out, because I have to call Eliot. But after ten minutes of ringing—he won't set up his voice mail in case Gabriel leaves him one—my shivery joy fades.

This is Eliot's worst nightmare, the world having an

excuse to treat him even more like an alien.

I'm dressed in a millisecond and at Rex's door. "Did you get your truck back?"

"You just evicted me five seconds ago!"

"It's an emergency. I need a ride to Eliot's."

He grumbles, but he gets dressed even faster than me.

He's incapable of driving fast enough, though, because that would be light speed. When we're halfway there, he remarks, "Your boyfriend mentioned that disease last night, didn't he? He didn't say it was a superpower thing. Can he sneeze on me so I catch it?"

I picture Eliot semiconscious on his kitchen floor. "It's not a superpower thing."

I'm expecting mobs of reporters, SWAT teams—isn't that what happens when something goes viral?—but we arrive to find his car alone in the driveway.

"This is where your boyfriend lives? I would have been way nicer to him if I knew he was loaded," says Rex, disgusted.

"Thanks for the ride. I'll see you after school."

I leave him before he starts pulling out and rush inside, where I locate Eliot draped on his couch as usual, eating a bowl of cereal.

What if I'm wrong and this wasn't his plan?

I'm panting. "Eliot, did you know that—"

"Come on, Sam. Obviously I know." He waves a spoon lazily at me. "Want some cereal? You did buy it, after all."

I sink into the couch next to him. "How the _hell_—"

"One of the guys who had his phone out during the fight has a YouTube channel. I may have suggested posting something attention grabbing for views. BuzzFeed only caught it last night. I was going to send the video to the school no matter what, but now anyone who ever googles 'Anthony Moore' will see this as the first result."

His look of self-satisfaction is truly spectacular.

"I knew he'd make people watch that fight," he adds. "And who'd watch a fight without recording it? It's always good to have blackmail material for a rainy day. Turns out it started pouring."

I stare at him openmouthed.

His smirk softens to a smile. "Now you won't have to worry about him anymore."

"Now I have to worry about you!" I cry. "You hate people knowing about your condition."

"Not as much as I hate Anthony." He checks his phone. "Oh, you called. I had it on mute. Gabriel won't stop trying to reach me, for some strange reason."

A horrible new possibility dawns on me. "He'll want to transfer you to a different school."

"I have years of practice preventing him from getting what he wants. Don't worry."

"You're sure?" His confidence seems unwarranted, but then there's the sound of a vehicle outside, and I look out the window. It's the van from our local paper, *Forest Hills Weekly*.

I whip the curtains closed. "We can't leave the house."

"And fail our education?"

He's up and propelling me out of the living room, through the doorway, where a woman in a blazer aims a camera at us.

"Are you Eliot Rowe? Would you answer a few questions?"

"Unfortunately I'm late for my daily campaign of dismantling the public education system from within." He sweeps past her, grandly opening my door for me.

"Is it true you can't feel pain?" she calls.

Eliot pauses halfway into his seat, considering. Then, so fast I can't stop him, he finds a penknife in his glove compartment and draws a red line on his arm, maintaining creepy eye contact with the reporter.

She shrieks. I lunge across his lap and slam the door. He drives off, chuckling.

"Don't ever do that again," I snarl, and inspect his arm. It's a faint scratch, but I slap a Band-Aid on it. I've learned to carry Band-Aids around Eliot.

"But I never get the chance to show off!"

As we walk into school, I remain directly in front of him. It's difficult since his legs work considerably better than mine, but I want to be well positioned to concuss the first person with something to say.

The first person turns out to be a tiny freshman with huge eyes, which get huger as he points at Eliot, but for some reason he's scared into silence.

"You're glaring," Eliot informs me.

I elbow him.

"Did you feel that?" the freshman blurts.

Then friends of the freshman feel safe enough to crowd around, and friends of the freshman's friends, all chattering at him excitedly as he stands there blinking.

I stress my way through my classes. Principal Chase calls his name over the speakers, and I guess he's still in her office during lunch, because I'm sitting alone when Kendra taps my shoulder.

"Hey," I say as friendly as I can on the off chance she can hear the apology in it. Although I should probably verbally apologize instead of trust people to psychically access the fact that I'm sorry.

"Listen, I didn't mean to get so pissy before." She twists the chain of her necklace like she does when she's nervous. "I just wanted to say, I don't care about BuzzFeed or whatever. What Anthony did was awful."

"Thanks—and you weren't pissy, Kendra, you were right." Once I say it, it's like there's less weight in the atmosphere. "I mean, you were right that I messed up, not that I didn't like you guys for who you were. I just figured you shouldn't have to put up with a downer who couldn't even play, so . . ."

"A downer?" she asks incredulously. "We have, like, a thousand-message-long thread about how to help you from a distance. If you'd wanted a shoulder to cry on, we would have high-fived and lined up."

My first instinct is to slink back from an apparent lie, but is that even surprising? It's so amazing when someone likes you, despite the parts of yourself you *know* are bad. It's even more amazing we don't default to conspiracy theories whenever a person wants to be friends.

Except I guess that's what I've been doing.

"Anyway, you were going through a lot." She bites her lip, then adds brightly, "But I meant it when I said I was happy for you. Even when I tried to be mad, every time I saw you guys together I'd go, 'Well, duh.' You two fit."

I don't want to blush, but that's what I do.

Fit is a good word—a neat and comforting click.

"I've been wanting to ask you something, only you were out." The fact that she doesn't ask why, though I'm sure she guesses it was the same reason as before, gives me legitimate hope for our friendship. "Today's my birthday."

Shit. "*Right!* Happy birthday!"

She beams, albeit nervously. "I understand if today is crazy for you, with everything happening with Eliot, but my party's at seven. The whole team's coming. The theme is prom rehearsal—we're going to try out prom stuff and see what works, since it's in May, but you don't have to dress up if you don't want."

"This isn't a great time for me to party . . . ," I start, but she's twisting her necklace so tight I'm afraid she'll strangle herself. After months of hearing no, she's still inviting me to things, like she knows I secretly pray she doesn't stop every time I turn her down. She's always finding new last chances for me. After I almost lost Eliot, I don't want to risk running out. Some people only give you one.

It's been more than half a year since Mom died.

Everything that died in the winter is being reborn, soft and green. I might not be graduating with everyone else in June, or going to senior dinner, senior night, prom, the last sports games . . . but I can go to this party.

"Never mind," I say. "I'll be there."

"Oh, shit." She laughs and releases her necklace. "I thought you'd say no."

"So did I." I laugh, too, just as breathless.

"You don't have to dress up," she says kindly, even though the most lavish thing I've worn to any of her themed parties was a pair of jeans that was only one size too big. "You should bring Eliot. It's mostly girls, but Amy's brother is coming and a couple other dudes. And I want to get to know Mr. Mystery. He must be a supergood climber if he got past your walls."

"You guys should hang out. Mr. Mystery's biggest secret is that he's a really good friend."

She winks. "Okay, Ms. Mystery."

Once he tries, it won't be hard for Eliot to prove his good side. People are unexpectedly willing when you try.

"I'm glad you're doing better." She pats my arm.

"I'm glad . . ." My face heats up.

"Hm?"

"I'm glad . . . it's your birthday," I tell her. "I hope you have a really good one."

When the bell rings, I meet Eliot in the parking lot and immediately scan him for bruises.

He swats me away. "You were obviously imagining some

nightmare scenario where people took turns hitting me to find out if I couldn't feel pain, now that they've heard about my condition."

"Basically."

"That's more or less what happened at my old school."

I groan. I didn't want to know that. "How were the people at this one?"

"Good," he says, sounding confused but tentatively pleased. "A few told me Anthony was an asshole. A lot had no idea that he and I had a problem, so they must have moved here yesterday in a mass exchange program."

It did seem like the whole school was against us, and all of humanity, but it really was just Anthony and his group.

I lean against his car and say with what I hope is nonchalance, "Now that you're making friends, you can come to a party with me tonight."

"I'll bring the piñata."

"I'm serious. Kendra Baker invited us to her birthday party, you specifically."

"There's a video of my ass getting kicked going around the internet. Now is the time I have least wanted to go to a party, and I spend a lot of time appreciating the fact that I'm not at a party. Parties are the natural antithesis to my ideal of a comfortable, productive environment."

". . . Please?"

He looks at me for a moment, then sighs. "Fine."

I try to act cool, not like I was terrified by the idea of going without him. "You can pick me up at seven."

"If anyone puts a lampshade on my head, I'm holding you responsible."

"You don't know what real parties are like."

"Neither do you."

"I do, too! I've been to parties. And I watched *Skins*."

Before he can make fun of me for that, I dive inside the car and lock the doors. Every time he hits Unlock on his keys, I lock them right back. It's not until he collapses against the window, snorting with laughter, that I finally let him in.

Even if it feels like a boulder lifted off my back, that Anthony has been miraculously arrested and punished without the police having to rip off my family's scabs, it's only half the weight.

I still haven't decided if I'm going to tell my family. Without question, they deserve to know. Telling them something they deserve to know has all the trappings of the right thing to do—and Dr. Brown loved the word *closure*.

But would it be *good* for them to know? Would Rex quit pills or end up in jail for attempted murder? Would they move on or move backward?

I can only find out by talking to them, but Rex is still the only one I've apologized to, and he was high. I want to turn my life back into a distant TV show so it doesn't matter if I don't sit down with Dad and Lena and acknowledge the horrible things I said. Or I could be despicable, play the accident card, and never bring up what happened, knowing they won't hold me responsible when I've been having a Hard Time.

It's fascinating, laying out all your defense mechanisms one by one, like scraping out the weird gunk that clots a sink.

I'll talk to them tomorrow, after the party. One cliff to jump off at a time.

It's three, so I have four hours to get ready. I dissect my closet and find, unsurprisingly, zero prom clothes. Mom never pushed girly stuff on me, but sometimes I'd secretly wish she was the type to drag me off for shopping and makeovers while I pretended to complain, because I was never going to *ask* her to do it.

Kendra's used to me ignoring her themes, but I want to prove I'm trying. I shove aside sheets and clothes, again unearthing the box of photos and knickknacks that Rex and I had rescued from Lena.

This time, though, I sit down next to it. It takes forever to pick off the tape.

Someone raps primly on my door.

I fling my arms over the box. "Don't come in!"

"I have decided we need to stop avoiding each other," declares Lena, coming in.

Then she spots the open box and loses whatever mental speech she'd prepared. "Oh . . . that's where these went." She kneels next to me and picks up a framed photo of Tito as a puppy licking Mom's face. "Were you hiding them?"

"No," I lie, badly.

She's stricken. "I wouldn't have thrown these out."

"You kind of went on a rampage," I try to say nicely, but it's hard to tell someone nicely that they went on a rampage. Especially when I should be begging forgiveness.

"Hey, Lena," I blurt. "I'm sorry about . . . you know."

"It's okay, Samantha. You were due for a rampage of your own."

Then she pretends to be distracted by the box.

"There's a lot in here. . . . Oh, look, it's that picture of your twelfth birthday party—that was the first vegan cake I ever baked. Mom showed me how. Did you know she worked in this hippie bakery in high school?" She smiles. "They called her the Flour Child. Like flower child, get it?"

The warm, heavy thing in my chest starts glowing. It's been there since Mom died, even if it feels like I acquired it that night at Eliot's, but the only difference now is that I hold my hands to the heat instead of suffocate in the smoke.

"She didn't tell me stuff like that," I say. "I never asked."

"I did," she says shyly. "I can tell you more, if you ever want. . . . I mean, it's better not to dwell, but . . ."

I'll never hear Mom's stories from Mom, but I'll hear them from Lena. The painful warmth inside me swells, cradling my heart. "You were smart to spend lots of time with her."

She rests her chin on her knees. When she has bad posture, her spine curves exactly like Rex's. "She was my friend."

The pain glows brighter, but it's a living sort of feeling. "I don't think we were friends. I think she was just my mom."

"You're not supposed to be friends with your mom. I just didn't have any other ones."

"What? You were in a million clubs in high school—"

"A million clubs doesn't mean a million friends. Frankly I was far more driven than most girls my age, and they found it intimidating."

I nod faithfully, but after a moment, she sighs.

"That's not true. I was just awkward. You were right about me not cutting it in Northton. My roommate hated me—apparently ten chore-reminder Post-it notes on her door per day is excessive."

"Well, she sounds . . . unreasonable."

"There's a thousand trip wires for setting people off, and I never notice them until it's too late." She droops but then ruffles my hair. "But here, you people have to put up with me."

"We do," I concede.

She smiles. "I've always been glad you had plenty of friends, Samantha."

BMD, I never thought of myself as someone with plenty of friends, even though I wasn't technically *alone*. I felt left over, the least special of anyone, like I'd missed the brief but key section of the friendship tutorial on evolving relationships from fake to real.

"Only because I'm boring," I try to explain. "People

don't mind having me around, but they don't get excited about it."

"You are not boring!" she says, affronted. "You're *nice*."

"Everyone's nice."

"They absolutely are not," she sniffs. "Samantha, you're nice, you're brave, you're . . . independent. . . ."

And suddenly she's stammering, "I was only babying you because I wanted us to be close, like you and Rex are. You've always liked him more than me— No, don't deny it."

She starts pawing furiously through the box again, her cheeks pink.

She had no one but our family, and even then, Mom was the only one she connected with. Mom probably spent so much time with her not because she needed a distraction from Rex but because she knew Lena needed a distraction from her loneliness.

I have no choice.

"Lena, I'm going to a party tonight." I summon all my strength. "Do you . . . have a dress I could borrow?"

She lights up like a firework.

"Of *course* I do! Come *on*!"

She moves to drag me upright, hesitating at my crutches but then tugging at me anyway, not enough to unbalance me but enough where I don't feel like she thinks I'm made of glass.

In her room, she flings open her closet. It's just as packed as mine, only organized. She never threw away her things—she just stored them.

After a long, intense search, she shoves a green dress at me. "This one! Mom got it for me because it matched my eyes, but it's your color. Your hair and eyes are nice earthy tones; you'll look like a garden."

"And in this garden metaphor, I am the dirt."

"Nothing beautiful could grow without a strong bed of soil," she says, which is a compliment only in her world. "Go try it on!"

The dress has a fringy hem. This reminds me of what I'd forgotten about dresses, which is that they show your legs.

"Actually I think I'll just wear jeans to the party."

The cry Lena unleashes is so devastated that our neighbor's dog howls in unison.

"It'll look *pretty*! All you need is some mascara to go with it—"

"It'll look stupid. Like I'm trying when there's no point." Even if I could have miraculously rocked a dress before, I missed my chance. I nod at my crutches. "Even if I wore a wig and six-inch heels and a ball gown, I'd still be on these."

She whips out her phone so fast she almost hits me in the face with it. She full screens a picture of a woman with shining black hair, a white dress, and crutches. "Solana Rodriguez, disabled model, flawless human being."

I push it away impatiently. "I mean, yeah, it'd be nice if I suddenly felt hotter because of her, but she's still gorgeous and I'm not."

"But you were wrong about there being no point if you're

on crutches," she declares. "No girl thinks she's beautiful until she decides to be. I just want you at the same starting point as everyone else."

She ushers me to the bathroom and shuts me in with the dress. Knowing I'm probably trapped until I put it on, I submit.

It actually doesn't look too bad. There's a ribbon around the waist that makes my boobs look bigger. It's my favorite kind of green, that sweet minty shade.

"I can't wear it," I yell at the door. "I'm taking it off. Don't come in."

She comes in immediately and gasps like it's my wedding dress.

"Those stunning Herring genes!" she cries. She glances at our reflections and double takes, like she's still not used to her new eyes or hair.

"I would rather have stunning Herring jeans. As in pants."

"Samantha, I do not accept a world where you don't wear this dress."

"It's too short," I mutter.

"It's *low thigh*! The concept of sluttiness is a patriarchal construct. You shouldn't be afraid to express your sexuality."

"No, I mean . . ." My face heats up. "You can see my leg."

I look anywhere but at her while she looks anywhere but at my exposed scars. BMD, I didn't know the ways skin could twist and pucker.

Lena opens her mouth.

I interrupt again. "I know what you're going to say about body positivity—"

"No, no, no," she says sheepishly. "I was just going to tell you I have tights."

The tights in question are just thick enough, and even though it's probably not a dress you're supposed to wear with tights, they match the dark-green ribbon.

Lena does my makeup while I pointedly squirm and make comments such as "Is face powder made of face?" and "Did you know they test this on baby mice?" But when she starts with the eye shadow, I'm glad, because I can close my eyes to enjoy it without looking like that's what I'm doing.

When she's finished, I say, "You'll make a good mom someday."

She turns red and spills face powder on her shirt.

I ask Lena not to tell Dad and Rex, so of course by the time Eliot comes, they're all lurking by the door with their phones out.

"I don't think we've met. I'm Samantha's sister." Lena lunges for Eliot's hand like there's a race for it. I guess she hasn't seen the video of the fight, probably due to her complex network of site blockers for content she doesn't consider "edifying."

Rex throws an arm around Eliot, who is staring straight ahead with an expression like a robot. "You haven't met my buddy Eliot? Sam introduced us ages ago."

"Hello, Eliot," says Dad cautiously.

I still haven't technically apologized to him, and the air between us is heavy, but he's following Rex's and Lena's leads.

"Reginald, doesn't Samantha look nice in my dress? She's like a mini-me!"

"Not in the tit section," says Rex under his breath.

I was worried about them judging Eliot, but it should have been the other way around.

Eliot nods stiffly. "It's nice to meet you. I have no intentions of impregnating Sam."

Rex and I choke. Lena's eyebrows shoot up into outer space.

"Well, that's good, isn't it?" says Dad politely. "Stand together so I can take your picture."

We frame ourselves in the doorway. Eliot looks like a katana in his slim gray suit. He doesn't comment on my dress, which I'm grateful for, but Lena gives a vaguely offended sniff, so I whisk him outside before any actual conversation happens.

In the driver's seat, Eliot stares dead ahead without starting the car. "Are these clothes okay? Does prom-themed mean fancy clothes or clothes that have literally been worn to a prom?"

His voice is slightly high.

"I don't know," I say, stifling a giggle. "My sister wore this to hers."

For a moment he looks stressed, and then he says, "Well, there's no way they can check."

He still hasn't turned on the car.

"You know what we could do instead?" he asks me suddenly. "We could go get some teeth pulled. Or watch a romantic comedy. Or see if any local raccoons want to give us rabies. I'm just brainstorming things that would be more pleasant than a party."

If I don't calm him down, he's going to bail on me, and I'll have to walk into Kendra's house, in a dress, by myself.

A stroke of genius hits me. "Let's bring Tito."

He lifts an eyebrow. "Girls would kill to see him in a tux, but reportedly you're not supposed to bring animals to parties."

"We'll leave him in the car. I only want to stay for a little while anyway. Afterward we can take him for a walk in our prom clothes and confuse the neighbors."

He glances uncertainly out the window, toward the doghouse.

"I want him to be my prom date," I insist.

It turns out that Tito is an effective social anxiety therapy dog. Once he's in the backseat, Eliot remembers how to drive.

"You're lucky I'm a genius, or I wouldn't have escaped the house," he says on the way. "Gabriel is threatening anybody in our driveway with a lawsuit, so I called every news source nearby and offered them an exclusive interview at my address. I slipped out the back in the pandemonium."

"Has he said anything about transferring you?"

He shakes his head, staring silently at the road.

He probably doesn't want to talk about his brother when he's been dealing with him all afternoon.

"You look nice," I say instead, keeping my voice light. "I bet someone makes out with you."

"I'm not interested," he says, his lip curling, "in that."

I'm relieved at first, until I'm not.

"Bet you feel different when someone goes for it," I probe.

He laughs. Which is completely unsatisfying.

We park on the side of the street from Kendra's house, her windows thick with silhouettes. Even though the lacrosse team is small, her parties end up overcrowded because Kendra invites everybody she's ever met.

I crack the window and kiss Tito's nose for luck. Eliot shakes his paw.

When we go inside, a Spotify ad for Walgreens is playing between songs. People in gowns and tuxedos are laughing, talking, not noticing us. Eliot draws closer to me, and I almost don't notice, but then I do and it makes me feel warm and stupid.

"Sam!" Kendra nearly bowls over three girls in heels on her way to us. She grabs at my arm to steady herself, her face as pink as her dress, but falters at my crutches and seizes Eliot instead.

"Hi!" she yips at him. "I'm Sam's best friend!"

He slides back into robot mode. "It's nice to meet you. I have no intentions of impregnating Sam."

I'm realizing Eliot genuinely doesn't know how to interact with strangers when he can't be cruel or condescending.

No wonder he's so nervous. This is a brand-new experiment.

"Ever?" She's so distressed. "But you guys would have the cutest babies!"

"Happy birthday, Kendra," I cut in. She squeezes my wrist like she's afraid I'm going to disappear, then swipes two Bud Lights from a nearby table.

"You both need drinks! I stole them from my brother because it's my birthday."

Eliot holds the can like he's not sure what to do with it. Kendra helpfully tips it toward his mouth.

I have to be not-nervous for both of us, so I down my beer and dunk a cup into the bowl of red stuff on the counter. It's sweet. I hand some to Eliot while he taps his foot irritably to Ariana Grande.

Eventually, predictably, everyone descends on him.

A girl from JV lacrosse in a bright-orange dress pinches his arm. "Did you feel that?"

Then a guy I've never met pretends to whack Eliot's head but doesn't touch him. "Did you feel that?" he jokes.

Eliot tenses, but I catch his eye and smile reassuringly, and the corner of his mouth quirks up.

The girl who pinched him does it again, giggling, and the guy gives Eliot a Guy Nudge. I am forgotten.

But then Eliot flashes me a this-is-your-fault look, and I return one that says *You're doing well*. Then I leave him alone so he can make friends and force myself to start talking to the three girls in heels by the counter. Their circle naturally widens to absorb me.

For the first time in months, I don't feel like the girl with the dead mom—just a normal girl with normal problems, like her best guy friend getting repeatedly pinched by another normal girl.

Now he's asking her questions, leaning forward intensely—trying to get to know her, for the experiment. She's laughing because it's weird but cute.

This is what I wanted, even if it means I won't be his only person anymore.

To stop myself from interrupting them, I go outside and take Tito to pee in the backyard. A circle of girls I've never met is smoking by the porch, and they crowd around me, cooing over Tito.

He drools in delight for ten minutes without peeing. I can't let Eliot get pinched to death, so I tie Tito's leash to the fence. He'll be okay out here for a little while, and he'll be happier than in the car.

"We'll look after him!" exclaims one of his new prom dates.

The instant I'm inside, Eliot materializes back next to me.

"Where were you? You were gone for ages," he grumbles, and I feel warm and stupid again.

The pinching girl appears out of nowhere and bops him on the shoulder. "We were just talking about that video, and I wanted to say that Anthony is such an asshole, honestly. I can't believe he did that to you."

"Fuck him," I agree. The enemy of my enemy is my friend.

She smiles at me, then whispers, "My mom knows his mom. She had to come back early from abroad to post his bail, and then she raided his room and found all his pills. She's sending him to rehab until he goes to trial for assault."

I search for Eliot to celebrate with. He's standing by the fridge, obediently opening his mouth as two girls aim M&M'S at it. Chocolate pings off his chest. I careen into him, the one who made Anthony not exist anymore.

"Oh, my God, this is my make-out song!" Kendra pelts toward us. "Somebody better make out with somebody else right now!"

I'm noticing how pieces of Eliot's hair curl over his ears, how his face is both sharp and soft, and I'm happy, I'm ecstatic, because neither of us is on the wrong side of normal anymore. We didn't fit in by ourselves, but we fit together; and somehow the circle was completed, and now we fit in everywhere else, too. We found each other and made our way back.

I say, "I'm somebody," and drag him forward by his tie so I can kiss him.

And he's not made of ice, or crystal, or glass. He's so human that it startles me. Warm, smooth, soft . . .

Candy explodes off my forehead as a bowl of M&M'S is joyfully dumped on us. Kendra's leaping up and down like a psycho. Panting, I let Eliot go. I had to do it then or it wouldn't ever have happened. Everything's okay right now, so this has to be okay, too, right?

But his expression is blank, and it's bad blank, every-thingness.

Without a word, he stumbles away from me.

A few people stare. I give this exaggerated shrug, *what's his problem*, and immediately hate myself for it.

I search for what feels like hours. He's not in the basement, the kitchen, or the living room. Finally I pass the long line for the bathroom and figure it out.

I cut to the front and knock. "Eliot, let me in."

"Can you guys use the bedroom?" a girl in a sequined gown whines behind me. "I have to pee."

I whack the door with my crutches until it opens slightly. Before Eliot can reconsider, I wedge myself inside, closing out the chorus of groans from the hallway.

Eliot's at the mirror, fixing his tie, even though it's already straight.

I want to drown myself in the toilet. "I'm so sorry."

He doesn't turn around. "You don't need to apologize."

"You're supposed to be trusting my intel on friendship, especially when we need to apologize."

"It's just that you don't have to make fun of me," he says a little coolly, but I see him swallow. "Everyone else has that covered."

"I wasn't making fun of you! That's not why I kissed—" Kissed. I kissed Eliot. Jesus. "It wasn't. That."

"It was a good joke, I'll admit. Humor is based on the unexpected. Nobody would expect someone like you to kiss someone like me."

He accidentally undoes his tie and swears.

I collapse onto the toilet. "Someone like *me*?"

A long pause. He determinedly avoids eye contact. "Someone beautiful."

"Eliot, *you're* beautiful," I yell at him.

"I have scars," he says.

"*I* have scars." I yank at my tights, but they end in socks because girl clothes are ridiculous. I'm not stripping in front of Eliot, so like the Hulk, I rip them open. "Look."

He looks.

"Let. Me. Peeee," the girl moans through the door.

I bash it with a crutch, my leg still stuck out. "My dog pees outside, so can you!"

Eliot bends down and runs his thumb over the big scar, the worst one. The warm-stupid feeling shouldn't be able to exist alongside this anxiety; they should cancel out each other, but they don't.

I'm sick of feelings. I either have none or all of them at once.

Gently he pulls the torn edges of my tights together and opens the door. Sequins-girl nearly mows us down.

The house is full of people, and I need to be alone with Eliot. I flag down Kendra and inform her of this in a whisper that strikes me as not entirely sober sounding.

She spends the next twenty minutes flying in and out of her bedroom, and it's not until she shuts us inside that I realize she probably thinks we're going to have sex.

Eliot sits on the bed, gazing around at all the lit candles.

293

"Was she preparing a séance?"

I blow out all the candles, and then I lie down next to him in the dark. It's the closest I've felt to being ready to be naked with someone. Instead of making me want to have sex, it makes me want to talk.

"Do you remember when you told me you took pills because you couldn't feel?" I say. "I was there, too. But not feeling anything *is* a feeling, I think. It's feeling everything at once, but in the background. Like how white is all the colors. Most of the time depression is really something specific, or a lot of specific things . . . but that's good—it means it's not actually nothingness; it's stuff you can work on."

He's silent. For a while he just watches me in the light of the one candle I missed, and then, shivering, he extends his hand until he's cupping my cheek.

I close my eyes. He trails his fingers down my neck and strokes my shoulder. "You are a person," he whispers. "A whole person."

"Are you going to kiss me?" I whisper back, terrified.

He takes his hand away, and for a while, he's just quiet in the dark. "I don't . . . I'm not . . . I've never felt . . . like other guys do, Sam. I've never been . . . interested in the end result of kissing."

"That's okay! Eliot, that's fine." I like him for his brain. "But just so you know, kissing doesn't have an end result. Doing it doesn't mean you're signing a contract to have sex or something. And liking kissing doesn't mean you have to like sex."

Another silence. "Then maybe I'll try it. Eventually. As an experiment."

"But not right now," I finish for him.

"But not right now."

I lean into his shoulder, and both of us stop talking.

I don't realize I've fallen asleep until I'm waking back up. Beside me, Eliot rolls over and mumbles something inaudible. The sole candle has burned out.

I stumble out of the room, letting Eliot sleep. I have the nagging feeling that something's off, that I forgot something important. Probably just the disorienting aftereffect of waking up in someone else's house.

Almost everyone has gone home. Empty cups litter the countertops, black and white streamers stripe the floor. The few people left are playing Magic: The Gathering in the living room.

Kendra materializes and lunges at me. "Well? Did you sleep together?"

"Yes," I say, because we did. But then she screams and I wave my hands frantically. "No, not like that."

Her brow furrows. "Maybe he didn't want to do it drunk. He did say he was worried about getting you pregnant."

I'm turning to go back to Kendra's room and wake up Eliot when I slam into eye contact with Trez.

She's picking her way over the streamers. When she sees me, her face contorts and she whips toward the door, the lace edges of her dark dress floating out. It plunges me into an ice lake.

I leave Kendra confused and chase Trez outside. I catch her leaning against the fence, clutching a broken heel.

"I'm sorry I came," she stammers, like I had her under house arrest. "I heard about Anthony, and it felt like a sign that today was the day, that you'd finally call the police and they'd show up at my door. I-I'm ready, but . . . I wanted to see people again, one last time, before they looked at me differently."

"Are you the one who's been bringing us all those lasagnas?" I have no idea why I say this, but the moment I do, I realize I'm right.

A breeze makes her shiver. "It's just lasagna."

We stand there in absolute silence like the last two people in the world.

"So are you going to?" she asks after a minute. "Call the police?"

"I . . . don't know," I say honestly.

"I'll still call them for you if you want. Tell them what I did." Her chin is delicate, but the way she sticks it out makes her whole face look braver.

I don't answer for a long time, so eventually she takes a shuffling step toward the road. But then she stops.

"What was your mom like?" she asks quietly.

I've spent so much time worrying I'd never know enough to answer that question. Maybe I don't know every little thing, but I do know the important stuff.

"She was sentimental, and smart, and creative, and somehow an optimist and a worrier at the same time; and she never tried to make anyone be someone they weren't."

"She sounds like a nice lady," Trez whispers, hugging herself in a way that makes her seem incredibly small. "I was just wondering. My mom's not a nice lady."

Something about the sight of her looks fundamentally wrong there, but she's only standing in the moonlight, her fingers brushing the edge of the fence. My skin prickles, not from the breeze. I stare at her until she backs away.

But then I realize it's not her at all. It's the unattached leash dangling from the fence.

Chapter Seventeen

I CAN'T FIND MY DOG.

We search all night. Kendra marshals the remainder of the party, and despite the presence of ten hungover kids in prom clothes combing a three-mile radius, despite yelling for Tito until the neighbors yell at us, despite how Eliot and Kendra and I keep hunting long after everyone else goes home, I can't find my dog.

"I'm really sorry, but I have to leave," Kendra says around four, near tears. "My mom's coming back from her night shift, and I have to clean up the house."

She keeps talking, but I fade out and turn away down a street I've checked twice—maybe Tito looped back.

Eliot jogs up to me. Before he has to apologize, too, I tell him, "You can go. It's fine. I'll walk home."

"I'm not going anywhere," he says calmly. "I was just going to point out it'll be faster if we drive, now that it's just us."

So we creep around the neighborhood at five miles per hour, calling out the window for Tito. My body is tight, like half of me is tied to him and I'm stretching as he gets farther and farther away.

Eliot maintains a stream of encouragement: "Even if we don't find him tonight, I've walked him around this neighborhood so many times that he definitely knows the way to my house. Stupider dogs have found their way home from farther away."

My brain feels loose and detached. "If we don't find him tonight, I have to explain to my family that he's gone because of me."

After only a moment of hesitation, he takes my hand.

Around six, the sun staining everything paler, we almost run over a thin shadow. Trez steps under a streetlight. She's barefoot, her ankles dirty, her one unbroken shoe hooked on her left pinkie.

"Did you guys go to Greenhorn Street?" she pants. "I checked it, but that was hours ago."

Greenhorn Street is four miles away.

"Trez, you can go home," I croak. "We'll give you a ride."

She backs away and cuts across someone's lawn. She's light on her feet in the early-morning grass, like a cross between a fairy and a witch.

"I'm sure Tito's at my house by now," Eliot promises.

But when we get there, his yard and driveway are empty except for Gabriel's car and Gabriel himself, standing on the front porch in a bathrobe with his arms crossed.

"Shit," Eliot mutters, then glances at me desperately as I gulp and blink because it's not Tito on the porch. "Sam, Sam, it's okay. Don't worry."

The reassuring phrases I've taught him to say don't feel reassuring now.

"I just have to deal with this"—he gestures at Gabriel, who is striding toward us—"but we'll look again later. We'll find him, Sam. I *promise*."

He grips my wrist like he's burning the promise into my skin, then gets out of the car.

Numbly I watch them argue in front of the house, Gabriel snatching Eliot's keys and pointing repeatedly at the door, until finally Eliot throws up his hands and storms inside.

Gabriel comes out to the car and drives me home, somehow managing to say a lot without me hearing a single word.

My family isn't mad, which is worse.

"I'll bet you a hundred dollars I don't have that he shows up in the night like the couch." Rex fist bumps my shoulder.

But Lena's eyes squish up, and she doesn't comment on the hole in her tights.

Unexpectedly, Dad is the one who launches into action, and his plan is so detailed it's like he took a workshop on locating lost pets.

"Your mother taught me Photoshop—did I ever tell you kids that?—so I'll design a flyer. Rex, you'll print three hundred copies at the library. Lena, you'll call every shelter within twenty miles and give them a description of Tito. Sam, you'll write a Facebook post and share it with all those lost-pet pages, and hopefully it gains some traction. As soon as Rex gets back, we'll hang so many flyers there won't be one person in the entire town who hasn't seen Tito's silly mug. He'll be back before dinner."

We all stare, speechless.

He blushes. "I always told your mother that if we had a dog, we'd have to know what to do when it got lost."

So Lena curls up in a chair and starts making calls, and I write the Facebook post on my laptop. When Dad hands Rex the flash drive with the flyer on it, Rex jumps in his truck and rockets off.

Then we just sort of sit around waiting for him to get back.

After a while, Lena's lip starts quivering.

"Do you think he'll get hit by a car?" she asks weakly, and for a brief and terrifying millisecond I genuinely wish I wasn't alive.

"He's only missing." Dad reaches over and gives her shoulder a firm pat. "If we do everything right, we'll find him. And we're going to do everything right."

None of us mentions it when 8:00 a.m. passes, which is when we usually give Tito his meds.

LOST DOG
Answers to: Tito (also "Tits" and "The Animal")
Description: Small mutt, 13 years old, brown with white-
tipped tail, NOT a stray despite appearance. Does not
bite. Has epilepsy, requires daily medication.
Reward offered.

After we hang so many flyers that the neighborhood
changes color, we stop by several nearby shelters, none of
which has Tito.

We go to McDonald's for lunch, except by then it's dinner. Instead of complaining about the fries, Lena eats hers
like a paper shredder, feeding them mechanically between
her teeth.

"Here's what's next," Dad declares. He said it after Mom
died, too, when we wanted to believe in a *next* even though
one couldn't be possible. "Good old-fashioned legwork."

"What about me?" I ask.

Lena surfaces from her cloud of despair. "It's too much
walking."

"I'm not—"

"—a helpless infant, I know," she says thickly. "But it's
too much."

I kick Rex under the table, but he looks away. Suddenly
he's on her side. Great. As much as I hate it, though, she's
right—my leg is already too sore from last night.

"I'll stay home with you, Sam," offers Dad. "They'll
leave me in the dust anyway."

"I'm not worried." Rex announces it like the whole restaurant is listening. "Tito is Tito. He couldn't disappear."

Legwork would work better with more legs, and I'm about to suggest they call some friends, but Rex's crew ditched him after he was expelled, Dad stopped going to his coworker's place for drinks, and apparently Lena never had friends to withdraw from. But I had ten people roaming the streets for me last night.

I can't believe I ever thought I was alone.

On the drive home, Lena is having an inaudible conversation with Rex in the backseat when, at the top of his lungs, he shouts, "HOLY SHIT."

Dad slams on the brakes and then twists to look apologetically at me, but I'm turning toward the backseat, where Rex is staring at Lena.

"You called me Rex," he accuses her.

I wait for her to deny it, but slowly she flushes.

"Well, that's your name, isn't it?"

He doesn't rub it in; but once we get home, he shoves all the McDonald's bags in his truck onto the lawn to make room for her.

Inside, Dad and I pour glasses of water and sit in the kitchen without drinking them.

"Are you okay, Sam?" he asks.

I put on the smile. "Yeah. We'll find him."

"You don't need to protect me," he says wearily. "I've let you do it for too long. If you don't want to tell me what your real feelings are, let me take a guess. You're sad and scared, and you miss your dog. Close enough?"

I nod, my eyes hot.

"Well, those were the easy ones. I'll try to guess right more often." He straightens his back. "There is a new therapist. I don't want to have another fight, and you don't need to confide in me about how you feel if you're not comfortable with that, but I need to know you're confiding in somebody."

"There is somebody."

He lifts a hand, silencing me. "He seems like a nice boy. But you still need a therapist."

"I don't care as long as it's not Dr. Brown."

I don't care about much right now, which is a good time to ask things I'd normally care about too much.

"Dad, do you remember when Dr. Brown asked us what we thought about the person who was driving the other car? You never answered."

He chugs most of his water before speaking. "After the third time the police questioned you, my thoughts were that finding this person wasn't worth causing you any more pain."

I dig my fingernails into my crutches. "But don't you wish you knew who it was?"

"I also wish your mom was still with us. You don't hang your life on wishes that won't come true."

Maybe my face shows how I feel about that, because he hastily continues. "Sometimes it's a relief, to be honest. It's a full-time job, missing your mother. I don't have the time to hate someone, too."

I keep pushing. "You don't think they should be punished?"

"They'll never forgive themselves, and that's a punishment, believe me." He wipes his damp forehead. "And when it comes to your brother, I personally think that hating someone he doesn't know is safer for him than hating someone he does."

We'd both heard Rex when he said he wanted to kill the driver.

Consequences don't occur to Rex like they do to other people. He doesn't understand that drinking too much means a hangover the next morning, or that not doing his homework dooms him to fail.

I finally get why Lena is always throwing consequences in Rex's face.

"What about Lena?" I ask.

"Lena is all about the future. Revenge is about the past." He yawns. "Try not to think about it too much, Sam. What you need to do now is go to sleep."

"You, too, Dad."

"You're not wrong," he says, but he doesn't move.

I go upstairs first so he can eat as many gummy dinosaurs as he needs without having to do it in front of me.

By Sunday morning, Tito still hasn't come back.

Nor does he return on Monday, Tuesday, Wednesday, or Thursday.

Eliot isn't at school all week. He texts me a halfhearted

excuse about Gabriel, but I'm too drained to take on another worry, so I spend lunch periods in the computer lab, making new flyers.

On Thursday, Kendra spots me through the open door. Within ten minutes she's marshaled the whole lacrosse team, girls drawing ads for the school paper and emailing shelters across state lines.

All these people care about finding Tito, just because he's mine.

Eliot texts me endless updates from his end:

Gabriel can confiscate my car keys, but he can't confiscate my feet. Last night I searched East Ave from Hardy.

That's miles though, I answer.

I ran into Trez. We split the distance.

I told her finding your animal wouldn't change anything, and she said she knew.

I think I finally understand why you hit people for me. If I could hit whatever's making this happen, I would. But I can't, so I'm just going to find the animal instead.

If I found the couch, I can find him.

Then he texts me a picture of a headline.

Boy Who Can't Feel Pain Seeks Help Locating Lost Dog

My Facebook post now has hundreds of shares. My chest unclenches.

It was a miracle that he found the couch. Maybe he has one miracle left.

★ ★ ★

On Friday, Rex lets me convince him to go with him as he searches on foot. We walk down our street together, shaking bowls of food.

"You're not overdoing it, are you?" he asks worriedly. "Ten minutes and we're heading back. Thanks to your boyfriend, the internet will probably have found him by then."

I crack a small smile.

"It'll be soon—I can feel it." His confidence is contagious. "The couch had to be a sign that the universe is giving things back to the Herrings."

He's been different since Tito disappeared. His skin has more color; his voice is stronger. He's not high, and he's not hungover.

My leg throbs, but it's just pain, no broken glass. I can handle pain. It turns out that without the anxiety, I actually have a pretty high pain threshold.

I stop by a neighbor's fence and take half a Vicodin, palming it so Rex doesn't see.

He sees. "I won't try to take it. I'm done, Sam. Don't give me any more, even if I ask. I'm . . . I'm gonna talk to the new therapist about antidepressants."

I feel like I'm inflating with pride. "Rex—"

"Yeah, yeah. I'm sorry, Sam. I never should have asked in the first place." He looks away and grimaces. "You were in so much pain after the accident, but the pills put you to sleep, and I was jealous. I wanted to go to sleep forever. I stole the first one—I never told you that."

It had taken me a good month after I'd left the hospital to realize I should be hiding them in my sock drawer. "Did you keep doing it?"

"Nah. Felt too much like a scumbag, stealing pain meds from my little sister. Had to ask. Still a scumbag move, but at least then I felt like I was getting the punishment I deserved, because you'd look at me . . . like you were disappointed."

The first time he'd asked, he said he'd pulled a muscle. The next time it was a migraine. Eventually neither of us bothered pretending anymore.

"At least you tried to feel better. It wasn't *good*, but you were trying." I let Tito's food bowl drop to my side. "I just sat there and felt awful because I thought the awfulness should be felt."

"At least neither of us went crazy and threw out all the furniture."

We both laugh.

Then I hesitate. "You know, Lena doesn't mean——"

"I know." He sighs. "She's like everyone else on this planet—trying to do the right thing, only she's too much of an idiot not to mess it up."

Late that night, I have to get out of bed to use the bathroom.

I find Rex sitting in front of the door, alone in the dark hallway. He jumps when he hears my crutches. Instead of saying anything, he looks back at the closed door. There are soft kitten noises coming from behind it.

"You'll have to go downstairs," he whispers. "Lena's crying in there."

I'm so tired that all I do is stumble down to the kitchen bathroom and go back to bed.

But I can't sleep, and when I peek into the hallway again half an hour later, the door is still closed and Rex is still sitting there, his back against the wall, elbows on his knees and hands dangling between them, staring at nothing in the dark.

Hours later, during that dull navy-blue sliver of time when it's impossible to tell if it's night or early morning, I'm woken up again, this time by a text.

I need to talk to you. Meet me in the McDonald's lot.

It's from Anthony.

I hurl my phone in my drawer, slam it shut, and curl up under the farthest corner of my covers.

But this could be my last chance to ask him why.

I get dressed, cold and shaking. The hallway is finally empty. I find Rex's keys downstairs on the kitchen table, and then I steal his truck.

The McDonald's parking lot is deserted, an expanse of nothingness only broken by the pale yellow pool beneath the streetlight. I park beneath it and lean against the pole, trying to calm my stomach.

Half a minute later, Anthony parks next to me.

He gets out of the car. He's disheveled and pale, thinner, his eyes puffy as he faces me under the light. His tiger smile is gone, just blank confusion.

It's impossible to be afraid of him like this. Like you can't really be afraid of a worm, only sickened by it.

"I know what you made Trez do," I manage.

And I'm going to ask why, the question big and bloody in my mouth, except I already know, don't I? Eliot already explained.

He did it because he thinks other people are lesser and worth sacrificing.

Because he was never brave enough to question what he was taught to believe.

He's not evil, and that's the saddest part.

Anthony doesn't seem surprised by what I've said, but the desperation in his expression deepens.

"You have to believe I didn't mean that to happen," he says hoarsely. "If you need to blame someone, blame *Trez*; she was *driving*. You can't want me to blame myself—do you know how fucking horrible that would be? I *liked* your mom."

But he already is, I realize.

He blames himself deep down, but he won't face it, so the guilt and sadness will stay forever as white noise that covers everything, and all he'll know is that something in him is broken.

"Say something." His voice cracks. He's begging. "God, Sam . . . you were the only one, you . . . and your dog, who ever liked the real me. That pathetic . . . I thought, if I could ever really have a friend someday, not a fake one, it'd be you."

I was friends with a little kid who snuck my dog home in his sweatshirt. Not him.

"But suddenly you were all about this Eliot *asshole*. . . ."

His hand spasms. "People like me when I pretend I'm someone different, okay? You and Rex were running around reminding everyone of the truth. I just wanted to be the version people liked. I don't deserve to suffer forever for that, right?"

I would have stayed his friend. But he won't even try to understand how badly he hurt me, my brother, my family.

I can't feel sorry for him when Eliot learned how to try.

"How can I have a chance with you if you don't talk?" He takes a jittery step forward, then back. "You were the only one who cared. You and your goddamn dog . . ."

He chokes on the word *dog*, and something shifts strangely inside me. It reminds me of Kendra's birthday party and how I felt the wrongness of the situation before my brain registered the dangling leash.

"He's missing, you know," I say dazedly. "My dog."

He's wordless for one second too long.

Then he rasps, "It's not my fault, Sam," and I fill with black horror. "I fed him, I gave him water. I don't, I don't know what . . . He had a seizure or something. I didn't mean . . ."

It's not fair.

It's not fair.

It's not fair.

"I was driving around, blowing off steam, and I saw him in that yard. . . . It was like I was meant to find him. He jumped on me, he licked he, he didn't care what I've done. He was just happy I existed. . . ."

It's not fair.

I repeat it like a prayer, but no one will answer it, because no one ever has.

And it doesn't stop Anthony from removing a blanket-wrapped bundle from the backseat of his car and handing it to me.

"I needed someone to be happy I existed, Sam," he moans. "I was going to give him back."

The bundle is the right weight, but not the right warmth or softness.

Another hole in me to add to all the others.

"The world thinks I'm psycho, I got kicked out of school, my mom's sending me to rehab, and I'm probably going to jail—my future's fucked, Sam. It's too much; I can't have you convinced I killed Tito, too. It was an accident! Like the crash. You understand, right?"

I clutch the bundle to my chest. I never realized how small he was. When someone is filled with so much love, it makes them seem bigger.

"Talk, for fuck's sake. Tell me you understand. Is this what you want, for me to sound as pathetic as possible, just like No-Moore? Everyone else hates him, *I* hate him . . . if you hate him, too . . ."

His face folds, and he starts bawling like a kid.

Which he is. He's only been eighteen for a month.

"*I didn't do it,*" he weeps. "*Please.* You can't not say *any-thing.*"

I lay the bundle tenderly on my passenger seat, and then I get in the car and drive away.

I can see him in the rearview mirror, sitting alone in the pool of light, surrounded by empty pavement.

Then I turn onto the main road, and I can't see him at all anymore.

We bury him the next day.

Dad digs a deep hole behind the doghouse, pausing only to wipe away tears or sweat, I don't know which.

We all wear black, and it's not until we're standing in a circle around the grave that I realize every one of us is wearing what we'd worn to Mom's funeral—except Eliot, who comes in the suit from Kendra's party.

Red eyed and sniffling, Rex carries out the box from my closet. We hung all the pictures back up, except for the one of Tito licking Mom, which we left in the box with his blanket-wrapped body.

"You Raise Me Up" plays on the phone tucked into Rex's breast pocket as he lowers the box into the ground. Then he pours in an entire box of Milk-Bones. They patter loudly on the dirt.

"Here's some snacks to bring to dog heaven, little man. I'd tell you to share with the other ghost dogs, but I know you will, because you're a good dog."

He retreats, blowing his nose.

Dad steps forward and drops several slices of Kraft cheese on top of the Milk-Bones.

"You didn't care for the pills, but you liked the cheese, and now you can finally have a piece without the pills."

There's a pause as he looks down into the hole, his shoulders slumped. "My wife once told me that the worst thing about life was having to outlive dogs. Now I'd argue it's having to outlive her, but you come in second, Tito."

Lena is crying harder than any of us. She wobbles forward and adds the leash she braided for him when she was in high school.

"I'm s-sorry I made you think I didn't l-love you anymore," she sobs. "You made me sad because you r-reminded me of Mom, but that w-wasn't your fault."

"Nah," says Rex gruffly, putting his arm around her. "He knew you loved him. He probably just thought you were on your period."

She buries her face in his shoulder.

Dad is blinking rapidly. I can feel myself trying to drift into numbness, but instead, I squeeze my hands into fists until my knuckles crack. I'm determined to stay here. This pain is mine, and I'm going to feel it now, not let it poison me for the rest of my life.

"You go," I whisper to Eliot.

He shuffles forward.

"I doubt dogs can learn to play the ukulele, particularly ghost dogs, because even if they had opposable thumbs, they would be intangible."

My family stares at him. He clears his throat and unzips his backpack, taking out his ukulele and a pack of cigarettes.

"You liked this when I played it for you, and I've been thinking it's time to get rid of it. Someone once told me a gift should have a piece of me in it. Good-bye, Tito. Now

I'm back to having only one friend."

Unsteadily he places the ukulele and the cigarettes into the hole.

"Also, the cigarettes are because I'm supposed to stop smoking," he adds. Then he moves back next to me and gazes at the sky with fierce determination.

The rest of them turn to me, but I'm not one for public displays of sadness. I shake my head.

So Dad fills in the hole, and Rex lights some discount sparklers and sticks them in the ground, and that is the end of Tito.

"Apparently I can only cry at dog funerals," notes Eliot suddenly.

I look at him, and his eyes are wet.

I take his hand and interlace our fingers. They fit like two halves finally coming together.

I can't say I don't consider the option of getting into bed and never coming out.

The urge is there.

But I have to reply to Eliot's texts, and Kendra's. I have to go with Dad to meet the new therapist, and help Lena pick a new color for the living room (we choose a sandy shade, like Tito's fur). I have to hover over Rex and count his push-ups, because he's decided that getting ripped is a better way to deal with grief than getting high.

And because I'm doing all those things anyway, I might as well wash my hair and eat breakfast and commit to being alive.

When Mom died, it booby-trapped the house with pits of absence. Simple things would trigger the sudden plummet in my gut—pouring an extra mug of tea without thinking, accidentally reaching for her tea tree oil shampoo bottle that had been there for weeks because there was some left but no one dared use it.

But then I memorized where the holes were and got better at avoiding them.

Now there's a whole new set.

I'll stretch my toes under the table in search of fur to bury them in, or drop bread on the floor during dinner that stays there until I sweep it up. No one head butts my leg when I walk through the door.

But by Monday night, I'm not dehydrated from crying anymore. And on Tuesday, I'm capable of collecting myself enough to sit down and write a short email to Trez.

Keep your future. Just do something good with it.

–Sam

Dad is probably right and it's a good enough punishment that she'll never forgive herself.

But I hope she does, someday. She used to be a shadow, but now she has bold edges. She paints her nails a different color; she's a stage manager. She planted things in her wreckage, and they're growing strong and fierce. I want to see what kind of fruit they bear.

It's a better legacy for Mom than suffering—people changing for the better. Mom would prefer it.

I don't know if it'd be the right thing to do for anyone

else, but it's the right thing to do for me.

I hit Send and go to sleep.

And on Wednesday, Rex asks me to help him study for his GED test.

And on Thursday, I don't hear Dad go downstairs for his usual midnight snack.

On Friday, Lena adopts a cat.

"His name is Keokolo!" she says brightly, struggling to keep the cat in her arms as its bottom paws scrape her legs. "It's a Hawaiian name—it means 'gift from God.'"

The cat is a rotting shade of orange, and its face looks like a carved pumpkin, missing teeth and all. Its escape strategy is apparently to go as limp as possible until Lena loses the battle with gravity. Then it droops into a puddle on the floor, meowing like a garbage disposal.

"What the fuck is that?" asks Rex from the top of the stairs.

"Our new cat!" she says happily.

Rex clings to the rail. "Sam, it's moving."

The cat is slinking across the floor. I hold my bag protectively in front of my chest.

Lena coos at it. "The Humane Society said he'd been there the longest, which means he needed love the most."

"You can't just *assign* us a cat," Rex says.

"Did you talk to Dad first?" I ask.

She opens her mouth to argue, but then she stops, probably because she didn't. "I was just missing Tito, and thinking about how pets can be a very calming, therapeutic presence. . . ."

She glances at the cat, whose left ear is missing. For a second she just looks at it. Then, suddenly, she bursts into mildly hysterical laughter.

"Oh my God," she gasps. "I bought a cat."

"They charged you for that?" Rex asks, sounding concerned. He comes downstairs, and I elbow him.

"There was an adoption fee." Lena sits on the floor with a thump. "Oh, lord. You're both right. What am I *doing*?"

Rex and I exchange looks.

"You're nobly saving a lost soul," I decide. "A lost cat soul."

"He's not the *ugliest* cat," Rex offers. "I like his . . ."

There's a very long silence as he struggles to think of something.

"His face," he says eventually, then peers at the cat to confirm. "Nope, his face creeps me out. But I'm sure he has a great personality."

"All he does is sleep," Lena says tearfully.

He pats her head. "All I do is sleep around, and *I* have a great personality."

We spend the next hour convincing Lena we like the cat. By the time Dad comes home, we're in too deep, and he's outvoted.

And then next morning when I come downstairs, Rex is asleep on the couch with Keokolo on his lap.

I don't see Eliot much over spring break. Every time I invite him to hang out, he makes mysterious excuses. At first I think maybe he's avoiding the outside world, thanks to that video, but the hubbub about that has already died way down. Apparently there was a baby born in Arkansas with two heads.

Finally I get fed up, steal Rex's truck, and head over myself. Knowing him, he's probably having a dire medical emergency and is afraid I'll call an ambulance. Which I will, next time. No more not calling ambulances.

When I pull up, there's a huge white vehicle in the driveway, and my heart stops. But it's not an ambulance.

It's a moving van.

I jump out of the truck.

"Sam!" Eliot is on the porch, holding a cardboard box. A moving box, like the ones we unpacked together. He ambles across the lawn toward me with nowhere near enough urgency or shame. "You didn't tell me you were coming."

"Oh, are we talking about things we haven't told each other?" I shriek. "What about how you didn't tell me that you're *moving*?"

He stops in his tracks. "Yes, I'm moving, but—"

"I know you're new to the whole friendship thing, but this is something you're *really* supposed to tell your friends!" If I hadn't sworn to myself I'd never hit Eliot, I'd probably slap him.

"Sam—"

"How could I have been so *stupid*?" I rage. "Of course you were lying when you said Gabriel wouldn't transfer you! How could he not transfer you, after that video? Jesus!"

Eliot puts down his box. I whack it with a crutch. Hopefully it's something breakable.

"If you would just—" he starts.

"I'm never going to see you again, am I?" There are tears burning in my eyes, no matter how much I wish there weren't. I can't lose anything else. "You're—you're—you're the only interesting thing in my life, you're everything, you're—"

"Can I shut-up kiss you?" he interrupts.

My skull implodes. "WHAT?"

"I need you to shut up for a second, so I was wondering if I could shut-up kiss you, since nothing else seems to be working."

"It's not a shut-up kiss if you *ask*, you idiot!"

"It'd be rude to do it without asking," he says, affronted.

"Well, the answer is NO! *No*, you cannot *shut-up kiss me* when I'm yelling at you about how you didn't tell me you were *moving*—"

"I'm moving six miles," he cuts in.

"Six . . . miles?" I repeat, a wave of dizziness washing over me.

"One school district over. You are correct; there was no way Gabriel wasn't going to transfer me after that video, but I figured that the benefits were worth the drawbacks. And I very successfully talked him down from Florida, so you're welcome."

"Six miles," I echo again.

"And when I say drawbacks, I mean significant ones. It doesn't matter where we live now, because he has a new remote job, which he'll be doing from home." He grimaces.

"As in the place where I also live."

"So you're not disappearing forever?"

It's still not completely easy to breathe.

He smiles. "Not disappearing even temporarily."

I hurry up the steps and peek inside the house. Everything we unpacked is packed up again.

"It's still farther away," I grumble, my cheeks warming as Eliot joins me on the porch. "And I won't get to see you at school."

"You have other people at school," he says simply. "Besides, if we're always together, I'll never end up getting to know anyone else, because I'll only want to talk to you. And as much as I like to think of myself as the only interesting thing in your life, I shouldn't be."

I won't be able to sit with him at lunch, but Kendra's table never filled my empty spot. I won't be able to ride home with him anymore, but Rex is sober now, and anyway he said I can borrow his truck for school once I get my license. Eliot won't be everything anymore, but he'll still be something.

But what happens when he graduates? He's never talked about his plans after high school. I liked that we were in the same vague state of not having any, but now it makes me nervous, the idea of him in a different school, bored and unfulfilled. Bad things happen when he's bored.

He needs a new hobby.

"Eliot," I say. "That is a very wise thing you just said."

He squints at me suspiciously.

"I know this is random, but did I ever tell you that I think you'd be a really great therapist?"

He laughs. "My own therapist won't even see me anymore."

My heart skips, but all I say is "You probably had a rough time in therapy because your brain is naturally trying to swap positions. Being a therapist is literally just your favorite thing to do, figuring out the patterns in people's lives, except you get paid for it."

"Yes, I'm sure many people would pay me to point out their problems as bluntly as possible."

"By the time you became a therapist, you'd probably be better at that part. But the point is that it's a job where you're *supposed* to say the stuff you think. Instead of making people mad, you'd be helping them." I'm talking faster by the second. "My sister says lots of colleges are still accepting applications for next spring. You'd have something to use your brain for, other than figuring out when people are going to break up."

He's lost in thought for a minute, but then he snaps back to me. "How about you? I hear lots of colleges are still accepting applications for next spring."

I shrink back. "I'm not like you. I don't have something like psychology I'm naturally good at."

"So become not-naturally good at something. If you don't know what, experiment. Join a club." He sits down on the porch. "I hear the Math Club is low in numbers."

I grimace. "That pun was so stupid I had to block out

everything you said from my memory."

"You shouldn't do that," he chides. "Once I'm an acclaimed therapist, people will pay by the hour for my advice. You're getting it for free."

The Math Club does always need new members. And one of the girls is in Calc with me.

He checks his phone. Now that I'm paying attention, I realize it's the third time he's done it.

Suddenly he hops to his feet and takes me by my shoulders.

"Sam, do you trust me?"

"No."

"Fair enough." He sighs. "Let me rephrase: would you like to make one thousand dollars?"

"What's happening?" I break away from him and check the bushes next to the porch. "Where are the secret cameras?"

He seems nervous, sticking his hands in his pockets and then pulling them back out. "It's funny how meeting someone makes you want to spend a summer doing something other than smoking on your living-room floor, for once. We could have a pretty awesome summer with a thousand dollars. We could take a road trip."

I blink. I have no idea what he's talking about, but whatever it is, it's important to him. "What do I have to do?"

"Nothing much. Just kiss me in—" He checks his phone again. "The next thirty seconds."

My jaw works. "Eliot, if you want to try your kissing

experiment now, you don't need to come up with these weird elaborate—"

"Twenty-five." He taps his watch. "Twenty-four."

"Quit that! What does this have to do with a thousand dollars?"

"Twenty," he says ominously. "Nineteen."

I'm starting to sweat. "The last time I kissed you I was drunk!"

"Fifteen. That's true, but we both know that between the two of us, you're still the only one brave enough to instigate a sober kiss. Ten . . ."

I'm struck by a wild suspicion that, as a misguided romantic gesture, he's rigged the whole house to blow if I don't kiss him, and that's the real reason why he packed everything up.

"Also, supposedly I'm not allowed to kiss you until I take you out to dinner three hundred times, so you have to do it," he says. "Five. Four . . ."

It's extremely unlikely, but those two words describe Eliot more than any others, so I play it safe and lean forward, bringing my lips to his.

He's a person, a whole other person.

"That wasn't so bad," he whispers.

We're interrupted by the sound of a door opening and a crash. I whip around.

Gabriel is in the doorway, standing over several dropped boxes. His mouth is hanging open.

"He said he'd be done packing up the things in his room in fifteen minutes, fifteen minutes ago," Eliot tells me.

"He's very punctual."

"You wanted him to see that?" I hiss.

Gabriel is making croaking sounds.

"He made a very interesting comment, namely there were a lot of things he had to worry about but never that he'd walk in on me making out with a girl," Eliot says, the smirk in full force. "I disagreed, and he bet me that if he ever found me making out with a girl, he'd pay for a summer getaway with her. You can give me the check later, Gabriel."

He storms off toward his car, leaving the boxes on the porch. When he passes me, though, I think I catch a smile.

I sigh. "I hate you."

"You can hit me if you like."

"I am never going to hit you," I tell him.

And then I kiss him again.

The next day, I sit with Kendra and the team at lunch.

It takes me a while to psych myself up for it. But Kendra just beams and slides her tray over to make room for me, like I've sat with them every day since the beginning of time.

It occurs to me that maybe sitting next to somebody at lunch isn't as big of a deal as it feels.

After school, Kendra offers me a ride, but I turn her down. The Math Club is meeting today. Maybe I'll be the girl who went from lacrosse kid to Math Club kid.

Or maybe I'll take a cue from Lena and be an Environmental Club kid. Or follow in Mom's shoes and be an Art Club kid.

Maybe I wasn't born with a list of things that make me special, like lacrosse, slots I can't refill if they're emptied. Maybe I get to choose what makes me special.

I can't remember if the Math Club meets in the library or the cafeteria. I loiter in the hallway for a while, and then I head toward the library, because picking a direction at random will take me somewhere faster than standing still.